BURRITOS AND GASOLINE

BURRITOS AND GASOLINE

A Novel

Jamie Beckett

iUniverse, Inc.
New York Lincoln Shanghai

Burritos and Gasoline
A Novel

Copyright © 2006 by James F. Beckett

iUniverse books may be ordered through booksellers or by contacting:

iUniverse
2021 Pine Lake Road, Suite 100
Lincoln, NE 68512
www.iuniverse.com
1-800-Authors (1-800-288-4677)

This is a work of fiction. All of the characters, names, incidents, organizations and dialogue in this novel are either the products of the author's imagination or are used fictitiously.

ISBN-13: 978-0-595-40912-9 (pbk)
ISBN-13: 978-0-595-85274-1 (ebk)
ISBN-10: 0-595-40912-1 (pbk)
ISBN-10: 0-595-85274-2 (ebk)

Printed in the United States of America

For Dylan, Nikki and Madie.

Acknowledgments

The process of writing can be an unforgivingly solitary endeavor. However, the process of making a book ready for public consumption is not. In the case of this particular book, the list of those who've been indispensable during its creation is long. Too long to fit here, certainly.

A truncated version of that list would undoubtedly include Jeremy Maready, a talented photojournalist who offered large doses of much appreciated encouragement when it was badly needed. Similarly, without the able assistance and valued support of Joni Fisher, who read and critiqued my early drafts, this novel very well may have languished on my desk for years, unfinished.

The cover art, toward which I offered only minimal input, is the work of my good and talented friend, Mark Potter. It pleases me immensely that after years of working independently of each other, his artwork and my words are once again featured on the same collection of pages.

Diane Dvorak of the Florida Writer's Association deserves a permanent spot on my Christmas card list too. Her infectious enthusiasm and dedicated support for writers who want nothing more than to find an audience for their work is inspirational.

Most especially I'd like to offer a belated tip of the hat to Mark Cohan, a remarkable educator who was charged with the almost impossible task of attempting to teach the intricacies of history to several hundred students at Glastonbury High School during my formative years. It was pure dumb luck that I was enrolled there and awake often enough to benefit from his guidance.

My life to this point has been enriched beyond description by fortunate twists of fate, friends with big hearts and family members with the ability to forgive the most humbling moments in life. To these critically supportive few, as well as so many others, I say, "Thanks for the push."

CHAPTER 1

Call me crazy, but I believe life comes to us preloaded with its own inertia. Think of it as Newton's First Law of Humanity. The point where science leaves the lab and delves silently, secretly, into the lives of each and every one of us.

Yes, its true. I'm sure of it.

There is most definitely a force that propels inattentive, unfortunate souls like myself through doorways we know we'd be better off not walking through. It pushes us to do things that are best left undone. Selfish, destructive things that can only backfire and do us harm. Yet somehow, against our own better judgment, we do them anyway. And we pay a high price for being so habitually reluctant to heed our own inner voices.

Fortunately, there is evidence that even the most self absorbed and blatantly arrogant examples of humanity can redeem themselves, given certain conditions and the proper motivation.

At least that's been my experience.

The series of events that initiated the end of my own carefully guarded existence remain crystal clear in my mind. Even now, years after the fact, I can still mentally run through the movie of my life in all its cinematic glory. Oh, what a ride it's been.

My all but unavoidable downhill slide began on an otherwise unremarkable Friday afternoon in an unabashedly blue collar town known as Manchester, Connecticut. The exact time was 5:05 PM.

Even before that much deserved dose of a reality bore down on me, I was suffering from a desperate case of the emotional blahs. Which, I freely acknowledge, was pretty much the norm for me in those days. Still, I didn't have the slightest suspicion about what sort of surprise might await me as I drove dejectedly to work that morning. In only a matter of hours, my less than vibrant outlook on life would be forced to change in a big way. And not for the better, I might add.

Manchester, like so many towns that came into their own during the golden days of the industrial revolution, can be viewed in one of two ways. How you choose to see it depends very much on your point of view. It could easily be taken as a lovely little working class town, full of charmingly narrow streets, majestic leafy trees, a multitude of tidy parks and several thousand residents who represent the salt of the earth. The place exudes a certain southern New England charm that cheerfully embraces and celebrates the town's hard working, mechanized roots.

Then again, it could be viewed as a prime example of urban decay, where the potholed and cracked asphalt streets are thickly lined by weather beaten, multi family homes inhabited almost entirely by families who are either too poor or too dumb to move somewhere more prosperous. Somewhere like East Hartford, perhaps.

In general, I subscribed to the latter opinion. A fact that I'm not the least bit proud of.

I lived nearby, in East Hartford, which borders Manchester to the west. I suppose you could say that my hometown was distinguished from Manchester primarily by being a more economically hopeful place overall. It wouldn't necessarily be true, but you could say it. Others certainly have.

I believed that degrading theory with all my heart in those days. Although if I'm being honest, I didn't have much heart left at that point.

Even further west, only one short river crossing away from my own apartment, was Hartford, the capital of the state. In Hartford there was opportunity. White collar jobs in government office buildings or the crisp, clean, modern glass and steel high rises of the insurance industry paid much better than most of what was available on the east side of the river. A certain measure of status was attached to having a job, or even better, a career, in the city. To be employed in Hartford was to be upwardly mobile. Those who were lucky enough to steer their cars west with the morning commute were seen as being headed in the right direction in life. Those lucky bastards had hope. A big, rosy, flashing neon sign that read, "Prosperity!" was on their horizon.

My drive to work took me the other way, to Manchester, which forced me to squint into the rising sun as I made my way. I lived in East Hartford, hardly more than walking distance from downtown Hartford and a substantially better life. As a matter of fact, I'd lived in East Hartford for the entire 42 years of my existence to that point. But I drove the wrong way to work. Each morning I steered toward that blue collar kingdom with a chip on my shoulder and a scowl on my face.

It was that fact more than any other that caused the color to slowly bleed out of my life. The act of driving eastward, away from the opportunities of the city, eventually caused me to become a shell of the man I was convinced I should have been. I'd achieved so little, my life was barely a thin shadow of what my boyhood dreams had suggested for my future.

To be blunt, I was 100 percent dissatisfied, disgusted and disinterested in any aspect of even my own life, let alone anyone else's.

Then the hands of the clock ticked over to 5:05 PM. Things were about to take a turn for the worse.

As I pushed my way through the door to the Personnel Department, which was my habit on Friday afternoons, I took three deliberate steps toward Mildred Hanrahan's desk and extended my right hand without comment or eye contact. This wasn't an expression of affection or gratitude or even basic civility. In retrospect, I have to admit a sense of shame that I never showed poor Mildred the least bit of courtesy. Back then I saw her as something of a human cash machine. For Mildred was the secretary to Ted Winters, the personnel manager at what I perceived as the dumpy little company where Mildred and I both worked. A company that shall remain nameless for fear of possible litigation. I'm sure you'll understand, considering the circumstances.

It was Mildred's sad task to hand out paychecks every Friday afternoon to a long line of hurried, haggard employees who wanted nothing more than to get their checks and hit the bars hard and fast. It was a duty she performed without the slightest hint of enthusiasm or charm.

Who could blame her, really?

My hand remained extended momentarily, but no envelope passed between Mildred and me as was usual. Instead she spoke, a fact that in and of itself should have tipped me off that something was wrong. Mildred never spoke to me. I never spoke to her either. All in all, we were even.

"Ted wants to see you," she chirped, chewing a wad of gum, big enough to choke a lesser woman to death.

"About what?" I asked. The suspicious nature of the moment began to dawn on me. Mildred looked up at me wearily, chewing to beat the band. She never got the chance to answer.

"Frank, come on in," Ted's voice called out from behind his half-open door. The entrance to his office was located only two short steps behind Mildred's desk.

With butterflies suddenly flapping madly in my stomach, I made my way into the personnel manager's office for only the second time in my life. My first visit had been eight years before, when I'd been interviewed, then hired to work for the company as a CNC router operator. Suffice it to say the firm was a leading manufacturer of circuit boards. I'd prefer not to be any more specific than that.

Over the course of the eight years I'd been a part of that organization, I'd seen Ted a number of times. Our paths had crossed in the hallways, occasionally in the men's room, and once or twice at the company Christmas party. We nodded in a familiar manner, of course. But neither of us had ever said anything of importance to the other since the day he'd clapped me on the back, shook my hand and welcomed me aboard as an employee of the company.

That was about to change.

"Have a seat, Frank." He waved a hand at the lone empty chair in front of his desk.

Ted was my age, but looked ten years younger. Skillfully placed dark curls hung gracefully across his forehead. His suit jacket hung on a rack in the corner, crisp and clean. Nobody who encountered him on the street would take Ted Winters for a factory worker. More likely they'd peg him as a stockbroker or a lawyer rushing to catch a quick lunch with a client.

His office was another story, however. The wallpaper was beige and unremarkable, the bookshelves dusty and unkempt. Aside from the empty seat he'd indicated, there was only one other chair in the room, his. I hadn't noticed it eight years before, but Ted's desk was one of those build-it-yourself deals you can pick up at discount stores for cheap. The room struck me as being every bit as depressing as the reason I'd been invited into it was curious.

Sitting down as instructed, the sudden movement caused a wispy cloud of fiberglass dust to shake loose from my rumpled work clothes. The tiny glass threads began dancing spontaneously, gently circulated by the air-conditioning duct blowing across the ceiling above my seat. Within seconds, gravity began to drag the delicate cloud of minuscule fibers earthward. While watching them fall I said the only thing that came to mind.

"Okay."

"Frank, we've got a problem." Ted was matter-of-fact. He didn't hem or haw or beat around the bush in the least. "I'm afraid we're going to have to let you go." The words rolled smoothly, effortlessly off his tongue. There was no emotion of any kind in his voice.

I returned his gaze with the blank expression of a man who's only recently received a sudden, debilitating head injury. "Huh?" I said.

"It's your attitude, Frank." Ted wasn't apologizing and he wasn't about to backtrack or try to rephrase the salient point of my visit to his office. He merely proceeded to form the news into neat little bite-sized portions that he no doubt assumed I would find more easily digestible.

When it came to personnel matters, Ted Winters was the consummate professional. He didn't show his feelings one way or the other. For all I knew, he was mentally working out the potential benefits of changing auto insurance providers while we were having our little chat. The man was that emotionally detached from his work. He was a wonder.

Ted continued, "Your productivity scores have been sliding for months…you've received three consecutive unsatisfactory reviews from your supervisor and from what I've been able to gather, you haven't made any effort to correct these inadequacies at all."

Throughout the entire exchange, brief as it was, Ted was polite, dispassionate and unshakable as he delivered the bad news. I, on the other hand, was having great difficulty getting myself mentally up to speed. I watched his mouth move for several more seconds, although not a word was sinking into my addled brain. By the time the gist of his message finally began to register, I realized that Ted was holding an envelope in his right hand, offering it to me. Slowly, unsteadily I took it. The envelope contained my paycheck. The one I'd expected to receive without comment from Mildred moments earlier. Now here it was, weighing on my mind far more than it did my hand.

As it turns out, the thin slip of paper inside that envelope represented the last paycheck I'd ever receive from an employer. No more would I take money in exchange for hours of mind-numbingly dull work each week. Not that I didn't want to. But in a tight job market, a man in my position was left with limited options.

I'd given so little thought to each of those previous 400 odd paychecks. The first one got me excited, I imagine, although I have no clear recollection of picking it up or feeling anything one way or another about it. The last one certainly caught my attention, though. My head was swimming. The rest of me was locked in place, not moving an inch. I was dumbfounded.

"Good luck, Frank."

Ted stood deliberately as he reached out to shake my hand. I rose unsteadily and shook the offered appendage, as much out of reflex as anything else. Then I turned to the open door and slunk out. Mixing among the throngs that were lined up to receive pay envelopes of their own from Mildred, I felt oddly out of place. For her part, Mildred sat as quietly as ever, diligently working her way through the pile of envelopes on her desk and the associated line of workers that stretched out through her doorway and into the hall beyond.

Shouldering my way through the crowd, I began making my way toward the main exit as best I could. The walls seemed to heave and swell as if they were attempting to expel me from the building. The floor beneath my feet felt as if it had softened to the consistency of marshmallows. Time lost all relevance, except for the fact that I wanted to get out of that hallway, out of the building and out of the company parking lot, as fast as I possibly could. Unfortunately, try as I might, I felt as if I was unable to move any faster than a hobbled octogenarian using a slightly irregular walker.

Finally, after pushing myself with great effort down the hallway toward the cold, bitter world that was no doubt waiting patiently to add to my humiliation, I reached the steel exit door. Pressing against the panic bar with my hip, I oozed out onto the damp sidewalk, confused, embarrassed and just beginning to realize exactly how deep a hole I'd stumbled into.

The sun was still hours away from disappearing behind the curvature of the earth. But it was shaded mightily by a steel gray Manchester sky that caused the look and feel of the whole day to run together.

The calendar suggested it was the middle of summer. But the sky above my head looked more like late fall. The thermometer struggled throughout that dreary afternoon to reach 70 degrees. Yet, even considering that relatively warm temperature, overtones of the chilly, depressing nature of autumn were pervasive. The atmosphere surrounding me looked and felt more or less the same as it had when I'd arrived for work at eight in the morning. At lunchtime the world had looked just as bleak. By five minutes after five in the afternoon, nothing had changed much. At least not in the meteorological sense.

A light drizzle teased my nose and beaded up on my eyebrows and hair as I trudged to my car. The damp air caused my blue jeans and cotton work shirt to feel tighter, restricting movement, making it hard to breathe. I tugged at my collar, to no avail. Air flowed to my lungs only with great effort. My scuffed, dirty boots weighed a ton. One shoelace had somehow come undone. Rather than stop to tie it again, I let it drag behind me. The boot loosened slightly with each step.

My only thought was to get away. If my boot had fallen completely off, I'm sure I'd have continued on with only a sock to cover my foot. My embarrassment was unimaginable in its enormity.

With considerable effort, I quickened my pace.

Around me were straggling bands of my former co-workers laughing, joking and enjoying the freedom represented by a Friday afternoon. I on the other hand was just at that moment coming to realize exactly how isolated I was from the 200 or so men and women I'd shared a working environment with up until only a few minutes before. Not one of them made my list as someone I would count as a real friend. Then again, I didn't really count anyone else in the world as having a solid spot on that list, either. I talked to no one as I made my way through the parking lot and no one talked to me. Much like my relationship with Ted's secretary, Mildred, we were even. All of us. I knew I wouldn't be missed on Monday.

The world and I were at odds. Yet even with that critical tidbit of information gnawing away at the back of my brain, it still hadn't occurred to me that I was rapidly making the transition from being a deeply troubled man to being a man in deep, deep trouble.

There is a profound difference between the two conditions. I didn't know that then. I also didn't know that I hadn't hit bottom yet. I'd find out, though. Oh, how I'd find out.

CHAPTER 2

The drive home should have taken no more than 15 minutes. But I needed time to think, so it took longer. As a matter of fact, it took a lot longer. I was still driving around aimlessly when my watch ticked past 6:30. You might say I was working up my courage, or that I was working out what might pass for a plausible excuse to explain the situation I'd suddenly found myself in. However I might paint my frame of mind, the fact remained that I still hadn't managed to point the car down Tolland Street toward the apartment I shared with Jackie, my longtime girlfriend.

To some extent, I was harboring a powerful sense of anxiety. Certainly I knew she wasn't likely to react well to the news that I was no longer employed. It was clear that I wouldn't be contributing to the general welfare of our life together for some time. The job market wasn't good. I knew it. She knew it, too. It was beyond reason to expect that I would find anything other than an entry level position in the food service industry for the foreseeable future. That wasn't good for a man on the far side of 40. Even if only just. It wasn't good for anyone, really.

Jackie and I had been together for years. How many years exactly escaped me. But our relationship predated the job I'd so unceremoniously lost, I knew that much. We'd been together long enough in fact that we'd discussed marriage for more than half of the time we'd been cohabitating. She was in favor of it. I continued to have my doubts.

We'd been a couple for at least a year when Jackie and I moved into our tiny four-room apartment that constituted the entire first floor of a broken down, mold-colored three-family house on Tolland Street. Like most single women who can see the big four-oh coming from half a decade away, Jackie had been making it clear for some time that she was more than ready to make our arrangement legal and permanent. The subject of children had come up only occasionally, and I think we were in agreement that neither of us was really ready to take that enormous, irrevocable step while we were still struggling with the idea of exchanging rings and taking vows. But like the marriage idea, Jackie was far more predisposed to the idea than I was.

By seven o'clock, the pall of the day was deepening enough that I decided I wasn't likely to come up with a story that sounded any less offensive than the truth. Certainly nothing believable enough to get me off the hook with Jackie. I couldn't reasonably expect to shift the blame to anyone else, or even deflect a reasonable-sized portion of it from myself. So I settled in as best I could with the shame of the moment and turned the wheel toward home.

Tolland Street was never a particularly upscale section of East Hartford. Not even in its prime, which was several decades past by the time Jackie and I had moved there. The apartment we shared was small, with creaky floor boards and rotted old window frames. But it was home. More often than not, I felt at least a little bit better about life when I pulled into my parking space on the dirt driveway and put the workaday world behind me for another night. At least I was free until the sun came up again. That's how I saw it anyway.

On that Friday night, I didn't feel better in the least as I rolled to a stop in the driveway. I think I remember feeling a bit nauseous actually. Which was hardly unwarranted under the circumstances. I'd already had a pretty bad day. The fact that it was almost surely going to be capped off by a night of angry finger-pointing, deep personal embarrassment, loud bickering and possibly even threats of abandonment left me feeling less than enthusiastic. It was with great trepidation that I slowly made my way up the wooden steps to the front porch and the entryway to our apartment.

Jackie had long ago given up any pretense of being the suffering, supportive wife type.

I took a moment before turning the doorknob to catch my breath, compose my first few sentences in my head and prepare myself for the onslaught that would almost certainly be coming my way. Jackie had been warning me for months to pull myself together and find a more positive attitude toward my life, my job and our relationship. I had no illusions about how she was going to take the news. From the moment I opened that door, I knew I was going to be in for a long and difficult evening.

I didn't know the half of it.

CHAPTER 3

A long, drawn-out screech of protest came from the hinges as I pushed the old wooden door open. My head was turned down toward the floor, in a naturally defensive position. My eyes were closed tight in a vain attempt to gather the last of my inner strength before the unavoidable verbal barrage tore me down and made me feel like even less of a man. Then, in a moment of bold action, I willed myself through the doorway, announcing my arrival loudly as I marched into the room.

"Jackie, I'm ho…"

The words died in midair. My foot swung into the apartment and froze to the floor as if Super Glued to the ancient pine boards on contact. I was flabbergasted.

The apartment was as clean as a whistle. Not a single article of furniture or clothing cluttered the room. There was nothing but floor, windows and walls behind our front door. The apartment had been emptied of every shred of evidence that living people inhabited that space. It had been swept clean of absolutely everything.

I recovered momentarily and began to slowly, suspiciously move through the front room in the direction of the dining area. Finding nothing there either, I crept into the kitchen and then the tiny bedroom behind that. There was nothing. Not a single item remained. The furniture was gone. The bedroom closet was devoid of clothing. The cutlery had been removed from the kitchen drawers. The pots and pans and dishes, even the drinking glasses had disappeared from the cupboards.

Wandering like a zombie through the empty rooms, mumbling nonsensical things to myself that even I didn't understand, I found myself back at the front door.

"She's gone." The voice shook me from my trance.

"What?" I asked, completely beside myself with confusion and a fast-growing sense of fear.

"She's gone. She left this morning, right after the van arrived." The voice belonged to Mrs. Wisniewski, who inhabited the apartment on the second floor. She stood in the hallway, just outside my front door.

"The van." I repeated her words as if saying them myself would make them more meaningful, somehow easier to understand. "What van?" I demanded.

"The moving van." She spat the words out as if she was talking to a complete idiot. "There were two men that came this morning with a moving van. She gave them some instructions and then she left." Mrs. Wisniewski craned her neck to see further into the apartment. In a self-satisfied voice, she intoned, "It looks like they got everything, all right."

"Where did she go?" I pleaded, my mental distress growing by leaps and bounds. The elderly woman from upstairs was smug, my fast-growing sense of confusion and discomfort seemed to please her somehow.

"Oh," she stepped back slightly, as if she was offended that I'd asked a rude question or impugned her reputation. "I don't know," she said. Then, steeling her gaze, she added with venom, "And if I did know I certainly wouldn't tell you."

"Why not?" I begged, incredulously. "What did I do?" I was on the verge of tears.

"Well, I'm sure I don't know." Mrs. W. absolved herself of all responsibility with the wave of a boney hand. "But it must have been something awful to drive away such a wonderful girl."

I stared at my upstairs neighbor in disbelief.

"You ought to be ashamed of yourself." Mrs. Wisniewski literally spat at me, little flecks of spittle spraying in a tumultuous wind as it escaped her mouth. Then she wrapped her tattered housecoat tightly around her emaciated frame, tottered around in a half circle and feebly marched back up the stairs. For a good minute or more, I could hear her shuffling up to her own apartment with as much indignation and rancor as a woman of her advanced years could muster.

I was alone. Completely, absolutely alone in the world. Standing in the middle of my living room, surrounded by nothing but memories, questions and doubts, I didn't have the slightest idea what to do. It was several minutes before I had even an inkling of what my next move might be. Finally, with no better ideas presenting themselves, I closed the front door and locked it. I moved myself to the kitchen. Doing something seemed preferable to doing nothing. Even if the something I chose to do was pointless and vague.

My emotional state was under heavy assault. I could feel my nerves fraying, even as my stomach lobbied for attention by making its empty condition known with a series of loud rumbles. I needed to eat something, anything, in an effort to get my mind working more clearly and focus on the dilemma at hand.

I inspected the refrigerator, only to find that my empty stomach would have to wait. There was nothing on the shelves or in the door to make a meal of. Even the small box of baking soda Jackie had religiously kept in the freezer was gone.

Spinning around the empty room, I felt dizzy. Whipping my head this way and that, I looked hopelessly for any sign of something familiar other than the general shape of the kitchen. I was stunningly unsuccessful. And so I stopped and began the process of consciously working to calm my nerves.

"It's going to be all right," I told myself. As if repeating that mantra over and over would help somehow. Looking back, I don't think I had any idea of what I was talking about. The magnitude of my situation had yet to sink in completely. But I knew instinctively that when it did, I would be in even worse shape for the realization of my plight.

It was getting considerably darker outside. The street light planted next to the driveway flicked on, casting its blue-tinged rays through the bare kitchen window. A sudden urge to cry passed fairly quickly.

My profound sense of confusion left me feeling moderately stoned. As if I'd smoked a joint, or downed half-a-dozen beers in quick succession. Not an ideal reaction, admittedly. But under the circumstances, it wasn't an altogether unwelcome sensation. I can only say that I was lightheaded, dizzy, and no longer acutely aware of any human emotions or desires that were recognizable to me. Save one. I had to pee.

The bathroom was small, located at the back of the house, just off the kitchen. It was there that I stumbled upon the only clues I would ever find as to what had happened over the course of that day while I was off losing my job.

An old, somewhat discolored, claw-footed tub took up the majority of the floor space in the bathroom. A shower head and curtain had been retrofitted to it long after the house had been built, but before Jackie and I had moved in.

The curtain had been pulled closed, which was unusual. So I pulled it back, half hoping to find Jackie curled up in the bottom of the tub giggling, as if she'd just pulled the greatest April Fool's Day joke of all time. But it wasn't April Fool's Day, and Jackie wasn't curled up, lovingly waiting for me to discover her.

The tub was full of water, almost to the point of overflowing. In the water were clothes. Lots of clothes. All of them mine. It seems that Jackie had taken a shot at making a statement of some sort as she left me. She'd opted to drown my clothes in the tub. Which in the scheme of things, was preferable to her having drowned me there, as I imagine she was hinting was her original impulse.

The other clue I found was equally personal. It was a note, unsigned, but clearly written by Jackie. I found it taped to the mirror over the bathroom sink. Like the drowned clothes, the note wasn't very specific, but regardless of what the long version might have said, the abbreviated text got the point across well enough. She'd written only one word, followed by an exclamation mark. Her thoughts were underlined twice. And brief as they were, her parting note was sufficiently straightforward for even for even a dunderhead like me to understand.

The note said, "Enough!"

"Okay," I whispered to myself as I reread the page over and over again. "I get it."

CHAPTER 4

Four-and-a-half months passed from the day I'd come home to find Jackie gone, along with everything I owned in the world. A pile of soggy clothes excepted, of course. I'd like to be able to say that I'd been doing something productive over those many weeks. But I hadn't. I was doing nothing, more or less. Although, on the day that presented me with my next open door, yet another all-important opportunity that I could either take advantage of or discard, I was finally doing something. Specifically, I was making a list.

Sitting at a folding card table in the dining room, just two short days away from officially being three months behind on the rent, I was writing out a list on a yellow legal pad.

Eviction was in the wind.

I was what you might call destitute at that point. Other than the card table I sat at, and the folding chair I was sitting on, I owned nothing.

Until those few months of dread and depression, I had no idea that stress could be so…stressful. I was learning though. Oh, yes, I was learning.

The only person I'd had any direct contact with over those four-and-a-half months was my upstairs neighbor, Mrs. Wisniewski. The same woman who had delivered the news about Jackie's unexpected departure. I think it would be safe to say that Mrs. Wisneiwski and I were not on particularly good terms. Although that didn't stop her from knocking on my door from time to time. Especially if she needed a fresh fix of joy, which seemed available to her almost exclusively as a result of her witnessing my despair first hand.

Mrs. Wisniewski was short, slight and decidedly unattractive. She didn't subscribe to cable television, own a DVD player or go out to the movies. Her idea of entertainment was limited to the act of spying on her neighbors and checking her mailbox for new arrivals every two to three hours from dawn until dusk. Looking back on it now, I don't think her amusement at my plight was really intended to be mean spirited. I think she may have been conducting herself in more of a misery loves company sort of way.

As I understood her situation, Mr. Wisniewski had left his wife years before I ever moved into the rundown apartment on Tolland Street. Why he left her was apparently as much a mystery to her as I found the enigma of exactly why Jackie had left me. Maybe that's the way these things work. There's no explanation, just action followed by either regret or anger or relief. A given individual's reaction to a breakup seems to depend largely on their role in the relationship as the events unfold.

I sincerely hoped I'd never become as bitter and lonely as old Mrs. W. was. Although the odds were that I would if I didn't do something to drastically alter my situation.

As fate would have it, I was at that very moment planning to make a change. A big change. One that would take effect quickly and permanently.

I'd wondered occasionally over the preceding months if people like Mr. Wisniewski and Jackie had some insight into the phenomenon of abandonment from the perspective of the party who hotfoots it out the door. But I doubted they'd be all that interested in talking about it. I suspected they'd rather put the whole episode behind them. Somehow, I doubted they even thought about us, the ones they'd left behind. I had no evidence to support the theory. But it seemed to me that when they packed their bags and went, in their minds they were moving on and moving up in the world. I wasn't entirely sure they didn't think of themselves as the good guys. At least from their point of view, they were doing something about the situation. Mrs. W. and I were apparently content to maintain the status quo, even if that meant perpetuating the strangulation we felt as a result of being tied down in a dying relationship.

I'm not saying they're good people, or bad people, mind you. Just that I think they see themselves as the better of the two people involved. In the end, maybe they were.

As it was, I hadn't slept well in months. Which is understandable I suppose. But I was finding my natural sense of melancholy had been exacerbated by a relentless case of sleep deprivation. The frame of mind that resulted was less than ideal, as you can imagine.

Laying before me on my pathetic little card table, which I'd bought at Wal-Mart a few days after Jackie pulled up stakes and hit the road, were a yellow legal pad and a growing pile of incoming mail. The most recent batch had been delivered earlier in the day. Those few, new envelopes sat on top of what was becoming an impressively large and persistently disheveled pile.

Taking a break from list making, I waded through the latest collection from my mailbox.

Almost all of the envelopes contained bills. Several of which I hadn't been bothering to pay, since they seemed so inappropriate under the circumstances. The most recent message from the cable company told me in no uncertain terms that they intended to terminate my service if I didn't pay up immediately. Which seemed fair enough. I hadn't paid them since Jackie left. Partly because I'd become increasingly morose and had no real interest in the day-to-day activities of life, like paying bills. And partly because Jackie took the television. My logic at the time was, if I'm not using the cable hook up I don't see why I have to pay for it. Certainly, the whole thing could have been cleared up with a simple phone call. But she took the phone too. And I'd be damned if I was going to spend any of my very limited legal tender on a phone that I'd only use to cancel my accounts.

The letter from the Southern New England Telephone Company made the whole situation moot. I apparently didn't have working phone service anymore, anyway. Although I did owe a substantial bill. Much of it resulting from a flurry of long distance calls made over the week preceding The Unpleasantness. That's the term I'd decided to use rather than explain the whole long story that begins with, "I got fired," segues into, "She left me," and gave every indication that it was headed for an ending that whines, "I've been evicted and have nowhere to go." Hence, I'd decided to go with The Unpleasantness. Not that I had anyone to share my story with. I was as alone on that November day as I had been every day since being let go by Ted Winters. I'd hardly had a conversation with another living human being since.

Alone among the bills and "Current Resident" mass mailing offers to refinance my home, or install vinyl siding, or buy a full set of replacement windows that incorporated the latest revolutionary energy efficient window technology, was a single hand-lettered envelope. It was significantly worse for wear, as if a postal employee had kept it in his lunch box for a week or two before actually dropping it into my mail slot. The handwriting on the envelope was strong and bold, made with black ink. Upon looking inside, I found the lettering on the page to be shaky, thin and weak. The ink was blue and very faint, in places it was nearly indecipherable. It was obvious the letter and envelope had been composed by different hands.

I read it twice, not really grasping the point of it either time. My head hurt and I was tired. Not tired in the sense that I could have used a nap. More like the tired you feel after you've been physically hurt in a sudden and violent manner. Tired like there's a truck parked on your chest and you just don't see the point of it all anymore.

Folding the letter up and putting it back into its envelope, I tucked it into my shirt pocket. And I'm not positive, but I think I must have fallen asleep for a little while right there at my folding card table, in the middle of my barren dining area, while uncomfortably perched on one of Wal-Mart's least expensive folding chairs.

When I raised my head back up, I felt a twisted sort of enjoyment at the totality of the failure my life represented. Virtually everything I owned was assembled within a few feet of where I sat. It could have all been neatly stacked into a single box, had I wished to. It was stunning to realize that I had so little to show for myself after 42 years of life. And I was alone to boot.

Strange things pop into your head when you're under significant mental stress. On that particular day, I remember thinking that when I was a kid, the radio used to broadcast a trendy slogan. It was a popular saying of the late 1960's and early 1970's that was often found on posters pinned or taped onto the bedroom walls of idealistic teenagers. The slogan was this. "Today is the first day of the rest of your life!"

If that was true, I was painfully aware that I wasn't off to a very auspicious start.

When I'd originally sat down, before the mail distracted me and an industrial-sized case of ennui had overcome me, my goal had been to do what I had always done when faced with a complicated situation that seemed hopeless. I'd intended to write out a list of the pros and cons of my current dilemma and see if that information, arranged in cold clinical terms, could possibly lead me in the direction of a solution. A positive solution, hopefully. A way out from under this total disaster that my life had become.

That sounds like a reasonably mature way of dealing with adversity, doesn't it?

What I was really doing, however, was splitting my time between doodling on my previously crisp, clean, legal pad, and seriously contemplating suicide.

Twirling my pen with my index finger on the flat, yellow lined surface of the legal pad, I found it difficult to concentrate. Had I been a braver man, I suppose I might have gotten up from my folding chair and begun a search of the apartment for methods that suited me. But as it was, I just sat there and doodled, absently spinning my pen with my finger while considering the relative merits of an overdose of various over-the-counter medications as opposed to asphyxiation or drowning. I guess you could say that I was lost in my own thoughts, misdirected and maladjusted as they were. If I had to pick a single word to describe my state of mind, I'd have to go with hopelessly lost. Which is in fact, two words. But you get my point.

In the olden days, I might have just cranked up the oven, closed all the windows and doors and taken a terminal nap. But of the many wonders of the modernized world, an all-electric kitchen doesn't lend itself to a clean and painless end. Drowning myself in the tub wasn't particularly appealing, either. Since that would require a fair amount of personal discipline, which I just didn't have much of at that moment.

The left side of my legal pad held the cons portion of my list. Below that heading were the words, "alone," "savings depleted," "unemployed," "hopeless."

As was the case four-and-a-half months before, my stomach began growling just as my despair was reaching a crescendo. That gnawing emptiness in my mid-section distracted me from the idea of ending it all and got me thinking about dinner. As luck would have it, I still had the proceeds of my last unemployment check in my wallet. It wasn't enough to put much of a dent in the bill I owed for my back rent. My impending homelessness was all but unavoidable and I knew it. But those few dollars certainly carried enough weight to fill my belly and get me through one more night. Tomorrow would have to find its own solutions.

The suicide brainstorming session could wait a day, but only a day. It was too cold outside to be homeless in Connecticut, and it was only November. Life was only going to get worse from here on out. Unless of course, I put a stop to it before things got completely out of hand.

Having resolved nothing, and yet wasted a whole day in the process, I got up. Time was slipping away and I was very aware that life was passing me by. No matter how you looked at it, the light at the end of my own personal tunnel was getting dimmer. Eventually I expected it to go out entirely. If I had anything to do with it, that day would come sooner rather than later.

Grabbing my wallet off the kitchen counter, I headed for the back door, through the empty kitchen. But before I got close enough for my hand to grip the knob, the doorbell rang.

The buttons that activated the chimes for each of the three floors of my building were located on the front porch. Which meant the two tenants who lived above me in that dilapidated three-family house had to lean out over their warped and swaying porch railings to see who was down below. Only then could they make an informed decision as to whether they would admit or reject their callers. As for myself, being the first floor resident, I alone had the dubious honor of greeting my guests face to face in order to answer the mystery of who was ringing my bell.

Oh, lucky me.

My instincts were to head out the back door and forget it. I hadn't had a visit from a friend in…well, I didn't have any friends left to tell the truth. And while I wasn't worried that it was a bill collector, I was cynically suspicious that the finger on the other end of that chime circuit wasn't likely to bring me anything but more trouble. Yet somehow, I found myself walking toward the front door, tentatively. I swung it open with only a second's hesitation and stepped out onto the porch. I don't know why I did it, as averse as I was to engaging any other living person in even the briefest of conversations, but I did. That's the truth of the matter.

What I found there on my porch, aside from layers upon layers of unsightly paint that was chipping and peeling off the decking and two badly torn screens lying there that should have been fitted into my front windows, was an absolutely pitiful man. If it's possible, I recall thinking, he looked even more pathetic than I did.

The vagrant's hair flew in a thousand different directions. No two strands seemed to be coordinated in the least. Even in the November chill of southern New England, he wore no coat. Instead he was clad in an oversized gray sweatshirt that was so ill-fitting I would have bet it came from either a Goodwill drop-off bin or an unguarded clothes line. The white T-shirt underneath hung loosely around his scrawny, chicken neck. His jeans were well worn and baggy. Not the stylish sort of designer baggy pants that kids wear. These looked more like hand-me-down baggy pants. The kind you wear because they're your only option, not because you like them. His eyes were sunken deep into their sockets and outlined by dark circles. He looked old and worn down. How old was anyone's guess. But he'd seen better days, that was for sure.

I determined right away that I was facing either a junkie, or a fearless panhandler who'd moved up from street corners to begging on the front steps of his potential benefactors. The thought occurred to me that he should have picked another neighborhood. A better one. He wasn't likely to find much sympathy here in the most run down, unemployment rich section of East Hartford. There was no doubt about that in my mind.

The two of us locked eyes for a moment, neither seeming to have any idea what to say or do. After a few uncomfortably silent seconds, I began to form the words, "Can I help you?" but the vagrant beat me to the punch. A short, sharp jab aimed directly at the center of my brain. He connected with the full power of a diesel locomotive, the formidable blow innocently disguised in the form of a simple question.

"Hi Frank, I'm Danny Loughman. Do you remember me?"

CHAPTER 5

For the moment I was caught in a mental loop. The mere mention of the name Danny Loughman brought back a flood of memories. However, the sight of someone claiming to be Danny shook me badly and pushed my mental faculties to their limits. My brain shifted into reverse and accelerated back through three decades of my life in a desperate search for solid recollections of Danny to compare with the feeble, wayward man unsteadily rocking back and forth before me.

I had known a Danny Loughman once, many years before. He was my closest friend from the age of 11 until we went our separate ways a couple years after graduating high school. We were inseparable in those days, Danny and me. But this man on my porch looked nothing like the Danny I remembered. It pained me to even entertain the idea they might be one in the same man.

"Danny Loughman?" I said, as much to myself as to anyone else. I hadn't uttered the name in so many years. Those syllables felt oddly foreign as they fell from my lips.

"Uh huh," the scruffy vagrant responded. He was avoiding eye contact, tucking his face downward to the porch floor. He was squinting fiercely too, as if bright sunlight was causing him pain.

It had been more than 30 years since the Loughman's had moved into the small ranch-style house across the street from the one my family occupied on Burke Street. They moved in the week after school let out. The magical attraction of summer was in full swing. Under normal circumstances, it doesn't take long for two boys with similar goals to become fast friends in the summer time. It took Danny and me no time at all.

Our section of East Hartford was a great place for kids to live. Only a block from our school on May Road, there were seemingly endless playgrounds along with a public swimming pool and ball fields nearby. Our whole world was within a five minute walk from our front doors.

The thing that bound us together initially was our mutual desire to spend as much time away from home as possible. We both had good reasons for wanting to stay out of our respective houses. Lots of kids do, I suppose. Luckily for us, we rarely had to suffer alone, dodging our families as much as we did. We had each other for company. During the formative years of a young man's life, that can be a big deal. Our friendship certainly became a big deal for Danny and me.

Danny's father had a drinking problem. Not that he was a raging drunk who beat his family and terrorized the neighborhood. He was a lot more subtle than that. A casual neighbor wouldn't, and as far as I know, never did notice there was a problem. It was invisible unless you paid close attention. Which almost nobody did in those days. Not in our tidy little suburban corner of the world at least.

Yet the Loughman's lived in an almost constant state of embarrassment, shamed at the thought of their neighbors finding out the sad truth about Danny's dad and his battle with the bottle. Theirs wasn't a happy home. But it was quiet. And we learned soon enough that the appearance of order was usually enough for most adults to assume all was well. A quiet block was a normal block.

Normal carried a lot of weight in those days. I guess it still does in some circles.

Mr. Loughman worked construction for a living. He was a heavy equipment operator. Filtered through the eyes of an 11-year-old boy, a man who can operate a back hoe or a bulldozer is just about as cool as a professional ball player or an astronaut. And that's just what Mr. Loughman was for us. Cool. So unbelievably cool.

When he was involved in projects close enough to home, Danny and I would ride our bikes to the work site just to watch the big machines do their thing.

Danny was awfully proud of his dad. At least he was during the daylight hours. He didn't talk about the man much once the sun went down, though. Nights were very different from the days at the Loughman house.

On summer evenings, when we didn't have to be up for school early the next day, our mothers would let us stay out late playing in the neighborhood.

Just on Burke Street, of course. We weren't allowed to stray any farther than the corner of O'Connell Drive or there would be trouble. At least that's what we were led to believe by our mothers.

Mr. Loughman stayed out of sight. Mrs. Loughman would tell anyone who might ask about him that her husband wasn't feeling well, that he had gone to bed early. In truth, he was drunk. Sloppy, whining, crying about his life and missed opportunities, drunk. On the really bad nights, Danny's mom would keep turning up the old black-and-white Magnavox television set in the living room, making it progressively louder and louder in the hopes of masking the sounds of Mr. Loughman wailing away in the bedroom on the other side of the wall.

"Hey Frank, wanna have a catch? We can still see the ball if we keep it under the street light," Danny would offer on such nights.

"Sure," I'd answer quickly, running to grab my glove in the twilight. Neither of us was oblivious to the situation. Although we both pretended to be just as hard as we could.

By the time we were 13 or so, Danny and I had developed an interest in music. Which is really just a euphemism for the fact that we had developed an intense fascination with girls. As dopey and slow as we were, we recognized that girls were drawn to boys with guitars like bees to honey. So we began to teach ourselves how to play. We were truly awful. But we had big dreams that somehow buoyed our spirits and inoculated us from the horrible sounds we made in Danny's garage after school.

In the beginning, we copied the music we heard on the radio. WCCC and WHCN were the big rock stations across the river in Hartford. Sometimes we'd hook up our little tape recorders and try to save snippets of songs we heard broadcast from New Haven on WPLR, which was the center of the galaxy as far as we were concerned. New York City was only 120 miles away, but it might as well have been another universe. We couldn't even imagine touching a toe in such a faraway and exotic land as New York City.

With lots of practice, by the time we entered high school, Danny and I had gotten a whole lot better at playing our instruments. Danny took to playing like a duck to water. He had a real knack for the guitar, although he took every opportunity to bang on a beat-up, well used and way-out-of-tune piano he'd bought at a yard sale. It didn't come as naturally to me as it did to my partner. But with enough work and determination, almost anyone can become passable at the guitar. Which was about the level of competence I eventually attained. I was passable.

In our sophomore year at Penney High, we formed our own band. Marc Patnoe, a classmate from up on Oak Street, played bass. When he started, I don't think he ever played any song the same way twice. But like Danny and me, he got considerably better over time.

We chose Bobby Yount from Eldridge Circle as our drummer for two reasons. The most important being that he actually owned a set of drums and as far as we could tell, he could play them without losing his sense of time. But maybe more important than that, he didn't mind helping us carry our amplifiers whenever we had a gig at a local school or church dance. These were the days before solid state circuitry transformed amplifiers into neat little packages as small and light as toaster ovens. Our amplifiers were back breakingly heavy Ampeg models. Even today I wouldn't be the least bit surprised to find that the main building material for those clunkers was granite, or possibly lead. Maybe it was a combination of the two.

Our band was called "The Mayfair's," although I can't for the life of me remember why. We developed a pretty fair local following too. A fact that I'm as proud of now as I ever was.

The more serious we got, the more gigs we picked up. And it wasn't long before Danny and I were letting our schoolwork slide in favor of writing together, trying desperately to produce a hit song that would take us far away from East Hartford, and the life we were trying so hard to avoid there. By the end of our senior year, I doubt any of our teachers at good old Penney High had seen us in a month. But amazingly, we both graduated. To this day, I credit that fact to a fortuitous clerical error. I can't imagine either of us really earned enough credits to be awarded a diploma on our own.

Danny and I continued to play almost every day after school ended. Neither of us were hanging our hopes on college. At least not to begin with. We limped along as a semi-working band for about a year, but midway through the following summer I had something of an epiphany; It was time to grow up and earn a living. If the band started bringing in some real money, well then my decision was made for me. If not, I had no idea what I might do.

"I'm not so sure about this anymore, Danny."

"Keep your shirt on, Frank," was my old friend's constant reply. "The Rolling Stones weren't built in a day."

Believe me when I tell you, The Mayfair's were nowhere near threatening The Rolling Stones' solid position at the top of the rock 'n' roll pyramid. We were good, but we weren't the sort of band anyone would camp out overnight to buy tickets to see.

The clubs in Hartford were only interested in booking bands that would play covers of the songs that were playing on the radio. We'd already been that route during our high school years and had no interest in repeating ourselves. Besides, we were far too impressed with what we might be able to accomplish as songwriters to be willing to go back to the days of playing other people's music exclusively. We stood our ground and remained gig-less until Marc and Bobby got so bored of doing nothing but rehearsing, they left the band for more lucrative employment in the food service industry. Bobby washed dishes at The Farm Shop in Glastonbury. Marc worked the fryers across the street at McDonald's. They were both 20 years old when we parted ways. I never saw either of them again.

Danny and I continued to write songs together and separately, doing our best to emulate the style and success of Lennon and McCartney while sweating up a storm in Danny's garage throughout the summer months.

The four of us were about to transition into adulthood. And the one thing I knew for sure was that none of us was handling that task particularly well to that point. It was quite a shock to consider all the decisions, compromises and disappointments that change was likely to entail for each of us. In all honesty, I found the idea of growing up to be terrifying.

Over the course of that summer of last hurrahs, I realized that the likelihood of my face being featured on the cover of Rolling Stone magazine was slim. Surreptitiously, I began looking at other, more practical career options for my future.

Danny did not. He was indefatigable. To his credit, he did his best to keep me focused, offering encouragement on an almost daily basis.

"You're a musician, Frank. You were born to be an artist."

"I'd like to believe that's true, Danny, but I just don't know any more."

Danny and I were drifting in different directions. It was a silent parting of the ways, without arguments, fisticuffs or tantrums. But we were clearly beginning to head down different paths in life. That fact was becoming increasingly apparent.

In the end, I was the one who irrevocably fractured our relationship. Without mentioning my intentions to my partner, my longtime friend, I signed up for technical school. My intention was to buckle down, become a regular guy and study electronics. At least then I might have a secure future ahead of me.

In retrospect, I don't know how much of that idea was mine and how much could reasonably be attributed to my father. I suspect I can only blame him for so much of my downfall though. So at least in this case, I'll take full responsibility for what I did.

I filled out forms and bought books and took out a low-interest student loan that was scheduled to take me 10 years to pay off. I was going to be somebody. Somebody who had control of his own destiny. I was going to have money in my pocket and a life I could look forward to.

At least that's the way I thought it was going to be. Admittedly, things turned out a little differently than I'd planned. Which is why I don't gamble. I'm just no good at it.

"You did what?" Danny demanded when I broke the news.

"I signed up for school. No biggie."

"No biggie? Seriously, that's what you're going to say at a time like this. No biggie?" Danny was apoplectic. He knew I wouldn't have time for building a band with him, rehearsing, traveling, doing all the things we'd need to do in order to make our teenage dreams become a reality.

"Yeah, I don't see what the big deal is, Danny?" Although I did. I knew perfectly well what the big deal was. Danny knew it too.

"Well, I guess that's it then isn't it?" Danny threw up his hands in disgust, then collapsed onto his piano stool in quiet despair.

"If that's the way you want it to be."

I put the breakup on him, coward that I was. Then I left the Loughman's garage for the last time.

No car had ever been parked in that space. The garage had served exclusively as our shared rehearsal and work space for the previous six years. And I walked away without another word. A decision I regretted immediately and for years after. So much so that I'd pushed it from my memory for the most part. But not completely.

The last time I'd seen or spoken to Danny Loughman was 22 years behind me. And this tired, wiry, weather beaten man on my porch didn't look anything like him. My old friend must have fallen on even harder times than I had, I thought.

"Yeah…I remember you, Danny." I looked up and down Tolland Street for a car, or a friend that was traveling with him. Nothing caught my eye. "Where'd you come from?"

"That's a pretty long story," he replied sheepishly.

"Well, what are you doing here?" I asked, keeping my distance. I didn't extend a hand or open my arms to offer a warm welcome. Nearly frozen to the porch by a combination of confusion and trepidation brought on by this shadow of my past swaying before me like one of Charles Dickens' ghosts, I was at a loss for words. I had no idea at all what to do.

Danny looked worn and weary. He looked like I felt, diseased and broken.

"That's sort of a long story, too," he offered hesitantly. Then he shuffled his feet nervously and looked up at me, gazing directly into my eyes for the first time. He maintained eye contact for a moment or two then hung his head again and said mournfully, "I'm sorry. It's been a long time." He heaved a heavy sigh and added, "Yeah, a really long time. I should go…"

His voice trailed off as he turned and cautiously put one foot in front of the other, carefully working his way toward the creaky wooden steps.

"No, don't go," I blurted out. "I'm sorry. You just sort of caught me off guard." I felt genuinely apologetic as I gingerly reached out to take his arm and guide my old friend back toward the front door. "Why don't you come inside?"

His arm felt even thinner than it looked under his baggy sweater. It brought to mind the image of a broomstick in a sleeping bag. Danny was truly nothing more than skin and bones.

He swayed slightly, caught off balance by my rapid change of heart. But he recovered quickly and with the aid of my grip to steady him, he accepted the offer to follow me back into the apartment. It wasn't until I was closing the door behind the two of us that I snapped back to my current reality. Which was that I had escorted Danny into an almost totally barren space, devoid of any furnishings save for the card table and the single folding chair in the next room. I steered him toward the chair while stumbling through a feeble excuse. There was no point. It would be impossible to gracefully extricate myself from a situation that I was both unable and unwilling to fully explain.

"Why don't you have a seat," I said softly. "I've just got to get something from the bedroom."

Danny slumped into the chair without a sound, his head turned downward as it had been outside. He made no mention of the apartment's lack of furnishings. As a matter of fact, he didn't say anything at all.

Not a single piece of framed art or even a clock hung on the walls. It was impossible for him to miss the obvious, no matter how badly he'd been mangled by life or drugs or whatever. And the obvious was this; I was a loser leading a 100-percent, dyed-in-the-wool wasted life.

I excused myself and walked through the small kitchen toward the back bedroom, feeling a growing sense of shame more powerful than I'd ever experienced before.

Three steps later, as I disappeared into my bedroom, I heard Danny's voice. It was soft. Just a whisper really. I could barely make it out above the sound of my own breathing.

"What's that?" I asked, spinning back in his direction.

"Thank you," he whispered.

I hesitated for a moment, not knowing how to respond, then stepped back into my room, closed the door and began to cry.

I hadn't cried when I lost my job, or when I came home to find Jackie gone. I didn't cry at my mother's funeral, only three days after the car accident that took her life. But now, with the realization that I was indeed a lonely, lost, beaten man, even when compared to a withered junkie, or whatever Danny had turned out to be, well, that was too much for me to take.

I didn't come out for nearly half an hour.

I guess I wasn't much of a host either.

CHAPTER 6

The problem with disappearing on a guest for a long period of time is that it's a bit awkward to reappear again without offering some sort of plausible explanation for your absence. To be honest, I hadn't really thought of that when I closed the bedroom door and had my little breakdown. But as I began to pull myself together again, it occurred to me that I'd been gone far longer than was reasonable. I didn't want to pop back into the room looking like I'd been crying. Teary, red, puffy eyes aren't a particularly manly look in the first place. And it's certainly not a look one wants to present when welcoming a guest into an apartment that looks about as lived in as an empty packing crate.

The next few moments were likely to be embarrassing, but I didn't see any way of getting around the inevitable. I stood with my forehead pressed against the bedroom door for a good minute or two. My right hand was poised on the knob, but somehow I found it difficult to take that first big step into acceptance and turn the handle. Eventually, I had to open the door and rejoin the emaciated man I'd left alone in my dining area. I knew that. But I was procrastinating until I could think of a way of returning with at least a modicum of dignity. In the end, my embarrassment at being gone for so long overcame my mental machinations. I threw open the door and walked boldly into the kitchen as if all was well with the world.

Danny remained, frail and gray, precariously perched on that rinky-dink Wal-Mart folding chair, just as I'd left him. He was deathly still. Maybe he really was a junkie? Junkies pass out all the time, don't they? Maybe they lose track of time too.

I could only be so lucky.

It dawned on me that my guest's apparent lack of awareness could work in my favor. So, I decided to ignore the whole disappearance issue and soldier on. It never happened.

"You want a beer?" I asked.

It was a reflexive sort of question. The words were out of my mouth and gone before I could stop them. The refrigerator was in very nearly the same condition as the rest of the apartment. For all I knew, I didn't have a single beer left, let alone two.

"Thanks," he replied quietly, "I'd like that."

Danny didn't move an inch. Even his lips were frozen, as if he were nothing more than a ventriloquist's dummy left unattended in the middle of my dining room. Where the man pulling the strings might be, was anybody's guess.

I pulled the refrigerator open and was relieved to see two Rolling Rocks in the door. How I'd forgotten about having beer on hand, I had no idea. It's not like I had anywhere to go or anything to do most of the time. I suppose I should be glad that I hadn't developed a drinking problem during the previous four months, like Mr. Loughman had years before. As luck would have it, my addiction was more of a staring at the wall and regretting my life sort of problem. To characterize the man I was then as suffering from an extreme lack of ambition would be kind.

I opened the two cold, green bottles and set one on the table in front of Danny. With no other chairs in the house I debated whether it was better to stand, or pace, or sit on the floor as I got reacquainted with this thin, pale shadow of my old neighbor, my long lost best friend. I shuffled around a bit, aimlessly. My feet grew large and unwieldy. My entire body felt awkward and ill suited for whatever purpose it was supposed to fill. I'll admit I was uneasy, but I tried hard not to show it. Really hard. And eventually, after several failed attempts, I settled into a reasonably comfortable slump against the kitchen doorway, which was as close as I could get to adopting an attitude of cool under the circumstances.

"So, how's everything over on Burke Street?" Danny asked, gazing absently out the back window of my apartment. The view carried his eyes across the street to a 7-Eleven. Not a word was spoken, not a single question raised, about my ultra-minimalist apartment.

"It's been quite a while since I've been back," I answered. I made a conscious decision not to mention that I'd been avoiding our old stomping grounds like the plague. "Eight or 10 years, I suppose."

"No kidding?" Danny perked up a bit, sounding truly surprised. He gingerly turned his head just enough to make eye contact. "You don't ever have an urge to go see your old house?"

"No," I shot back gruffly. The truth was I didn't even like thinking about Burke Street. As a matter of fact, I didn't like thinking about it so much that neither the topic, the house nor the neighborhood had passed through my waking mind in years. Even though it was all still there, not five miles away, on the other side of town. To me it was as far off as a distant galaxy, light years away from the life I chose to live. Burke Street represented a period of my life that I'd just as soon forget altogether if I could. No sir, I had no interest at all in walking down the memory lane of Burke Street and life with the good 'ol Stevens family.

While the Loughman's were an unapologetically blue-collar group, my own family, the Stevens, had white-collar aspirations. My parents held nothing so dear as their desire to move up and out of their little ranch house, into a home of greater size and status across the river in Wethersfield. Aspirations that would never be fulfilled, I might add. Not that every moment of the day and night wasn't dedicated to the proposition that we, our little nuclear unit, shouldn't have to live in the midst of laborers and high school dropouts.

That was my father's view, in any case. Which in those days meant it was the shared view of the family. Or, at the very least, the shared view of my mother. A woman who stood solidly by her man in good times and in bad. Just as the marriage vows she'd taken said she would. Even if that steadfast support resulted in occasional unexplained bruises and a never-ending stream of harsh words and personal attacks.

Tears weren't at all uncommon in the Stevens house.

It seems that for my mom, and a whole lot of women very much like her, a life of secret misery wasn't too much to endure in return for a secure home and a dependable income. I'm sure that wasn't the plan they had when they married the men they chose to spend their lives with. But it sure seemed to work out that way for an awful lot of them.

There's far more sorrow in the world than is visible to the naked eye. I wish that wasn't true, but it is. It most assuredly is.

Across the street, Danny's dad might have been a secret, nocturnal drunk, but he loved his family and did his best to provide for them with the skills he had. Danny loved his dad. And I envied Danny.

Things were a bit different on my side of the road. My father did his best to provide for himself. If that meant the rest of the family got to come along for the ride, so be it. But he made damn sure we knew how much he hated crunching numbers as a mid-level executive at the insurance company in Hartford. He was an actuary. A job I didn't understand as a kid and one that I don't care to understand much better as an adult. My father, the ever-oppressed and overlooked Warren Stevens, certainly had nothing good to say about it.

Five days a week, he'd drive his white Chevy Corvair across the river into Connecticut's capital city to add up columns of numbers, or whatever it is that actuaries do. Then he'd drive home again every week night with a plan to do nothing more constructive than to mentally beat down the wife and children who were unlucky enough to share his house with him.

I always found it ironic that we had the obligatory needlepoint wall hanging in the kitchen that read, "Bless this happy home!" I think my mother bought it at a yard sale, for cheap. It was certainly out of place, tacked up over the stove at our house.

Oh, yeah. We were thrilled to be together.

"I've always sort of missed the old neighborhood," Danny said, dreamily.

"Not me."

"Not even a little bit?"

"I don't even think about it anymore," I lied.

Granted, for all my anger and resentment, I never strayed far away from the home I loathed so much. I'd never traveled far from East Hartford in all my life. As a teenager, especially during my senior year of high school and that short period after when Danny and I were having our brief delusions of grandeur, I'd jump at the chance to go to a concert at the Coliseum in New Haven. Occasionally we'd pile into the car and head north to the Civic Center in Springfield, Massachusetts. It seems ridiculous now, but I thought New Haven and Springfield were far off exotic locations back then. I felt like I was seeing the world.

I did stay close, but I continued to spend as much time as I could out of the house. The older I got, the longer those periods of absence became. I nearly always ended up in my own bed at night. But the temptation to delay my arrival back home until as late as possible was irresistible. In retrospect, maybe that's the one advantage of having a parent who sees you as a true loser. They have so few expectations for success from you that if you were to stay out until the wee hours of the morning on the night before your SAT's, it wouldn't really surprise them.

I did that, by the way. And I performed as miserably as you might expect, bleary-eyed and sleep deprived as I was.

"So what have you been up to for the last…however many years it's been?" Danny queried.

I didn't want to get into a conversion about my current situation any more than I wanted to talk about the old days. This wasn't a conversation I wanted to have with anyone, let alone a desperate-looking junkie who I hadn't seen or heard from in two decades. Debating my options quickly, I blurted out, "Nothing much. How about you?" The words came out forcefully, with far too much intensity to be considered a conversational exchange.

Danny considered for a moment before replying in a slow, tired voice, "Yeah, I don't really want to talk about it either."

We sat in silence for a long time. If I had a timepiece to gauge the passing minutes, I might have been able to quantify the interminable delay in our blundering social intercourse. But I didn't even have a simple, two-dollar plastic clock.

"So are you back for good?" I finally asked.

"No."

"Are you staying with somebody in town?"

"No."

Our discussion was turning out to be not only somewhat forced and unnatural, but it wasn't looking like it was going to be very productive, either.

"How long are you going to be here? In town, I mean." I was stumbling through the conversation like a drunken talk show host who'd lost the will to carry on. With no idea what I was doing I began feeling increasingly self-conscious about the whole experience. I was convinced that I was mere seconds away from a verbal land mine that would go off without warning. The results would be debilitating, I was sure. An unrecoverable situation was about to occur. I could just feel it. Some might call it a psychic phenomenon. Personally, I think it's more a matter of being smart enough to recognize that you're digging yourself a really deep hole, but not smart enough to put down the shovel. Once you've had the experience, you can see it coming around on you again. The problem is you just can't seem to put your finger on exactly what's wrong until you've gone too far to prevent the impending train wreck you're about to be a witness to as well as the cause of.

"Not long, I hope. I'm sort of…passing through, more or less." Danny seemed to be fading in and out of consciousness. Long pauses strung out between his words, making it difficult to understand his meaning at times.

"Where are you passing through, to?" I asked. Surprisingly perhaps, I was finding myself to be honestly curious.

"Home," he said with some satisfaction. He smiled weakly. The younger version of Danny had often worn a big, wide-open smile that stretched across his whole face. His bright blue eyes would crinkle up in the corners. This grin was a much abbreviated version of the one I remembered, but I had to admit, it was familiar. Mine were deeply faded memories, but this hobo in my dining room had a distinct resemblance to the handsome, hopeful young man Danny had once been. He straightened himself in the chair, pulling himself more erect than he had been and announced proudly. "I'm going home, Frank."

After a short pause of my own to organize a few thoughts, I asked the pivotal question of the day. The answer to that question seemed simple enough. But as sometimes is the case with simple, unassuming questions and the answers they elicit, this one proved to be the first undeniable indicator of a major turning point in my life.

It seemed like such an innocent question at the time.

"So what brings you to come see me after 20 odd years?" I asked. I was running out of small talk and couldn't think of anything else to say.

"A ride, Frank. I'd like you to give me a ride." Danny was upbeat and surprisingly matter-of-fact about the statement, as if my answer was a forgone conclusion.

"Home? You want me to give you a ride home?" I asked with some reluctance.

"Yes, I would. If it isn't too much trouble." He sounded sincere, as if he was concerned that he might be putting me out by asking.

What could be the harm, I thought.

"OK. I guess I could give you a ride. I was just going out when you got here, anyway."

I was getting off easy. Danny was looking awfully weak and pale and I'd been starting to worry that he was going to hit me up for a place to stay. The last thing I needed was a junkie going through withdrawal on my bare floor. Yes, I can recall being filled with a sense of relief that the day wasn't going to get any worse for me. All I had to do was drop good ol' Danny off at his place and I'd be back to dealing with my own pathetic problems and their secret solutions in no time.

Taking another slug from my now warm Rolling Rock, I tried to move the conversation along and end the visit before Danny asked me for anything else, like a loan.

"We can get going whenever you want, Danny." Then, as I slipped an arm into the sleeve of my worn denim jacket I asked, "Where do you live, anyway?"

"Florida." The answer hit me like a middle linebacker.

"Florida?" I was incredulous.

"Florida. Gainesville, Florida." He said this as if it was the most natural response in the world. Danny locked eyes with me and spoke very slowly and distinctly in a soft voice, almost hypnotically. "You're sure it's not too much trouble." He was telling me, not asking my opinion. It wasn't a question.

"I...I...Ah...um...I." Try as I might, no intelligible sentence came to either my mind or my mouth. I did my best, but it just wasn't going to happen.

"Why don't you finish your beer and think about it," Danny suggested. "I'm not in any rush."

And with that Danny Loughman slumped down in my Wal-Mart folding chair, bowed his head, crossed his emaciated arms over his chest and promptly fell asleep.

CHAPTER 7

I was floored. I may have been within a few days of being homeless and destitute, but at least I had the good manners not to show up on the doorstep of an old friend I hadn't seen since the first Reagan administration, drink half his beer supply and nonchalantly ask him to drive me home. Especially when home is over a thousand miles away.

I was livid. Well not exactly livid, but pretty damned mad. What the hell was he thinking? That I would just drop my life and drive through 10 states to drop him off? What was I going to do then? Even if I did take him home, and that was one hell of a big if, I'd still have to drive all the way back to Connecticut again. By the time I got home, I wouldn't have a home to go to. My landlord, old man Peterson, would have changed the locks on my door by then for sure. I'd be out on my ass, with no place to go and no money to get there with. And who could blame Peterson for locking me out? I hadn't paid a dimes worth of rent in three months as it was.

It was at about that point in my thought process that my view of the world and my place in it began to change. If I could put aside my astonishment for a moment, it began to dawn on me, this situation might actually work in my favor.

The tea leaves were there. All I had to do was read them.

I was about to be homeless, and I was in Connecticut. Added to those two irrefutable facts, I considered quickly that winter was on its way and there was absolutely nothing I could do about forestalling the bone chilling weather that was headed for my rundown, dumpy neighborhood. So I began to wonder; Would it really be all that bad to face the same fate in Florida? At least it's warm there.

Sheepishly, I began to feel my tattered old friend out for signs of financial support.

"I'm a little tight on cash right now, Danny. Can you cover gas and meals for the trip?" Even as the words left my lips, two mutually exclusive thoughts passed through my head. One, that I couldn't believe I was even considering this idiotic idea. Second, that this was the first time I had felt excited and the least bit optimistic in a long, long time. It was just a hint of excitement, but there it was. I could feel it. A small, glowing coal of euphoria buried deep down inside. Small enough that it would require a fair amount of tending to bring to fruition. But still, it was there.

"Actually, I don't have any money with me at all," Danny replied. "But I can make it up to you when we get there." He must have sensed my lack of optimism at the thought of footing the bill entirely on my own, because without missing a beat he added, "Really." He looked sincere.

I knew that if I was going to jump in with both feet on this deal, I had no choice but to take him at his word. Which isn't an easy thing to do when the lifeboat you're hoping to grab a seat in is captained by a man who just might be in worse shape than you are. Junkies, and Danny certainly looked every bit the addict, tend not to be the most trustworthy people in the world. But all things considered, I wasn't in a position to quibble about minor details, like which one of us had the more serious debilitation. I opted to climb aboard.

It was clear to me that I was being presented with what was essentially, the last favorable option for an otherwise drowning man. I could stay put, deny Danny the ride and end up out on my ass looking just as penniless and broken as he did by the middle of next week. Or I could pack up and head for Florida on a moment's notice, spending the last of my meager savings to get from here to there.

It really wasn't that hard a decision to make.

I did a little mental math, figuring the approximate distance, the mileage my old heap was likely to get and the price of gasoline. Then I figured in 10 or 15 dollars for tolls and probably 50 bucks or so for food. We could get there, I guessed. We wouldn't be traveling in style, but we'd probably make it, provided we didn't encounter too many unexpected obstacles along the way.

"We'd have to sleep in the car," I admonished. "I can't afford any motels. And I'm not 19 anymore. There's no way I'm going to drive straight through." I wasn't trying to dissuade him as much as I was laying the facts out for both of us to consider before it was too late.

"I understand," he nodded absently.

I was about to ask if he was willing to share the driving, reasoning that we actually could drive straight through if we drove in shifts. But then again, did I really think I was going to be able to sleep with a man as unfit as Danny appeared to be manning the wheel? Whatever was wrong with him, he didn't appear to be in top form. The man could hardly stay awake long enough to participate in a conversation, let alone safely drive a couple hundred miles down an interstate highway. No, that option probably wasn't in either of our best interests. I let the idea pass without mentioning it.

If I was going to do this, I'd have to drive the whole way myself. That meant two, maybe three days on the road. We'd be eating bad food, dealing with lousy, cramped sleeping arrangements and more than likely showing up on the other end with an empty wallet. Still, it was a new lease on life. Even if it did lead me directly into the unknown. The very place I'd spent the majority of my adult life avoiding at all cost.

"Give me a couple minutes to tie up a few loose ends," I said while heading for the bedroom. "I'll take you home." Then, under my breath I whispered to myself, "What do I have to lose?"

I threw a couple handfuls of rumpled clothes into a gym bag that was lying in a heap on the closet floor. A few more handfuls went into an assortment of paper bags from Stop'n Shop. I cleaned out the bathroom cabinet, taking my toothbrush, deodorant and razor, dumping them into the same bag with my slightly ripe clothes. As I surveyed the nearly barren apartment, I was surprised to find that I was feeling a welcome sense of relief. An enormous burden was being lifted from my shoulders. I was almost giddy.

Simultaneously, I was also experiencing a twinge of melancholy as I came to the realization that my life here really was over. Jackie wasn't going to be coming back. She was gone for good, and in a few minutes, I would be too.

It had come to this. All the work, the dreams and aspirations for a brighter future were gone. I was only a few minutes away from being what I'd always feared I'd become most, a desperate, homeless loser.

An emotional wave broke over me as I realized that this wasn't a joy ride. I was running away. I was about to become a grown man who'd willingly made the conscious decision to live in his car, even if only temporarily. And as if that wasn't bad enough, I wasn't even going to be living in my car in privacy. I was going to have a roommate. A roommate who gave every appearance of being a hopeless drug addict. For all I knew, Danny was one fix away from heaven. The thought worried me, but I shook it off and finished packing.

In a flash, the obvious thought crossed my mind. What if he didn't have any money. What if Danny was as financially destitute as I was? What if he couldn't put together two dimes and a nickel when we got to Florida? It was entirely possible that I was only a few days, and eleven-hundred miles away from being a true homeless wanderer with no hope or prospects. It hurt a bit to realize that if disaster was to be the eventual outcome of this road trip, there wasn't a single person in the world who gave a rat's ass one way or the other about it, or about me.

"I'll just be one minute," I shouted over my shoulder as I lugged my mismatched and predominantly biodegradable luggage out to the driveway. Throwing my few belongings into the trunk, I twisted the house key off my key chain. Rubbing it like a talisman between my thumb and index finger, I climbed the back stairs to Mrs. Wisniewski's apartment.

My excitement had me taking the stairs two at a time, feeling more enthusiasm for living than I'd experienced in years. I knocked hard with my right hand while fingering the key in my left. Mrs. Wisniewski shuffled to the door and peered through the window for several seconds. Her expression told me she was debating whether or not she should open it. Finally she did, slowly and only as far as the safety chain would allow. Squinting disapprovingly, a long, suspicious, question escaped her paper-thin lips.

"Yyyeesssss?"

Mrs. W. was ancient and bitter beyond belief. The woman had neither trusted nor befriended anyone in all the time I'd known her. Bright red lipstick was slathered across her mouth. She applied it often and well beyond the borders of her natural lips in an attempt to make them look fuller and by extension, herself more youthful. The desired effect was entirely in her mind. The attempted ruse merely made her look clownish and silly.

My mind raced at a breakneck pace. Until that very moment, I hadn't given a single thought to what I was going to say exactly. My intention had been to simply turn in the house key and get out of Dodge before I had the chance to reconsider and waffle over the decision.

"Mrs. Wisniewski, I'm so glad you're home," I said breathlessly. In fact, in the years I'd lived in the building I'd never been aware of her not being home. She ordered her groceries by phone and had them delivered. For all I knew, she hadn't been farther than the front porch since Elvis was a boy.

"Umm humm," she replied dubiously.

"My sister Sharon…You remember me telling you about Sharon, don't you? She's the one who moved to San Diego after college. Well, she called last night and told me about a terrific job opportunity that she'd found for me out there…in San Diego…in California." I was babbling, but the story sounded reasonably good to me, so I kept going with it like a freight train on a long, downhill grade.

"Anyway, I've got to go right away because she says they won't hold the position for more than a few days. So could you please return my key to Mr. Peterson and give him my apologies for not talking to him myself? I'd really appreciate it." My feet were itching to move again. "Thanks, Mrs. Wisniewski."

I'm pretty sure I was hyperventilating. My fingertips were tingling and I felt a little wobbly.

I beat feet down the back stairs, leaving Mrs. Wisniewski standing dubiously at her door, peering through the open slit at the madman stumbling down the stairs. I grabbed Danny from the landing behind my former kitchen door and guided him toward the car. Two steps before reaching the Taurus, I heard Mrs. Wisniewski calling down shrilly from above.

"What kind of job is it that you have to leave in such a hurry? Without even a good-bye to your landlord?"

I couldn't think of anything. Sharon hadn't lived in San Diego for years. The story was a total fabrication and I was out of ideas. My mind was blank. Yet, I felt like I needed to complete the lie for some reason. I couldn't just jump in the car and disappear. Not that it would have made any difference either way.

What kind of work would I be doing if I moved to San Diego, I wondered? Where would I work if Sharon had indeed found me viable employment…in San Diego?

"The zoo," I shouted back. "She found me a job at the San Diego Zoo."

It was all I could think of. And as goofy as it sounded, I thought it was as plausible as anything else I might have come up with.

Slamming the door, I cranked the old Ford up and threw it into gear. The car was more than a decade old, but it had been a reliable ride for me to that point. Sure, it had some dents and dings. That comes with the territory. But I was confident the car would last for years to come. Certainly, it had enough oomph left in it to get me to Florida. What's another thousand miles or so to a car with more than a hundred times that many on the clock? Nothing. This would be a breeze. I felt a peculiar sense of confidence that I had no basis for. Still, it was good to feel something other than miserable again. Even if my emotions were totally unwarranted, I felt good. Sometimes, that's all you need to get up and get going.

Ten minutes later, Danny and I were motoring across the Connecticut River, with the capital city of Hartford looming on the other side. I merged smoothly from Interstate 84 onto Interstate 91 at the interchange. The traffic was still fairly light so early in the afternoon. Rush hour wouldn't be under way for at least another hour.

Danny kept himself occupied by lazily playing with the radio. He punched the preset for WPLR in New Haven and The Rooks came blasting out of the crackly speakers in the rear deck. The song was "Reasons," which seemed remarkably apt for the occasion.

Michael Mazzarella, the driving force behind The Rooks, had grown up in East Hartford, not far from my recently vacated apartment.

"I've got reasons, You've got reasons too."

The unmistakable sound of Mazzarella's voice took me back to a live show. I'd seen him perform at the Agora Ballroom in West Hartford years before. He hadn't formed The Rooks yet at that point. He was in another band, the name of which I couldn't remember. It was a good band though, with poppy three-part harmonies and a set of all original tunes. The band was a four-piece, but Mazzarella was the standout performer. All eyes were on him as he beat the hell out of the strings on his Rickenbacker guitar and wailed forlornly into the microphone.

Danny and I had set our sights on playing the Agora ourselves one day, but we never got that far. The dream of taking the stage at the most popular club in the area, which had been built on the bones of a deserted bowling alley, turned out to be beyond our reach.

I considered mentioning to my traveling companion the coincidence that the singer on the radio, Danny and I were all from East Hartford, but thought better of it. There was no point in bringing up potentially painful memories now that we were trapped together in close quarters for the next few days. Instead I sat back, kept the Taurus in the right lane and softly sang along with a song I hadn't heard in far too long.

My caution didn't matter much as it turned out. It was only a few minutes later when I realized that Danny, thin, frail and worn down as he was, had fallen asleep before we could even get clear of the city.

I was alone with my thoughts as we rolled down the highway on a trip longer and more intimidating than any I'd ever taken before. New Haven, WPLR and eventually Connecticut would be behind us as we slipped across the border, passed through a tiny corner of New York and continued south. Interstate 95 would take us all the way to the Sunshine State. I knew that from years of studying Rand McNally maps of the United States. It may not be glamorous or exciting, but everybody has to have a hobby I guess. Reading maps is mine.

There were fewer than 15 miles behind us as we cruised through Hartford's southern border with more than a thousand yet to go. But for the first time in longer than I could remember, I was excited. I was finally leaving my home state for a life that might offer me nothing, or everything. And I had absolutely no idea what I was going to do when I reached my destination. All I knew for sure was that for the next day or two, all I had to do was drive. Which is exactly what I did.

CHAPTER 8

The traffic was heavy, slow moving and seemingly endless. Our 55 mile-per-hour pace soon dwindled to 45 among the thickening mass of cars, then slowed even more. What appeared to be a difficult driving experience gradually became worse, then worse still. After three hours of driving, we were still in Connecticut. I'd expected to be in New York at least by that time. But I was mired in a slow-moving stream of steel and glass flowing ever so slowly southward, past road construction signs, heaps of refuse and the occasional abandoned vehicle.

The elation of adventure gave way to tedium one creeping car length at a time. As the sun set behind the trees to the west of Bridgeport, it became obvious that my imagined worst-case scenarios for the journey ahead were woefully inadequate. The greatest challenge didn't appear to be coming from physical discomfort as much as from mental fatigue. There, simultaneously trapped in and protected by a cocoon in the form of a mid-level sedan, so painstakingly manufactured by the Ford Motor Company of Dearborn, Michigan—I'd have given up and gone home but for one small detail. I had no home to go to anymore. I was committed. That fact alone kept my nose pointed south, as I inched ever closer to my ultimate destiny with each agonizingly slow turn of the Taurus's 15-inch wheels. My passenger was looking like a rumpled old beggar in the right seat. His feet were pulled up close, putting him very nearly in a fetal position. His arms were tucked tightly against his sunken chest and his head was bowed into a pair of folded knees. Danny looked a lot like I imagined those sacrificial mummies in the mountains of Peru must have looked before centuries of exposure to ice, wind and sun tanned their skin and dehydrated their bodies. It felt a little eerie being in the car with him.

Ahead of me, a tractor trailer displayed a prominent "How's my driving?" sticker plastered across its left-hand back door. Honestly, I had no way of answering that simple question. We were parked as often as we were driving. And when we did move, it was so slowly that there was no way to judge a given driver's ability at the wheel with any level of accuracy. The situation was maddening.

"Come on, come on," I found myself muttering in frustration to the traffic ahead of me, as if the endless line of nearly stationary cars and trucks were an independent entity. The left lane appeared to be moving much more frequently and freely than the right lane was. I was of course, stuck in that right lane. Try as I might, I was unable to extricate myself. So forward we crawled. Slowly, a few measly feet at a time, my lane mates and I crept along at a snail's pace. We were all attempting to put Connecticut behind us and we were doing a piss-poor job of it so far.

"Come on!" I silently screamed in frustration. No one heard. For all I know, the other drivers were experiencing the same frustrated, internal tantrum I was. Like me, they showed no outward signs of distress, however. Our cocoons continued to protect us from each other, even while they prevented any meaningful interaction from occurring between us. Just as they were designed to do.

Danny continued to sleep. If only I hadn't wanted someone to talk to so badly. Someone to help distract me from the nagging feeling that I had just committed myself to a horrible tactical error by leaving home so impetuously. Temporary and barren as it may have been, home is home. If I had somebody to talk to, I reasoned, I might have been less prone to anxiety as we made what little headway we could. But he slumbered away, peaceful as a baby. I, on the other hand stewed in an exhaust-rich atmosphere that I was finding increasingly detestable.

"C'mon, C'mon, C'mon!"

The traffic refused to move faster than a moderate walking pace. Long periods of immobility punctuated each brief forward movement.

Mentally reviewing the events of the day, I was struck by the irony of it all. I was terribly lonely and without a doubt a complete failure in life. I could admit that to myself, at least. But here I was, having made my big breakout move only hours before, yet I felt more lonely and isolated than ever. Even surrounded by hundreds, perhaps thousands of other drivers and passengers who were just as trapped as I was, I found no relief.

The traffic continued to advance at a painfully slow pace. The possibility of driving to Florida at 20 miles per hour or less was becoming a very real concept to me.

"Let's Go, Go, *Gooooo…*!"

I wouldn't be eating a hot meal that night. That fact was becoming increasingly clear as time ticked by so much faster than the miles did. I wouldn't be sleeping in a warm bed either. No, I'd be spending my entire evening behind the wheel, accompanied only by my own thoughts and a slumbering addict. My short-term future was assured. There was nothing left to me but the realization that I would be making a long solitary drive on that roadway and spending my last remaining dollars along the way on microwavable burritos and gasoline at a series of uninspiring roadside convenience stores.

I nudged Danny in the shins, that being the only part of his body that was accessible while he was all balled up on the seat beside me.

"Hey, are you going to sleep the whole way?"

My query was met with silence. He didn't move. He didn't even flinch. Danny was as still as a dead man, which led me to wonder if I had been unknowingly transformed from a volunteer cabbie into the driver of a bargain basement hearse.

The idea scared me. Danny had been looking a little better when we'd gotten into the car. Which is to say he didn't look as likely to fall face down on the floor as he had at first. But he didn't look healthy in terms of any accepted medical standard. I was sure of that. If he died, I wondered, how was I going to explain my situation to the authorities? There would almost certainly be authorities involved, I reasoned. You can't just pull into the Vince Lombardi Rest Stop on the New Jersey Turnpike, gas up, drop off your dead passenger and head on down the road without somebody in an official looking uniform asking a few questions. Those questions were likely to be asked in a fairly stern tone of voice, too. I was sure of that.

"Hey, Danny!" I smacked him a good one and shook his knee with my outstretched hand for good measure. "Wake up, will ya?" I shouted at him. We were stopped, still shadowing the tractor trailer with the "How's my driving?" sticker. There was no danger of going off the road due to driver inattention.

"Mmmpphhff," said Danny. He balled up even tighter and made not another sound.

He wasn't very good company, but at least he wasn't dead. Not yet at least. That was one worry off my mind.

Long stretches of silence gave me time to develop concerns about the state of the Taurus and whether or not it really could make a trip of so many miles without breaking down. I wasn't at all sure how much gas we'd need, or food, or money for tolls. The calculations I'd done mentally before leaving the apartment were all based on guesswork. In truth, I had no idea how much it might cost to make such a long trip. I had no previous experiences to base my estimates on. As time passed and the miles didn't, I became increasingly concerned about the very limited supply of dollars available for the trip. The last thing I wanted to do was run out of gas, money and luck a couple hundred miles short of our destination. But at least Danny wasn't dead. For me, that one fact became the bright spot in my world. A signal that there was at least the possibility of the beginning of a good luck streak stretching out before me.

I looked straight ahead, staring lazily at the tractor trailer's back doors, waiting for the traffic to start moving again. We were four hours into our journey and I hadn't even made it to Stamford yet. We were still in Connecticut, a state so small that it generally has to share a page on road maps with Rhode Island, its even smaller neighbor to the east.

It was going to be a long night. That much was obvious.

CHAPTER 9

Traffic was flowing reasonably well by 10:00 PM, although we'd only gotten as far as New York. Danny and I were just one state away from our starting point and several hours behind the pace I'd anticipated. I continued to be frustrated and antsy, hoping to get miles behind us as quickly as possible. Danny continued to sleep with an inspirational resolve. Nothing, it seemed, could rouse him.

I hadn't touched the radio since Danny had set it back in East Hartford, on the short stretch of Interstate 84 that took us across the Connecticut River into Hartford. Somehow the music kept playing. A hundred and fifty miles after leaving home, and without anyone changing stations, the music still poured from the tattered Taurus's speakers. The reception was clear as a bell. I chalked that peculiar detail up to some odd atmospheric anomaly, like sunspots in reverse.

Deep down, I think I knew that sunspots had nothing whatsoever to do with the phenomenon I was experiencing. But like a small child who suffers chills from an inescapable inner fear when confronted with the idea of entering a strange, dark basement—it's often easier not to think too hard about what might be hiding in the shadows. Instead, you just run out of there as fast as you can and keep on running. Logic and reason have nothing to do with some of the more important decisions we make in life. Fear, lust and greed are far more powerful motivators.

"Deep Blue Sea," by the Hometown Rockers, was playing as we rolled through the southeastern corner of New York State. Danny and I had seen them once, the Hometown Rockers that is. They were the opening act for Greg Kihn when he played Hartford. That gig was at the Agora Ballroom too. The same room where we'd seen Michael Mazzarella play with his first reasonably successful band.

Kihn was from California. He was more of a regional favorite than a national act, but he'd had a couple hits, and Danny and I agreed that his talents were generally underrated. Years later, Greg Kihn went on to host a popular radio show on KFOX in San Jose. Unlike most musicians, Kihn found a way to stay in the music business and still earn a living at it. He certainly gave the appearance of being one of the lucky ones.

The Hometown Rockers were from Providence, Rhode Island. A six-piece band, they were led by an energetic blond singer named Tom Keegan. They had a great sound and a good selection of original material that was nothing short of infectious. They wore street clothes. But they had something. Something I knew I wanted to have too.

On the one night when Danny and I had seen them, I bought a single they'd put out on their own label, Rocker Records. The identifying sticker on the 45 RPM disc was as black as the vinyl the recording was pressed on. And while it was a very low tech recording, it was well worth whatever I paid for the disc. The cut on the back side, a tune called, "Night Watchman," was just as good.

"We ought to make a record too," I announced to Danny in the garage one afternoon. I'd been playing Deep Blue Sea for days and couldn't find anything about it that made me think my best friend and I couldn't come up with something just as good.

"Yeah, we should," Danny agreed.

But we never did make a record. I learned young that there's an enormous chasm between the statements "We oughta," and "We did." That leap was one I'd never taken in my life. And so for many years, I paid dearly for my cowardice.

The idea of having our own record out impressed me. It was almost beyond my comprehension. I didn't have the first idea where to start. Danny didn't either. But we dreamed of the day when we'd make that transition from wanting to be someone special to actually being someone special. We imagined the thrill of walking into a record store in our hometown and finding the shelves stocked with our records. The idea of our own faces smiling back from the covers in those bins was electrifying.

Who could have guessed back then where Danny and I would end up a couple decades later? Here we were, cruising the highway late into the night. One of us homeless, the other a completely useless waste case who couldn't manage to stay awake for more than a few brief moments at a time.

Impossibly, Danny was still asleep. He hadn't spoken two words in hours.

My rancor remained hidden, but damn it, I was getting pretty steamed at my unsociable passenger. All that time alone with my thoughts, my only company was the music that thankfully continued to flow from the car's speakers. I was lucky on that one point. Every song I heard was one I'd had a love affair with at some point in my life. Each and every one brought with it a long forgotten memory or an emotional reaction I'd cherished at one time, but long ago forgotten.

If I ever see Danny again, which may or may not be a possibility, I really don't know, I'm going to have to remember to apologize for my attitude that night.

As tired as I was, it seemed to me a good idea to establish short-term goals for myself, checkpoints to reach before quitting for the night. With any luck at all I reasoned, that little game would help the time pass more quickly and provide me with a much needed sense of accomplishment as we motored south. The New Jersey Turnpike was my short term destination. I knew I was too tired to drive straight through the night, but I was certain that I could make my way into Delaware. Maybe we'd even cruise through the cool, clear night all the way to Maryland before the need for sleep overtook me.

The traffic wound freely through concrete canyons, across roads pockmarked by heavy use and plagued by infrequent maintenance. New York City was out there all around us if the road signs could be believed. From my vantage point on the Cross Bronx Expressway, it didn't strike me as particularly glamorous, though. All in all, the city was a disappointment. After all those years of building it up in my mind as a brilliant, glowing example of what the pinnacle of success would look like, actually seeing the city up close was anticlimactic. Depressingly so.

"So this is it, huh?" I said to myself as we rolled along, surrounded by concrete and asphalt on all sides.

"Mmmph," Danny responded.

"That's an excellent point. I hadn't thought of that," I responded sarcastically. It's entirely possible I was getting a little punchy from lack of sleep.

The traffic gradually slowed before coming to a full stop ahead of us. A short line of cars stood between my weather-beaten Taurus and a toll booth, erected especially to welcome traffic to the Garden State, and the wide open New Jersey Turnpike. The roadway that stretched out on the other side cut a wide swath from one end of the state to the other. At least that's how it looked on the Rand McNally map I'd dug out from underneath the front seat. With all that time I'd spent sitting in stalled traffic through southern Connecticut, I'd fished it out of its hiding place and spent a fair amount of time studying and memorizing our probable route. As with life in general, there were a variety of options to choose from. I opted for the easiest, most direct choice, as was my habit in those days.

There's a lesson in that. In a perfect world, I would have learned from new experiences and observations as I encountered them and revised my opinions accordingly. But as with so many people who are full of themselves, as I most certainly was back then, I believed my own theories and superstitions were so universally valid that I clung to them as if they were my most valued possessions.

On that note, let me urge you to consider this little piece of advice; Be careful what you assess great value to. Not everything in life is as it might first appear to be. The corollary to that is, of course, take great care in the things you put little value on, too. Over the course of your life, you may very well find that your estimations were 180 degrees out of whack at certain points along the way. Mine certainly were.

With one car left between my own and the toll booth, I took a quick look over at the sleeping lump that was my passenger. With nothing important to say and no burning questions that needed an immediate answer, I left him alone to sleep for as long as he needed to. I probably wasn't very good company anyway.

If I'd let my emotions run away with me, I think I might have turned around and headed home again. I might have done so even before I remembered that I had no home to go to. Luckily, I wasn't quite that brash. I kept my head and my place in line until I came alongside the toll booth where a sullen, middle-aged woman, dressed in a bland, state-issued uniform handed me a ticket. She extended a boney hand toward my open window, her palm facing downward. She offered the all-important paper coupon in her claw-like fingers without making eye contact or uttering a sound. She made no attempt to engage me in any way.

"Thank you," I said dispassionately as I slipped the ticket from her fingers and rolled slowly forward.

The woman said nothing. She retrieved another ticket and held it out for the next driver reflexively. The woman might as well have been a machine.

Her name was Lois Hunt, as it still is. I had no way of knowing it then, but the day would come when our paths would cross again, albeit under very different circumstances. In truth, I've come to learn quite a bit about Lois and her life by now. But at that moment, on the occasion of our first and only face to face meeting, I would never have guessed that Lois had at one time been a very beautiful woman, with high hopes and an eye on the future. But that was before she hooked up with her oh-so-handsome ne'er-do-well boyfriend, Eddie Donnigan.

As is so often the case with humans, a love affair gone awry became a stumbling block in Lois' life. She still hadn't learned how to move on, and so she suffered for holding her romantic nostalgia so close to her heart.

"You're the tops," Eddie would say to his young girlfriend. "Where would I be without you?"

He continued to whisper sweet nothings in her ear for several years. Over the course of their time together Eddie gave Lois three children, along with plenty of headaches, heartaches and late night worries. Chief among the things he never gave her was a ring, a wedding or even a modicum of respect. He uttered his majestically beautiful words to her less and less often until one day, he stopped entirely. That day was February 14. Lois remembered it bitterly as the day her true love offered to go to the store for bread. While he was out, he apparently had a change of heart. Instead of shopping for staples as he said he would, Eddie emptied their bank account and never came back.

Lois hadn't seen her great lost love in more than seven years when I rolled through her toll booth. Unbeknownst to me, she was thinking of Eddie as she handed me my ticket. A fact that I know now only because it has come to my attention that she'd spent virtually every waking moment of her life since he left thinking of that long-gone man. Lois Hunt was torturing herself. I'm sure she didn't see it in quite those terms. But that's what she was doing. Torturing herself, nothing more.

Lois the robotic toll booth attendant was thinking about how handsome Eddie had been, and how hurt she was that he'd left her and the children without a word. The specifics of why Eddie had left her were as much a mystery to her as Jackie's departure had been shocking to me. Had we decided to commiserate and incorporate, Lois could have qualified as the third member of our club, along with Mrs. Wisniewski and me.

Lois's dreams of a bright future were gone, as her working days got longer and her cost of living grew inexorably along with the kids. During the day, she worked as a waitress in a small, undistinguished diner in Hoboken. At night, she handed out toll tickets on the New Jersey turnpike. The woman had pride and a good working brain. But it was all slipping away one dead-end day at a time. Her sense of humor and all hope for a better tomorrow were long gone by the time I rolled through her booth.

"Thanks," I said again, sincerely, hoping for some kind of human reaction. Lois stared straight ahead, saying nothing.

It's a terrible thing to lose hope. I know.

There are a lot of people like Lois in the world. I've met quite a few by now. If not for Danny and our impulsive excursion south, I might never have realized that I'd become one of them. Lois hadn't realized how far she'd fallen either. Although if I've learned nothing else in the time between then and now, I've learned this. It's never too late to turn your life around. It really isn't.

I accelerated onto the turnpike, leaving Lois to deal with a line of cars that wouldn't end before her shift did. Down the road I flew. The Taurus humming and clanking and creaking away as it accelerated to 65 miles per hour. That was the fastest we'd been able to run since we started. I might have gone faster too. I was sure I could have. The traffic was light and the weather was good. There was plenty of light on the road shining down from rows of street lights flanking the sides of the highway. There was a full moon filling the night sky with a soft wash of light, too.

I'd have liked to get as many miles behind me as fast as I could. But I was pushing the Taurus pretty hard at that speed. It wasn't long before I began to fear that we might break down and end up stuck on the side of the road if I pushed any harder. So 65 miles per hour became my target for a time. Faster might be foolhardy. Slower was a waste of time.

In all honesty, I wasn't just afraid of breaking down and getting stuck. Like Lois Hunt, and so many others, I was just flat out afraid. Life intimidated me. I'd been beaten up, disappointed and slapped down enough times that I'd stopped trying to get up anymore. I'd stopped living, just like Lois had stopped living and began merely going through the motions of having a life, serving coffee and handing out toll tickets. I was going through the motions too. We'd both survived our major upheavals. At least we thought we had. But food, drink and a covered place to sleep isn't what it takes to make a life. Neither of us had learned that yet.

CHAPTER 10

Exhaustion was getting the better of me as midnight closed in. My head ached from hours of exposure to carbon monoxide gas and thousands of pairs of halogen-bright headlights shining in my eyes. I knew it wouldn't be long before I would be having real difficulty keeping the Taurus between the painted lines that stretched out ahead of me. I needed to rest.

The lump next to me was still snoozing away, showing no signs of stirring even after hours upon hours of uninterrupted sleep.

"You wouldn't by any chance like to take a turn at the wheel, would you?" I asked sarcastically. Wind whistled through the dry-rotted weather stripping that very nearly sealed the car's windows shut. The radio was turned low, but strains of "Stage Fright" seeped out of the speakers behind me just loud enough to identify. Robbie Robertson's classic song about a young musician with frayed nerves and big dreams was a favorite of mine since the first time I heard it. I'd always loved Rick Danko's fragile voice, breaking and straining to reach the high notes, but never completely giving out.

Danny remained silent.

"I didn't think so." I answered my own question. A clearly discernable tone of defeat tinged the words.

I slapped my face and rolled down the window, encouraging the chilled night air to refresh me enough to get to the next exit. Neither ploy worked for more than a few seconds. So I struggled and slapped my face again and even drove with my head hanging out the window for a mile or two. I was lucky that it was dark. At least nobody could see me acting like an idiot trying to stay awake enough to drive. I was equally fortunate that no New Jersey State Troopers were on the road behind me.

I managed to stay on the paved surface somehow, my fenders never once coming in contact with the barriers on either side of the highway. Which is a miracle since I have no doubt I was weaving from one lane to another like a drunken teenager returning home from a keg party.

A sign for the Walt Whitman Service Area loomed into my line of sight. It caught my attention and forced me to rouse myself from my stupor for long enough to navigate the exit. "This is us," I announced boldly, turning the wheel and coasting toward the expansive parking lot hidden behind a clump of trees.

Finding most of the spaces empty, I chose one far from the main building, threw the gear shift into "park" and turned the key to the "off" position.

"Finally," I said, heaving a sigh of relief.

Sliding out of the driver's seat, I closed my door quietly so as not to wake my passenger. Popping open the back door just as stealthily, I successfully climbed into the back seat without rocking the car too violently on its worn shocks and creaky springs.

Attempting to stretch out and get comfortable in the back seat turned out to be an exercise in futility. I couldn't straighten my legs completely and realized far too late that I hadn't packed any blankets or pillows that might comfort me, increasing my likelihood of getting a restful night's sleep. Tossing and turning and twisting in place, I finally gave up and succumbed to the probability that I'd be waking up in a few short hours. More than likely I'd be cold and sporting a stiff neck too. I was wallowing in self pity.

For a moment, I lay quietly, mentally reviewing my situation. Before I could come to any conclusions, I was overcome with a powerfully familiar and most welcome sensation that told me in no uncertain terms, I was falling asleep. It was very nearly an out-of-body experience. The most powerful I'd ever had, unless you count that time in Springfield at a Blue Oyster Cult concert. I'm almost positive somebody spiked my drink that night though, so that doesn't really count. This was similar, in any case. It was pleasant though, too. So I let it happen and drifted off for as long as my body and brain would let me.

The dreams that invaded my sleep that night were as vivid and colorful as any I'd ever had, to that point in my life at least. Over the course of those dreams, I enjoyed an absolutely wonderful dinner with my parents. Something that certainly never happened in real life. The three of us chatted amiably, truly appreciating each other's company as we devoured steak and potatoes at the kitchen table. Our old house on Burke Street never looked so good, or felt so sunny and warm.

"More pie, Dad?" I asked with a smile.

"No, no," the old man joked. "I think I've had enough for one sitting."

"You certainly have," laughed my mother, patting her husband's belly affectionately as she draped her arms around him.

None of that could ever have happened in the real life version of the Stevens house. But it felt so good to be a part of in my dreams.

One vivid dream replaced another. I found myself with Danny again. We were back in the Loughman's garage, rocking out with The Mayfair's. The whole band was there. It was a wonderful moment.

I also had a dream in which I was a much older man. This older version of me was driving a recreational vehicle through the desert. Something I'd never done and somewhere I'd never been. It was a huge machine, far more comfortable and welcoming than the rank apartment I'd left behind earlier that day. The sky was a brilliant blue with only the thinnest wisp of a cloud beginning to form over a ridge far off to the north. An unfamiliar but sweetly melodic woman's voice called out in my dream, "Do you want to stop on our way through town, or on the way back?"

I had no idea what any of that meant, if anything. But I can say without the slightest fear of contradiction that sleep is indeed an all too often underappreciated state of mind.

CHAPTER 11

The sun rose in the east, extending its warm yellow glow across the landscape. Unprotected by curtains or window treatments of any kind, the Taurus willingly accepted every available ray. Thankfully, the warming beams of light quickly went to work taking the early morning chill off the interior of the car. Unfortunately, they also robbed me of the ability to sleep any longer. I would have loved to snooze for several more hours.

The windows were damp all around, frosted over with a thin layer of condensation. Periodically, small droplets would break away and wander aimlessly down the length of the glass, producing tiny rivers of clarity as gravity pulled them earthward. I entertained myself by watching them for several minutes. As you might imagine, I was in no rush to get anywhere or do anything. For those few precious, peaceful moments I was at ease. The experience was blissfully serene.

"Hey, you want to grab some breakfast?" I queried blindly from the back seat. While waiting for a response I continued to lay still, watching tiny drops of water stealthily trace their erratic paths down the length of the back windows. Hearing nothing, I smacked the seat back with my palm and called out, louder this time. "Hey, Danny. You awake?"

The droplets of water continued their journey toward the earth. Danny said nothing.

Sitting up I peered over the front seat. He was gone. For the moment at least, I was alone. The sun continued doing its fine work, heating up the car and the wide, black sea of asphalt surrounding it.

I guessed that Danny must have headed off to find himself a spot in one of the finest restrooms New Jersey had to offer, as so many itinerant drivers and their passengers do. He might have grabbed a bite to eat at Roy Rogers, too, I surmised. Not that I thought all that highly of Roy's. But while camped out at the Walt Whitman Service Area alongside the New Jersey Turnpike, it was necessary to accept certain culinary limitations. The guarantee of nothing being available but a warmed over, fast-food breakfast was just one of the realities I had no choice but to accept.

Oh, well. It could have been worse.

I pushed the driver's side door open with one foot and began to slide out into the world. Standing up straight and stretching hard to get the kinks out, I realized with some satisfaction that the parking lot was nearly devoid of people. There were a few pedestrians scattered along the sidewalk outside the main building, quite some distance away, but there were no real crowds to contend with. I was glad of that. The idea of exchanging cheerfully mindless jibber jabber with perfect strangers didn't appeal to me at all as I made my way across the parking lot. I was in the midst of one of those moments in life when you realize your belly is empty and your bladder is full. Standing around chatting on the sidewalk wasn't on my agenda.

"Let's move it," came a belligerently booming voice from up ahead. "I'm not fucking around, here."

Looking up I was confronted by an undeniably well fed family man as he prodded a young boy through the glass doors of the rest stop with his foot. "Get going…I mean it," the big man scolded. The boy couldn't have been more than four years old. He looked afraid. Not terrified, but not at all comfortable with the way things were going.

The man berating the boy was red in the face, breathing heavily and easily pushing 300 pounds, maybe more. He was obscenely wide for a man of his height.

Behind him through the doors, flowed an equally belligerent mass of humanity that bore a striking family resemblance. Two more boys, not yet in their teens by the looks of them, swore and kicked at each other playfully as they trailed after the round man and the little boy, who was scampering across the parking lot as fast as he could, attempting to stay out of range of the big man's foot. I guessed this group constituted a family unit. An idea that was reinforced by the sight of a harried woman bursting through the doors several steps behind the rest.

She struggled to move as quickly as she could, although she looked tragically comical in the attempt. Her puffy, powder blue, down-filled coat made her appear even more rotund than she actually was. A wild shock of mousey, brown badly permed hair alternately flew or squeezed its way around her head, held tight in places by a pair of white, imitation rabbit earmuffs. She was weighed down by an armful of Roy Rogers paper bags.

By the look of things, she was almost sure to lose control of her burden before making it across the parking lot. The sugary soft drinks she carried sloshed back and forth precariously as the poor woman struggled to balance the fast drooping corrugated paper tray that held them together. The image gave every indication that her situation was one of immanent disaster. It seemed to be only a matter of seconds before she was either on her butt in the parking lot, covered in spilled beverages and burgers, or worse yet, trapped inside a closed car with this odious bellowing man and the handful of misbehaving boys in her life.

"Louise, are you coming or not?" the big man shouted over his shoulder. He was closing rapidly on a well-worn station wagon that was parked directly between me and the rest stop.

"Oh great," I remember thinking to myself. "This is just what I need right now."

"I'm coming, I'm coming," Louise's high-pitched voice responded in a voice that sounded like she was regurgitating a mantra forced upon her against her will. Her breath came in great gulps as she hurried to catch up. The hulking mound of flesh I assumed was her husband let out an audible, "Aarrggghh," as he fumbled in his pockets for a set of keys. He ultimately selected one from a large ring and pressed it into the lock on the driver's door.

The three boys continued to run and jump and generally behave like bad monkeys. All three appeared to be oblivious to their poor mother's plight. None signaled any interest in attempting to lighten her load as she waddled at top speed across the tarmac, doing her best to catch up with them. The woman reminded me of a bowling pin skittering across the lane after receiving a glancing blow. It defies belief when the pin doesn't fall, but somehow it doesn't.

Louise didn't fall either. Although the embarrassment of landing spread eagle on the cold, hard pavement couldn't have made her fate any worse than it already was.

"Jesus Christ, Louise," shouted the bloated man from behind the wheel. "You're takin' forever. Let's GO!"

The kids squealed and squirmed uncontrollably, but somehow they managed to squeeze all five bodies into their faded green wagon and get all four doors closed at one time.

The car rocked and bounced and heaved itself frantically back and forth and up and down like nothing I'd ever seen. It shook and rattled like a clown car that was ready to dispel its riders. For three, maybe four minutes, the activity was ceaseless. Then, without the slightest indication of a change, when it seemed like the poor machine could barely survive the commotion that was coming from within it, the rocking stopped. The station wagon settled and sat still for a moment, completely motionless.

I ached to get to the restroom before my own growing discomfort turned into a memorably humiliating experience. But like a rubbernecker at the scene of an accident, I just had to see what was going to happen next. The fortunate accident that caused my voyeuristic tendencies to reward me in such a tangible way was a complete surprise.

Luck is like that. I can't explain it.

Without a sound the driver's side window eased down slowly, exposing the ample silhouette of the big man and little else.

"Shut Up!" The words exploded from his mouth. "I said shut up, goddamn it." His massive frame was far too big to allow him to turn around and confront whichever child had offended him. But judging from the sudden return of the rocking motion to the car, he was trying awfully hard to do just that.

Giving up a moment later, no doubt from exhaustion, the big man started the car. The motor shrieked in metallic protest. An impressive puff of black smoke from the exhaust system followed before the car settled down to a soft purr. The gear shift clunked into action and the car began to roll forward.

"Not another word, Joey. I mean it," hollered the beefy driver as he heaved a substantial pile of garbage out the window. A second later, the heaving green car with the ill-mannered family stuffed inside it slid out of the parking lot. The tinted driver's side window silently raised up again as the machine moved forward, rendering the occupants anonymous for all time.

I sneered at them as they went. I'm sure I did. The man at the wheel disgusted me as much as the collection of garbage he'd ejected onto the blacktop. Walking past it, I toed through the remains of the Roy Rogers bags and wadded up napkins, wrinkling my nose, making my displeasure obvious for all to see, had there been anyone there to witness the incident. But there wasn't. There was only me, the garbage and…green paper?

A tightly packed wad of green paper caught my eye. Looking up, I scanned the parking lot to see if anyone was watching. I wasn't in the mood for practical jokes, reality TV gotchas or Alan Funt wannabes. Seeing no one, I knelt down to pick the wad of green from the rest of the trash. Recognizing the collection of tender for what it was, I stuffed the notes into my jacket pocket and immediately began gathering the trash from the parking lot. Carrying it in both arms, I headed for the closest trash can.

My pressing need to visit a rest room was quickly becoming urgent. Pushing the paper bags and wadded up napkins down into the top of the can, I spun on my heel and headed off at a good clip toward the same doors the high-volume family had so recently emerged from.

"Just disgraceful, that's what it is," said an elderly woman as I brushed past. She was headed out while I was headed in. My eyes scanned the walls for an indication of where the Men's Room was. I was in no position to stop and pass the time of day with anyone unless I was prepared to change my pants, too.

"Yes it is," I answered, without losing a step. I found my destination just inside the glass doors and picked up the pace as I pushed my way past a couple teenagers and an older gentleman, diving into a stall and whipping my pants down in almost the same motion. Seconds later, disaster was averted.

I stayed in that stall longer than I had to. With the emergency past, I had time to tally the bills I'd so fortuitously found in the trash outside. I counted those bits of green paper over and over again, just to be sure I wasn't hallucinating. My good luck came to a total of $264. All thrown out with the trash in a frenzy of chewing, swallowing, shouting and putting miles behind them. The big man had made a tremendous error. One that I was going to make good use of, thank you very much.

I let out a long, high-pitched whistle as I carefully folded the money for safe keeping.

"Keep it to yourself," said a phantom voice from the stall next to mine.

I slipped out, washed my hands and headed for the food line at Roy Rogers as quickly as I could.

"I guess my luck's beginning to change," I chuckled to myself while selecting two practically fresh breakfast sandwiches and placing them on an orange plastic tray.

CHAPTER 12

Danny was back in the passenger seat when I arrived. Overall, he looked better than he had the day before.

"You want some breakfast?" I asked rhetorically, offering a sausage and egg sandwich in his direction.

"No, thanks, I'm good."

"You sure? Lunch is quite a ways off." I was prompting him, teasing, almost begging him to take the sandwich. But Danny held his ground, rubbing his stomach lightly with one hand and gazing out the window absently.

"Yeah, I'm OK without it. I do appreciate the effort though."

I didn't trouble him with my observations of the big, round loudmouth and his dysfunctional family, or the found money that was bulging in my pocket. The financial end of this trip was my responsibility. I'd known that from the moment we got into the car. There was no point in bringing it up, so I didn't. The story of how I came to be in possession of $264 more than we'd started with was a secret I never mentioned to anyone. Until just now that is.

Giving up on convincing my partner to eat, I settled for stuffing the key into the ignition and turning it. My reward was the short, high-pitched shriek of steel on steel as the starter motor brought the engine to life.

"We might as well fill up while we're here," I suggested, nodding toward the gas pumps positioned off to our left. The Taurus's fuel gauge needle was banging on the bottom peg. If we didn't buy gas there, I had no doubt we'd run the tank dry long before we got to the next gas stop down the turnpike. That would be the Clara Barton Service Area, which lies 21 miles further south. That interesting and useful fact was gleaned from a quick look at the information printed on the toll ticket I'd snatched from Lois Hunt's hand the night before.

Danny didn't respond. He was still rubbing his belly absent mindedly while otherwise appearing to be engrossed in something invisible, far off in the distance. No matter. He was awake and lucid, which was a considerable improvement over the day before.

Gliding slowly over the warming black pavement, I guided the Taurus up to the multiple rows of gas pumps and chose an empty space at the far outside pump. There weren't any cars in line there, which I took as a good sign. At least tanking up wouldn't take long. We'd be back on the turnpike in no time, I figured, putting mile upon mile of New Jersey behind us with every revolution of the ancient Ford's tires.

Slipping the gear shift into park, I eased open the driver's door and climbed out. Then automatically, like I'd done a thousand times before, I popped open the fuel cap and pulled a hose pumping 87 octane juice from the island. Inserting the nozzle into the fuel tank, I was about to squeeze the trigger when a flurry of shouting and the sound of scampering feet attracted my attention.

"Hey, hey...Hey! *Hheeeyyyy!*" two attendants were running toward me, waving their arms and yelling as if they were trying to protect innocent orphans from a madman who'd just pulled the pin from a hand grenade and was waving it around maniacally.

"You can't pump your own gas here, buddy!" hollered the first attendant to reach me. He snatched the hose out of my hand and clamped it back into the pump housing as if he'd been highly trained in the technique. The second attendant, a short, tubby sort of fellow, saw that his compatriot had taken control of the situation. No longer needed in the rush to disarm an unauthorized fuel pumper, he turned his attention to other things. Although he took the time to shoot a look over his shoulder as he strutted off that left little doubt about his feelings toward this interloper from the north.

"What?" I asked, as confused as could be.

"This is New Jersey!" the faster, surly attendant mouthed loud and slow, as if he was addressing a developmentally disabled child.

His name tag identified him as Sal. His eyes betrayed a deeply fermented anger, indicating that Sal was no stranger to the concept of a street fight. His crooked and flattened nose suggested he was reasonably familiar with what it felt like to be on the receiving end of a vicious beating when his temper brought him to blows, too.

"There's no Self Serve gas in New Jersey, Mac. It's the law."

That was news to me. "Self Serve is against the law here?" I smirked in disbelief. For a moment I wasn't entirely sure that Sal wasn't having a bit of fun with me, pulling a bad practical joke. And I certainly didn't know if the shift from "buddy" to "Mac" was an upgrade or a slip in rank. Whatever the case, Sal wasn't making a lot of points with me just then.

"It's a law, we don't do no self serve here so as to protect jobs, pal." The man's condescension was palpable. Sal stared into my eyes with an intensity that indicated he was also trying to communicate with me telepathically. The message was probably a fairly simple one. I imagined it could be conveyed with a basic hand gesture involving only a single finger. He clearly considered me to be on an intellectual par with a sea sponge.

"So *you* have to pump my gas, and I can't. Is that it?" I asked as sarcastically as I could, putting extra emphasis on the word, "you."

"Yeah, I have to pump your gas, snapper head." Finally, the idiot from Connecticut was getting it. I just knew that's what he was thinking.

Feeling somewhat indignant, highly insulted and maybe even a little amused by the situation, I pulled forty dollars out of my newfound batch of greenbacks and tucked the two bills into Sal's greasy blue shirt pocket, saying, "Fill 'er up." I said it as slowly and distinctly as I could. My eyes were locked on his as the two of us engaged in a rousing demonstration of male domination techniques.

Two, maybe three seconds passed before Sal, who was noticeably agitated, did an about face and stalked back to the pump to retrieve the hose. I opened my door, trying hard to look as casual as possible. Settling back into the safe confines of the Taurus, I waited.

My hands were shaking, so I held the wheel to hide the fact. My heart pounded out a beat so hard, I was surprised that my shirt wasn't fluttering from the furious impacts on the other side of my rib cage. But for the moment at least, I felt like a winner.

Danny didn't give any indication that he cared one way or another how gasoline found its way into the tank. He was pressing his mouth flat against the passenger side window and blowing hard to puff his cheeks out, fogging up the glass. Not five feet away at a parallel pump was a little girl no more than five or six years old. She was sitting in the back seat of a red Hyundai SUV, hiked up in a car seat that looked like it had been designed for NASA. She was doing exactly the same idiotic thing Danny was. I guessed they were playing a game of some sort, but I didn't ask. One confrontation at a time was plenty for me.

Sal, who worked with the dexterity of a slug and at roughly the same speed, finally finished filling my tank. He snapped the lid shut, then grudgingly shuffled up to my window and began counting out my change without comment. I used that moment to start the car and slip the transmission into gear.

"Fuck New Jersey, Sal," I taunted as he pressed the change into my hand.

"Yeah, fuck you too, asshole," Sal spit back.

I stepped on the gas pedal and the Taurus rumbled forward, toward the turnpike and our ultimate destination. Sal took a swipe at the rear bumper with his foot. I didn't care. We were moving again.

"OK," I shouted. "We're southbound once more."

"Uh huh," Danny responded with no apparent interest. He was using the sleeve of his shirt to clean the streaked and blurry window, seemingly lost in thoughts of his own.

CHAPTER 13

Danny and I didn't speak for a long time as the rust-bucket Taurus covered ground. Delaware was inching closer by the minute. The buzzing drone of tires on asphalt mixed with an occasional clank or groan from the aging Ford. That cacophony of sounds conspired to keep my mind engaged and my nervous system on edge, alert for the first signs of the breakdown that would almost certainly come. It was unavoidable, I reasoned. Increasingly I found myself working hard to push thoughts of failure and desolation from my mind.

The radio played on, impossibly, emitting one memory-rich tune after another. They were all reminders of better times, long ago. Periodically I'd sing along, but for the most part, I just listened and relived the memories as those melodies brought them back to me. If not for the radio, I think I might have lost my will to continue. Looking back on that tumultuous week, I can say with total honesty now that I was really touch-and-go for a while there.

"Papa Gene's Blues" was playing. One of my favorites from the Monkees, a band that figured prominently in my childhood. Written by Mike Nesmith, the made-for-television band's guitarist, I always credited that song as absolute proof the Monkees were no more fake than any other band of their day, which seems obvious in retrospect. But in their prime, the band took an awful beating as little more than a manufactured entity with no actual musical talent.

How wrong that assessment was.

Monkee Mike's voice sang along blissfully, thick with his distinctive Texas twang. The gist of the song was basic enough. In essence, Nesmith was singing about his satisfaction with the emotional component of his life, rather than bemoaning the tangible things he lacked.

If only it was that simple, I thought, not yet aware that life is in fact *exactly* that simple. Perspective. Life is all about perspective. Apparently, Mike Nesmith knew that decades before I did. Or, at least he gave a convincing pretense of understanding one of the great truths of life.

Danny was silent, still saving his words as if they were priceless gems, dear to his heart but far from his lips. However he appeared to be substantially more upright and aware than he'd been the day before. Ever since our foray into the industrial comfort zone known as the Walt Whitman Service Area, Danny had been awake and apparently cognizant of his surroundings. I wouldn't describe him as alert, since that would imply an energy level that he just hadn't displayed at all. But his eyes were open, and he gave every indication of being conscious of the sights and sounds surrounding him as we cruised ever southward.

After a time, I noticed he'd lost interest in whatever far off thing had held his attention at the service area. Now he seemed to be looking at me more than he was taking in the surrounding countryside. Which I must admit, was considerably more densely forested and pleasant looking than I'd expected it to be. After all the jokes I'd heard about New Jersey over the course of my life, I expected the Garden State to be much more dilapidated and urban. But instead of the dull, colorless landscape filled with belching smokestacks and acres of pavement I'd anticipated, I found central and southern New Jersey to be surprisingly attractive.

The end of the turnpike loomed ahead. One more state would be behind us in short order. A minor detail that felt like quite an accomplishment at the time.

Sliding into line behind a shiny white Cadillac pick-up truck, I fished my toll ticket out of the overhead visor where I'd stowed it the night before. Pulling another of the found twenties out of my pocket, I waited patiently to pay my toll and gain passage to the wonderland beyond the barrier known as Delaware. A postage stamp of a state that neither asks for nor receives much respect from its neighbors.

The toll booth was manned by a pasty-looking white man with enormous round spectacles. He was impossibly thin and looked to be quite a bit taller than average. The combination made his glasses seem ridiculously oversized, perched as they were on the bridge of his long thin nose. His physique brought to mind the image of a giant bird

I handed him the twenty before he could recite his state's price for using their fine roadway. With a quick, smooth motion that gave me the impression he must have been a dancer in another life, he returned the correct change to my outstretched hand.

"Have a safe trip,"he said, in a voice so resonantly deep and sincere that it startled me. The sound escaping his vocal chords was as mellifluous and pleasing as any I'd ever heard. The accompanying solemn facial expression he wore sold the line as totally genuine. I knew instinctively this man wasn't merely repeating a phrase he parroted all day long to a never-ending line of vehicles. He was addressing me personally, taking a moment from his day to connect with me.

I instantly liked him.

"Thank you," I said sincerely, before pressing on the accelerator and leaving the toll booth behind.

With the birdman's admonition to be safe rattling around in my head like a loose penny in a jar, Danny and I cruised across the state line toward the Delaware Memorial Bridge. The sun was shining, unimpeded by clouds of any kind, turning the autumn sky clear and bright.

Danny was looking at me again, or maybe he was *still* looking at me. I'd become so taken with the toll booth attendant that I'd lost track of Danny for a short time. I'd become engrossed by the road and my hands on the wheel instead. It was several minutes before Danny became my primary focus again.

We were climbing the bridge, arching our way up over the water below, staying in our lane and maintaining the speed limit as the lighted signs over the roadway instructed.

"How're you feeling?" I asked, being careful not to take my eyes off the road. I was attempting to fill an uncomfortable silence that was growing between us with something, anything, that would relieve my suddenly powerful sense of discomfort. I felt self-conscious. The sense that my traveling partner was staring at me left me cold. As if he saw me as a biology experiment he was anticipating some alteration to occur in.

After a long pause Danny said, "You've changed." He spoke slowly, with a hint of amusement in his tone, almost as if he was pleased with the discovery.

We crested the hump in the middle of the bridge and started down the other side.

"Of course I've changed," I shot back, feeling wounded by the remark. Immediately, I took Danny's observation as a personal attack. I became angry and defensive. Unnecessarily so, but angry nonetheless.

"It's been more than 20 years, for Christ's sake."

"Yes, it has," Danny said with some satisfaction. "But you've still changed, there's no doubt about that."

"Wha...how...In what way..." Offended, I stammered pathetically, sounding a bit too much like Tommy Smothers vainly attempting to counter his brother Dick's intellectually superior argument than I was comfortable with. I switched gears, going on the attack myself.

"Well, you've changed too, you know."

"Oh yes," Danny nodded almost imperceptibly, "I've changed. There's no denying that."

"Well, how come my change is bad and yours isn't?" I challenged, defiantly.

Danny grinned subtly and shifted his gaze away from me, back to the far distance. He scanned the horizon ahead of us as if he expected to see something specific. When he spoke, he sounded confident, but tired. Painfully, crushingly tired.

"Change isn't good or bad, Frank. It's just change." He turned toward me again, his voice soft as a whisper. "In nature, change is constant. The landscape, the shoreline, the path of a river, they all change constantly as outside forces affect them. Sometimes they change a little. Sometimes they change a lot. It's not good or bad. It just is."

"You smoke a lot of pot, don't you?" I queried sarcastically, suddenly full of myself for no good reason. "Just yesterday you were out of it, dozing and dragging your ass. Now all of a sudden, you sound like a new age motivational speaker trying to hook the assembled masses into buying your new three CD set on, *Oneness and the Cosmic Miracle of Is.*"

Danny laughed hard. His mouth burst open wide and his head flew back against the grimy headrest. His laugh was loud and powerful, exhibiting a burst of energy that took me by surprise. Tears welled up in his eyes. Even as he began to regain his composure, he retained a broad smile that indicated he was happy, truly happy. For the first time since he'd shown up on my porch the day before, I realized that of the two of us, I was the more damaged man. I had the steeper hill to climb in life and wore the bigger chip on my shoulder.

"I've missed you, Frank," Danny said with genuine affection. "I really have."

"You too," I replied after a short pause. My tone was far less convincing than Danny's was.

"I think you should pull over up here."

Danny gestured out beyond the windshield toward the road ahead, lazily, with an arcing wave of the hand.

"Pull over?" I didn't see any reason to stop. We hadn't been driving for more than a couple hours. The car had plenty of gas and there was nothing in our line of sight that indicated any reason to pull off the road.

"I think we're needed," Danny said simply.

The road ahead was wide open with only a smattering of traffic. There was nothing to see but a mass of trees to the left and an almost identical mass of trees to the right. Most of them had lost their leaves to the season, although a few colorful strays still clung tenaciously to their branches. Soon a stiff fall breeze would knock them to the ground too. Freezing winter temperatures would eventually turn them brown and brittle.

Another mile clicked by, followed by two more. A speck came into view on the side of the road, well ahead of us. As we closed the distance between ourselves and the speck, I could make out a dark blue vehicle pulled over on the right-hand side of the road. The driver was out of the car, standing in the grass behind it.

"Right here," Danny said as we drew closer.

I pulled over without an argument, rolling off the pavement and onto the grass a few yards behind a dark blue Chevy Envoy. The driver shot us an uncomfortable look as I brought the Taurus to a stop. She appeared to be in her mid-forties, was well dressed and talked excitedly into a cell phone. She may have been calling a tow truck, or her employer to explain why she was going to be late for work. I have no idea, really. Whoever she was talking to, she was telling her story with tremendous animation. Her free arm flailing wildly as her left foot stomped the ground for emphasis over and over again.

I wondered how Danny had seen her so far out ahead. I had good eyes back then, better than I have now, but even now I see better than my average peer. Yet, Danny had apparently been aware of her plight almost four miles before we actually encountered her.

The question was a good one. I filed it away to ask later.

Just as I shut the engine down, Danny slumped heavily back onto the passengers' door with his right shoulder. He was awake, but not quite bursting with energy.

"You can handle this," he said. It was a statement, not a question. Clearly, he wasn't going to be competing with me for brownie points or this woman's attention. I guessed he figured he'd done his good deed for the day by spotting the damsel in distress. I would have to do the actual rescuing, if there was any rescuing to be done.

I slid out my door, checked for traffic and made my way toward the Envoy. The driver was climbing into her own driver's seat by that time. She didn't look the least bit relieved that help had arrived. If anything, she looked nervous as if she was on guard, expecting something awful to happen.

How much help I might actually be able to provide was a mystery, even to me. True, I had a tool box in my trunk. But it was small and sparsely populated. I owned a pair of slip joint pliers, an adjustable wrench and some wire cutters. I knew that for sure. I was almost certain that I had a claw hammer and a medium-sized ball-peen hammer in there too. But the truth was, I hadn't used any of those tools in quite some time.

A well-worn Stanley ratcheting screwdriver with six replacement bits hidden in the handle was included in the kit, too. The screwdriver was the only tool I owned that I knew the manufacturer of. Sharon, my younger and much more stable sister had given it to me as a Christmas present when she was a teenager. I'm sure I thanked her for it, although I have no recollection of actually doing so. It was my favorite tool, having been with me for years and years. That screwdriver had successfully tightened doorknobs and switch plates around the house without ever letting me down. I'd even used it to fix a leaking radiator hose on the Taurus only a month or two before. Financial constraints had rendered buying a new hose a luxury I just couldn't afford.

The owner of the Envoy slammed her door shut just as I came near. She slammed the door hard, too. It was just a guess, but I didn't get the impression that she was particularly glad to see me.

Completely ignoring me otherwise, she continued yelling into her cell phone, filling the air with a grating, nasal voice that made me sorry I'd stopped. But then I caught my reflection in her tinted window and got a glimpse of the situation from her point of view. Under the circumstances, I couldn't blame her for locking herself in the vehicle and trying hard to ignore me. While I felt like the good guy who'd come to save the day, my reflection said otherwise. I didn't look like a friendly, innocent roadside assistance guy at all. Instead I bore a remarkable resemblance to the sort of shifty vagrant parents warn their children to stay away from. I imagined that if asked to describe me later this woman just might illustrate my appearance by saying, "He looked like Nick Nolte's mug shot." She wouldn't have been far off either.

I wasn't feeling all that well, suddenly.

"Do you need help?" I yelled though the tightly closed window. At that moment, a semi truck drove past, flinging my already unkempt hair in a thousand different directions, throwing it into a ballet of snarls. The effect didn't do my mood or my otherwise inadequate attempts to appear less threatening any good at all.

She looked at me through her tinted window with a mixture of shock, horror and pity as she insistently remarked to whoever was on the other end of her telephone that she was on the highway. Those were the only words I could make out from her conversation.

"I'm on the highway," she bleated out, then repeated "The highway!" slower, but with more emphasis and indignation.

She was more or less oblivious to my presence. Or at least she made a serious effort to be. Eventually, perhaps sensing that I wasn't going away until she acknowledged me, she nodded in my general direction and waved me off. This wasn't intended as a gesture to signify that she welcomed my help. It was employed more as if to indicate her feeling that I was a hobo who'd moved a little too far into her personal space. Which I guess I had, if you look at the situation in a particular way. I was nobody to her. I was barely there as far as she was concerned.

"If you'll pop the hood I'd be happy to take a look," I yelled back at my reflection in the glass, cupping my hands around my mouth as if she was far off in the distance. I have no doubt that I looked like a raving lunatic.

She leaned down and pulled the hood release while keeping the phone to her ear. I heard her demand tersely, "What is your name?" and so I told her. A moment later I realized she was talking into the phone, not the glass that separated us. I gathered her conversation wasn't going well. Which eased my embarrassment about shouting my name through a closed window to a woman who didn't have the slightest interest in knowing who I was.

The wide blue hood opened easier than I guessed it would, exposing a massive engine that must have sucked down gasoline at a phenomenal rate. It was both impressive-looking and hot to the touch. The woman screaming into the phone hadn't been stuck here long, that was for sure.

I began by looking for obvious signs of trouble. Broken fan belts, loose wires and large puddles of liquid forming underneath a vehicle can be a dead giveaway to what's gone wrong. Since the driver hadn't provided me with even the slightest clue as to what her problem was, I cast a wide net in my search. But I didn't see any telltale signs. In fact, the engine compartment was as clean as any I'd ever seen.

It occurred to me that there couldn't be many miles on a vehicle looking this good under the hood. It was new, or at least new-ish. It had air-conditioning that gave every appearance of working just fine. Condensation was dripping freely off the unit under the hood. I thought it odd that she would be running the air-conditioner on a day when the temperature probably wouldn't get any higher than the low 60s. But that was none of my business, and it didn't matter much anyway. Engines rarely quit because the air-conditioner has been working overtime.

I poked and I prodded and I stretched to get a look at the back of the engine compartment, but I couldn't find anything that was out of place. I was reaching for the hood, intending to close it up and admit defeat when I finally caught a glimpse of something that very definitely shouldn't have been there.

From the opening of the air cleaner inlet fluttered a piece of thin, blue plastic. It was much lighter in color than the truck itself and very much out of place in the black plastic and steel confines of the engine compartment. I popped the air cleaner top off and found, much to my surprise, a discount store shopping bag almost completely sucked into the intake manifold side of the engine. It was tattered, having lost most of its original shape due to its ordeal. But there it was.

"Got 'cha," I exclaimed, my chest swelling with pride.

Carefully, I pulled the bag out of the inlet piece by piece. I couldn't tell if I had the whole bag for sure, but I certainly got most of it out of the dead engine. I'd never seen or heard of anything like that happening. I still haven't. I mean, what are the odds that a plastic bag, a worthless bit of leftover refuse blown out of a garbage can or the back window of another car, could be sucked into the intake side of the engine, effectively starving it of air?

The engine was fine. It had merely been suffocated into submission. But I saved it. I revived it and brought new life to an unworkable hunk of metal and plastic and glass that had stranded its owner on the side of the road. I had done something of real value and I'd done it in less than five minutes. Now that's something to feel good about.

My elation at having solved the problem of the stranded woman was so complete that I slammed the hood closed harder than I'd intended to. The driver looked up, startled by the heavy metallic whunk of her hood pounding down onto the latching mechanism. She was still talking excitedly into her phone, but we had at last made eye contact. She was staring right at me.

"Go ahead, crank her up," I shouted, while making good eye contact and smiling like a drunken baboon.

She looked at me quizzically and shrugged her shoulders, mouthing the word, "What?" Her expression indicated she wasn't thinking of me as her savior as much as she was thinking I was an irritant. She didn't want to have to deal with me at all if she could help it.

"Crank it," I said again, exaggerating the movement of my lips and pointing toward the engine. I also made a circular motion with my finger, the internationally recognized signal for "start it up." At least it was the internationally accepted signal at George J. Penney High School back when I took auto shop class there a quarter century earlier.

She looked at me like I was a bug. An ugly bug, too. Then she turned the key. The Envoy leapt back to life with a rumbling roar before settling down into a powerful purr that fit the personality of the woman at the wheel perfectly. She cocked her head and listened for a moment. I smiled broadly and gave her a celebratory thumbs up. I was justifiably pleased with myself. The moment felt good.

While I was feeling all warm and gooey inside, the driver apparently decided she was back in business. She clapped her cell phone shut, pulled on her seat belt and threw the big cruiser into gear. She was looking over her left shoulder for an opening in traffic when it dawned on me that I was in real danger.

Relieved of the major obstacle that had put her on the side of the road in the first place, the driver was ready to go and nothing was going to stop her. She didn't bother to communicate with me directly. Not by giving me the international signal for, "Get out of the way or I'll run your ass over." Not even a friendly wave as a sort of "Thank's, now get out of the way," before she pressed down on the accelerator and raced off. It was as I was I diving into the grass beside the suddenly moving Envoy that all this ran through my mind. She missed me by inches. A couple tons of dark blue Chevrolet raced into the right lane and motored on down the road, oblivious to everything in sight.

I watched her go, never thinking to write down her license plate number and file a complaint. What difference would it make? She only considered me insignificant because I was insignificant. Humility came crashing down on me like a ton of bricks, replacing the warm fuzzies that had so recently been trying to take up residence in my psyche.

I picked myself up and slowly began brushing the dead grass and twigs from my clothes as the SUV flew out of sight. She moved from the right lane into the left almost immediately. She didn't use a blinker. Neither did anyone else apparently. The unexpected lane shift pushed a hapless Honda Accord into the median as the driver of that vehicle struggled to keep from being flattened, as I'd nearly been.

Danny was smiling and cheerfully awake as I slid back into the Taurus' driver's seat. He closed his eyes and curled up into a tight ball as I buckled my seat belt, totally deflated and in no mood for jokes.

"Don't you say a fucking word," I mumbled as I turned the key in the ignition. The Taurus shook and rattled back to life with considerably less grace than the Envoy had. I slipped the gear shift into "drive," and after a brief period of slippage due to excessive age and wear, we were rolling again.

Danny just kept smiling as he slunk down into his seat. I think he fell asleep again, too. I can't be sure.

CHAPTER 14

Diminutive Delaware was passing by without the benefit of conversation. Danny was holding his tongue, although I suspected the silence wouldn't last. He looked far too invigorated to remain quiet.

Wearing a smug little smile that indicated he was itching to begin jabbering away at the first opportunity, Danny had adopted the appearance of a man nearly bursting with pent-up ideas and feelings he couldn't wait to get out. Which was understandable, since he'd been either asleep or mentally detached for most of the drive.

I was the one in no mood to talk for a change.

As we rolled farther south, it became apparent that Danny was gaining strength, becoming more vibrant. His outward appearance continued to brighten with every turn of the rickety Taurus' wheels. His energy level rose in equal proportion to his overall look. If anyone was fading now, it was me.

The irony of this turn of events didn't completely escape me, considering how lonely and desperate I'd been for so long. Now, here I was with a perfectly good, warm body next to me, a friend with whom I had a significant shared history. One who was more than willing to talk on almost any subject, probably for hours on end from the look of him. Yet I was the obstacle now. Sulking and licking my emotional wounds after suffering another episode of rejection, this time at the hands of a total stranger in a hulking blue Chevrolet, I took the position of being a rock solid impediment to normal social intercourse. Not wishing to be totally antisocial, I comforted myself by employing one particularly general communication skill. I heaved a series of powerful sighs in Danny's general direction. Not that my method was particularly succinct or productive. In fact, the expulsion of each intentionally explosive breath failed to do me any good at all. The exercise seemed to provide Danny with mild entertainment, however. To his credit, he refrained from making any derisive comments about my childish behavior.

Eventually my thoughts and concerns shifted from the emotional to the physical. As each passing mile fell behind us, I felt at least some satisfaction that we were closing in on our goal. At the same time, I was becoming less and less sure the once mighty Taurus would actually hold together long enough for us to be successful. The clunking, creaking and occasionally shuddering car was rapidly becoming a prime source of worry. As sure as I'd been at the start that we'd complete the journey without incident, I was now just as certain that a breakdown of epic proportions loomed unavoidably in our future. As worried as I'd been about a breakdown in New Jersey, that concern had easily doubled by the time we were halfway though Delaware.

I was beginning to consider that if things kept going the way they were, I'd be suffering from a stress-induced ulcer and a persistent nervous tick by the end of our trip. And that was if I was lucky.

Added to all that, somewhere in the back of my mind, I was still stewing over my early morning altercation with Sal at the Walt Whitman Service Area. The fact that I'd had a nearly fatal road service experience only a short time later wasn't doing my frame of mind much good either. Considering the fact that Danny continued to stare curiously in my general direction from his side of the car, it didn't take much of an imagination to realize that I either had to confront my foul mood or continue to suffer from it. It was no secret, even to me, that I was running a very real risk of my emotional funk deepening into a truly self-destructive depression. Throwing caution to the wind and bracing myself for the worst, I gave Danny the green light.

"Go ahead," I mumbled.

"Really?" he teased back.

"Go ahead! I know you've got something to say, so you might as well go ahead and say it."

"Let the healing begin!" Danny shouted, his hands raised toward the car's roof like a revival tent preacher. He was so pleased with himself.

"What are you talking about?"

"You feel better." He said these words as if they represented an undeniable observation that not even the dimmest village idiot could miss. "You've been all down and cranky since we left East Hartford. Then you helped that poor woman back there. Now you feel better."

He was nuts, that much was obvious. Just plain nuts.

"Go ahead, take a minute to relax and take stock of your own emotions. You can sense it, can't you? You feel better?" His query came gift wrapped in a soft, warm, supportive voice.

"Feel better?" I shot back. "You mean after the nice lady locked herself insider her truck for protection? Or do you mean feel better, because I lived through squeezing myself between her vehicle and the road without getting run over by oncoming traffic? Or maybe you're thinking I feel better after dodging the bitch and her big ugly boat when she hit the gas and gunned her way right over the spot where I'd been standing? Maybe that's how they say, "thank you," where you come from. But where I come from, a smile and a handshake are a whole lot more appreciated."

I was shouting. The outburst shocked me, coming on as abruptly as it had. Only a moment before I'd considered myself to be slightly depressed, a willing victim of self-induced isolation. But as I was becoming embarrassingly aware, that wasn't even close to my actual emotional condition. Apparently my mental state was far closer to teetering between rage, rebellion and complete humiliation. I retreated back inside my shell for a moment to reconsider my situation, but Danny refused to give me even the briefest private moment to sulk.

"Now Frank," his voice had the same tone my kindergarten teacher, Mrs. Perkins, had used when she lectured me on the finer points of sharing with my neighbor. "You know I come from the same place you do."

"You know what I meant," I answered in a much more conversational, but embarrassed tone.

"All I'm suggesting is that you're starting to feel a bit better about yourself. That's all. You just are, and that's OK. As a matter of fact, it's sort of the point."

"What point?"

Danny sighed softly and leaned his head back on the grimy headrest.

"There are certain basic rules in life, Frank. With luck, you'll learn them all in time, or at least most of them. Chocolate is good. That's a rule. Mixing beer and wine in large quantities, that's bad. That's a rule too." His expression showed real compassion, while his tone of voice suggested he was speaking from a position of knowledge and authority. The actual words he was speaking struck me as gibberish, though.

Danny went on with his dissertation, listing what he referred to as the "rules of life." They were all simple, straight-to-the-point sort of guidelines that everyone already knows. As a matter of fact, his rules were so obvious that anyone overhearing our conversation would assume Danny was merely listing behaviors that constituted good old common sense. For all his bluster and increasingly theatrical delivery, he wasn't divulging any deep dark secrets that were known to only a select few.

"One of the most basic rules of life is this; When you're feeling bad, when you're down, or depressed, you can always make yourself feel better by helping somebody else. Even if it's somebody you don't know." Danny was really getting into his explanations, waving his arms and gesturing wildly. "Even if it's someone you have no reason to believe you'll ever see again." His face beamed with a smile that rivaled the Dali Lama's. "More often than not, the best way to help yourself out of a bad situation is to help someone else get out of their own predicament." He paused, leering at me with that ridiculous smile still plastered on his face. "It's true!"

My eyes stayed on the road for a good long time before I answered.

"That's the stupidest thing I've ever heard in my life." Sure, it's not the most eloquent thing I could've said. But it was my sincere appraisal of the situation at the time.

"Maybe so, but it's still true," said the philosopher in the passenger seat.

"So I feel better?" I queried.

"Yes, you do. If you take a moment to reflect on the morning and the direction you're headed in, you'll realize that you really do feel better. Your life is improving. You're improving." As if he'd just exposed me to one of the great secrets of the cosmos he shouted, "Things are looking up, Frank!" Then Danny fell silent. He spent the next several minutes doing nothing but looking me over, gauging my response to the revelations he'd just apprised me of.

So I sat and I thought. Not about anything in particular. Just harmless, random thoughts for the most part. But I did consider for a moment or two what an idiot Danny had turned out to be.

One more day and I'd be rid of him, I consoled myself. Just one more day, unless everything went to hell in a handbasket. In that case, I didn't even want to think about the myriad ugly possibilities our respective futures held.

We'd be crossing into Maryland in a few miles. That would put one more state line behind us, which I viewed unequivocally as good news. We'd be one state closer to our destination.

I tried to put Danny's nonsense out of my thoughts. But surprisingly, his lessons on life proved to be harder to ignore than I might have imagined. I found myself questioning my own feelings, trying to put a finger on my emotional state and apply it to some sort of mental chart of defined contentedness. It surprised me to find that such a seemingly simple task was actually quite difficult. I found that I was having quite a bit of trouble attempting to identify exactly how I felt.

Curious, isn't it?

What is *better*, anyway? Better than what? I felt better than I would have if the woman in the Envoy had hit me, sure. And I supposed it was possible that you could make a reasonable case that I was feeling better than I would have if I'd carried out my original plan to end it all. But there was no way Danny could have known I was thinking seriously about doing away with myself when he showed up. I was only thinking about it. I hadn't confided in anyone about my plans. So that didn't count.

All that thinking about how I felt brought to mind an interesting morsel of personal history I hadn't considered before. Jackie had often complained that I was distant or cold whenever she'd try to steer us in the direction of any long-term planning. Throughout our relationship I'd always dismissed her criticisms as girly bullshit. But what if that wasn't it? What if I was missing some critical intellectual or emotional component that prevented me from being a complete human being? I mean, I felt like I was a pretty normal guy. But Ted Bundy probably thought he was a pretty normal guy too. Normal is a fairly useless yardstick, I realized, especially when you're dealing with a subject as flaky and weird as the emotional make-up of the human race.

"Man, it's getting hot in here," I said while reaching for the window crank.

"You think? It seems OK to me," answered my passenger.

My chest was beginning to feel tight. Air moved in and out through my nose and mouth, but it didn't seem to make the slightest bit of difference to my body. I felt like I was drowning, gasping for air and not finding sufficient quantities to satisfy my needs. A tremendous feeling of lightheadedness swept over me. Waves of nausea clawed at my belly and throat as I began to fear that I might lose control of the car. I struggled to fight back against an invisible force that was so thoroughly beating me into submission. Panting like a St. Bernard on a hot August afternoon, beads of sweat formed on my brow and rolled down into my eyes. The salt stung and affected my vision. The road became distorted and blurry. Moisture oozing from my pores made my hands slick on the wheel.

"It's OK," Danny reassured me. "You're fine. You're having perfectly understandable doubts about yourself." His tone was as soothing as a cool glass of sparkling water.

"I don't know what's happening," I said breathlessly. "I think I might be having a heart attack."

"No, you're not having a heart attack," he chuckled. "Settle down now. You're going to be fine." His voice was oddly comforting, even as I felt the world crashing in on me. Danny's presence was a welcome, calming force. One that was thankfully slowing my breathing and heart rate back in the general direction of normal.

I didn't want to be alone anymore. I knew that immediately, even as my chest ached and I thought for an instant that I might die at the wheel. I was tired of the pervasive sadness, the anger and the sense of loss that never seemed to leave me. I wanted to live again. Not just be alive, but to really live.

"You're just having an anxiety attack. It's going away now. Everything's going to be just fine, Frank."

I didn't know what an anxiety attack was, but it didn't sound good. It's hard to believe that anything that can be termed an "attack" is no big deal, especially when you're in the middle of it. However, Danny assured me that all was well. And true enough, it was.

As the seconds ticked by, Maryland grew closer, my heart rate and breathing slowed to only a little faster than the speed of the Taurus. My chest no longer felt like a fat man was sitting on it. Danny was making progress.

"You're just a little tense. Now take a good, deep breath and let it out slowly. Go ahead, blow it out. You're doing fine." He was speaking in such a melodious, smooth voice. The situation somehow brought to mind the married guys at work who'd told stories of how they'd learned to talk to their wives during the delivery of their children. It sounded like new age nonsense to me at the time. But it was working. The tightness in my chest was going away. The light-headedness that had been making my brain swim as if the car was spinning slowly on its axis was abating too. Within another mile or two I was feeling like myself again, and Maryland was on the horizon.

"Do you want to pull over, Frank? It's OK if you do. We're not in any rush."

"No, I'm OK. I think I'm OK now," I answered, honestly feeling better.

Hey, I felt better! And not just because the tension of the anxiety attack was perceptibly oozing out of my chest and head. Danny was right. I did feel better. I could honestly feel less tension in my body than there had been. My mind was less troubled and had begun working at a more even pace. I don't know if it was the Lamaze method Danny used on me, or if my suddenly elevated spirits really did have something to do with helping the ultimate Type A woman in the Envoy, but I really was feeling better. Only slightly perhaps, but noticeably so. And when you're at the absolute bottom of a long, dark hole, even a half step up toward the light feels like progress.

"Hey…" I started to say.

"See. You're feeling better aren't you?" Danny continued, smiling.

"Yeah, I am," I admitted with some satisfaction. I took in the sights around me as I answered him, no longer limiting my gaze to just the two lanes of pavement ahead. "I really am feeling better." Then almost as if to negate the moment, I added, "But I'm not sure it has anything to do with the woman in the broken-down Chevy."

"It does, and it doesn't." Danny waved off my cynicism as if it was no more significant than a single gnat buzzing around his head. "The important thing is that you're feeling better, and you know how to continue that process."

"Process? I'm just driving the car, man. I don't have a process."

"Recovery from any damage requires a process," he explained. "It doesn't matter whether the damage is physical or emotional. If you follow the process, the healing continues."

"But I haven't suffered any damage," I protested. "She missed me. The Chevy missed me completely."

Danny cocked his head to one side and threw a look my way that reminded me of a wise old man looking over his reading glasses at a beloved but young, ignorant student. He didn't need any words to convince me that he could see right through any defensive facade I might put up between us.

"OK," I said in resignation, "I may have picked up a few dings along the way."

"Um hum," said Danny with some satisfaction.

CHAPTER 15

The Taurus continued southward, almost as if it had a mind of its own. The weather was warming noticeably, which was a welcome change. The chilly morning had given way to a comfortably cool afternoon. It was the sort of weather that makes driving with the windows open enjoyable. Not so much to rid the car of unwanted heat as to enjoy the sensation of fresh, cool air rushing past your face, surrounding your frame.

I was keenly aware of the changing meteorological conditions, but I was hardly overjoyed about the changes occurring within me. I was at long last beginning to be observant of them. Connecting the dots in life was a skill I was still far from mastering.

Danny had slunk down in his seat and taken another nap after my anxiety attack subsided. The experience had apparently been a difficult one for both of us. Although, my old friend was showing distinct signs that he was continuing to gain strength as the miles rolled by. His appearance was more vibrant and lively, his mind more alert. Our conversations were still sporadic. He only engaged me in short bursts. But those bursts of energy were becoming more and more frequent. Peculiar as it may sound, even his clothes seemed to fit his body better.

Danny was very definitely on the mend.

I on the other hand, was in less than tip-top condition. When left to myself, which I was for much of the time as we drove on, I recognized that my mood was flip-flopping back and forth at an alarming rate as I suffered through bouts of emotional confusion. Momentary glimmers of hope were beaten back by a sense of impending doom that frankly scared the beejeezus out of me. Danny's attempts to soothe the nervous strain helped, there's no doubt about that. But the long stretches of silence while he slept allowed my mind to wander without direction, seeking out the darkest thoughts and the most hopeless possibilities for me to consider, alone.

The radio was my only saving grace. Again and again, I was dragged out of a gloomy funk by a tune, a phrase, or the rip-snorting scream of a well-loved and long forgotten guitar solo. Without the radio I'd have been lost. Whenever Danny was unavailable, the radio filled my need for distraction from my personal woes.

I'd always been under the impression that FM radio signals were relatively weak. Although, never having been far enough from home to test that theory, I didn't really know for sure. With several hundred miles behind us, I was surprised that the nondescript, factory-installed radio in the Taurus continued to provide a never-ending stream of audio accompaniment. I hadn't touched the thing since leaving Hartford. As far as I knew, Danny hadn't either. But there it was, playing away. The miracle of Marconi doing its thing.

A loud, warbly yawn signaled that Danny had risen from the great beyond again.

"Ooohhhh, that was good," said my passenger, assumably referring to a dream he must have been having. He stretched his arms and squirmed in his seat to get the blood flowing again. Squinting through the windshield, Danny inquired sincerely, "Where are we now?"

Somewhat sheepishly I answered, "I'm not sure, exactly. Maybe Maryland, or Virginia, I guess." Truth be told, I hadn't been paying attention. The road was rolling by without much of a need for my input. I'd been daydreaming while Split Enz played "I Got You" in the background. The band was from New Zealand, or Australia. I'm embarrassed to admit that I've never really been able to distinguish between those two countries for some reason. In any case, two brothers named Finn led the group. I think "I Got You" was their only hit here in the States. Whether it was or it wasn't, it was the only song I knew by them. And I loved it.

The infectious chorus rang out, swimming around in my head like a round robin of, "Michael Row Your Boat Ashore."

"So you never got married, huh?" Danny was apparently feeling inquisitive.

"No, I didn't," I answered flatly. "How'd you know that?"

"Well, the decor in your apartment was a pretty good indicator that you're single. And, of course, the fact that you were willing to drop everything and launch off on an impulsive road trip is a solid tip-off."

"Hey, you asked for the ride," I shot back, too defensively.

"I know, I know," Danny chuckled. "But you stayed single all these years, huh?"

"Yeah, I did."

"Never found the right woman?"

I could have answered in the affirmative. I thought about doing that for an instant. It would have been the easy answer. But it would have been dishonest too.

"Actually, I found the right woman a couple times. I think I did anyhow," I admitted truthfully. "It's probably more accurate to say they just weren't lucky enough to have found the right guy."

"Ouch," Danny winced. "That's a painful admission."

"Yes, it is. But I'm pretty sure it's the truth."

We drove on in silence for a short time. My thoughts drifted to Jackie and the total failure our life together had turned out to be. I harbored no animosity toward her, even if she did drown every piece of clothing I owned in the bathtub. I deserved it. I was sure of that. Although, I wasn't exactly sure why.

"So we'll let all that go for the moment," said Danny. "It seems like a touchy subject anyway."

"OK."

"How are your folks doing?"

"They're dead."

"Both of them?" he asked, noticeably surprised.

"Yep, both of them."

"Wow," Danny whistled long and low. "What happened, if you don't mind me asking? I mean, they weren't that old."

"No, they weren't that old at all."

"That must have been devastating."

I shrugged and did my best to push the memories from my mind. We'd never been close, my parents and I. Not even toward the end of their lives. In all honesty, we were barely even speaking to one another anymore. Once my younger sister, Sharon moved to California, we didn't even share the pretense of visiting each other for the holidays. It's true, we resided in the same town, my mother, father and me. But we lived in different worlds. We were a classically dysfunctional family, divided by choice rather than by circumstance.

I never asked her, but it seemed reasonable to assume that Sharon had moved to the other side of the continent in an effort to start over with a clean slate. She got as far away from her nuclear family as she could. Three thousand miles and a handful of mountain ranges separated us. From what I'd been able to glean over the years, the move had worked out in her favor. At least Sharon had a life, a husband, a daughter. She was the lucky one.

"Was there an accident?" Danny nudged me again, pushing for details. Considering how distant we'd been in life, I found it surprising that the memory of my parent's deaths was far more emotional for me than I could comfortably deal with. Time had done little to ease that pain.

Still, I had no qualms about telling Danny that my father had suffered a massive heart attack and done a face plant in the middle of the living room in our old house on Burke Street. He died as he lived, blaming someone else for his failings and errors. At his funeral, my mother told me he'd been yelling at the television when it happened. Neal Cavuto had apparently been relaying some unwelcome news about a plunge in the Dow Jones Industrial Average on Fox News. My father took offense, having invested the bulk of his retirement funds in a handful of highly volatile stocks he hoped would skyrocket and finally make him the wealthy man he thought he deserved to be. In the midst of what my Mom described as a "hissy fit," the old man turned beet red, sputtered like a motorboat and dropped face-first onto the well-worn wall-to-wall carpeting. By the time the ambulance arrived, he was already long gone.

"No, I don't think you could call their deaths an accident," I admitted.

"Disease then?" Danny kept pushing.

"No, neither of them died of cancer or a runaway infection or a burst appendix or anything like that," I answered.

While brutally final, at least those deaths were unavoidable. Deaths that came about after valiant battles against powerful forces, fought with the aid of medical professionals. My father's death was more or less self-induced. Which is nothing to be proud of. My mother's demise, only four days after my father's, was a suicide, plain and simple. A fact that hadn't struck me as nearly so personal and understandable until that moment. Did my mother feel the same despair I'd felt only a day or two ago? Why did she carry out her plan to end it all, while I'd chickened out?

Danny! He was the difference.

My mother was alone. Unimpeded by outside forces, she'd had both the opportunity and the motive to be the agent of her own death. I'd been interrupted before I could act on my impulses.

I shifted my gaze to my old friend, sitting only inches away. Even in his increasingly rejuvenated state, he was still a long way from being mistaken for a man of great power and consequence. I knew better though. I owed my life to this rumpled bit of human refuse. And I was far too ashamed to admit it out loud.

"I guess you could say bad luck had a lot to do with it." It was the only thing I could think to say that didn't dishonor my mother or expose me as the fraud I was.

The truth was, my mother had left the minimalist funeral service held for my father, alone. Sharon and I rode together in a limousine supplied by the funeral home. We'd expected our mother to join us. But as we waited for her to leave our father's casket and climb in beside us, she walked across the parking lot to her own car, a used Cadillac Sedan DeVille. She started the car and in a style very uncharacteristic of a diminutive woman in her mid-fifties, lurched out of the parking space in a burst of smoke and squealing tires. While the rest of the small funeral procession waited for the traffic on Silver Lane to offer us an opening, my mother rocketed into the street and careened down the road apparently with no regard for lanes, standardized driving rules or her fellow motorists. She was headed in the wrong direction too, away from the cemetery.

Sharon and I dutifully stuck with the plan for the funeral. We escorted our father to his final resting place, on a grassy hillside in Manchester where he still rests today. We never saw our mother again.

Two days later a Sedan Deville was discovered on the muddy bottom of the Connecticut River. It was hers. Two young boys on a fishing trip hooked her rear bumper. Only their zeal to recover a lost lure led to the discovery of our mother's Cadillac. Otherwise it might have been lost forever, or at least a long, long time. Probably until a drought lowered the water level enough for the roof to pop out above the surface. It had apparently sunk almost as soon as it hit the water. Which occurred right after she launched herself and that behemoth of a vehicle from the ferry slip in neighboring Glastonbury.

In warmer weather, the ferry would have been running. There might have been a chance of her being rescued. But in the frigid waters of early spring, the ferry hadn't been fired up for the season yet. The area was deserted. Nobody heard her call for help, if she did in fact call out. Not a soul was on hand to see a well-dressed, middle-aged woman emerge from a submerged but otherwise perfectly good, pre-owned luxury sedan and float downstream with the current. Where her body ended up is anyone's guess. Long Island Sound I would imagine. As far as I know the only witnesses to my mother's death were the fishes. And whatever they might have seen, they weren't talking.

"Yeah, bad luck pretty much sums it up," I said absently as the North Carolina state line rolled beneath our tires and disappeared behind us.

"So you're alone then. An orphan, more or less," Danny observed.

"I guess so."

"What about Sharon?"

"She's an orphan too. It was sort of a package deal."

"No, I mean is she doing well? Is she OK?"

"Yeah, she's doing fine. Sharon is the only one of us who seems to have gotten it right." I grinned with the knowledge that emotional termites and dysfunctional dry rot hadn't destroyed our entire family tree. Sharon's life was our one great success story. She'd done just fine.

"But you don't see each other very often?" Danny continued, pressing me for details.

"No, we don't. She writes from time to time and I get a Christmas card from her every year. But California is far away. Our paths don't cross much."

"Do they cross at all?" Danny asked skeptically.

After a moment or two of reflection, I admitted, "No, they don't."

"Why not?"

"I told you why not. She lives three thousand miles away." The implication that the distance between us was more than geographical irritated me. We hadn't seen each other in years. Not since our father's funeral, six years before. And unless I either won the lottery or she moved east, it wasn't likely that we'd be seeing each other in the near future either.

"Is she all alone, too?"

"No, she has a family." I knew that was true. Sharon had sent me pictures of her husband and the daughter they'd adopted four years earlier. They gave every appearance of being a happy, healthy family unit. Still, I'd never met the people who'd made my sister's life complete. Not in person anyway. Which was probably for the best. There wasn't much point in showing up and tainting the well she was drawing life from now.

"And how do you feel about having a family of your own one day?" Danny inquired sincerely.

"That seems unlikely," I replied. "Considering how things have gone up until now, I'm pretty sure I'm the antidote for love and affection."

"Well, maybe that will change. Maybe you could change."

"Maybe," I said, "but it still seems unlikely, if you ask me."

"How unlikely would you say it is, exactly? As unlikely as putting a man on the moon, or as unlikely as the Red Sox winning the World Series?"

"Very funny, Nostradamus. Look, if you're just going to rag on me the whole time, you might as well go back to sleep." I was trying to sound playful, needling Danny in return for the way he'd been pressing me for a reaction. But I failed miserably. I don't know if my tone of voice was off or if the words I chose conveyed a different meaning than I'd intended. Either way, I ended up sounding bitchy and bitter rather than pithy and humorous.

"OK," he said, closed his eyes and fell asleep almost immediately.

Harry Nilsson's sweet, sensitive voice flowed from the Taurus' speakers. "Without You," washed over me like soothing rain. Harry's touching lament about the crushing emptiness of living alone and unloved struck a powerful chord deep inside me. I was glad Danny had fallen asleep. I wouldn't have wanted him to see me crying as the sun set over the North Carolina hills to the west.

Loneliness is a terrible thing.

CHAPTER 16

Darkness enveloped the landscape surrounding us, bringing the sky alive with thousands upon thousands of tiny pinpricks of light. A multitude of stars stretched from horizon to horizon. There were more than I could ever hope to count. Far more than I'd ever known were up there, out there and scattered in every direction all around us.

The greenery of North Carolina had disappeared with the setting sun. Only the two beams of light radiating from the front end of my increasingly dilapidated Taurus penetrated the nothingness of night. Occasionally, opposing headlights would flicker through the trees to our left. But not bright enough or for long enough to break the almost magical spell the darkness had cast on the land. Somehow, the traffic headed south was all so far ahead of or behind us, the distance made their lights inconsequential. Without that distraction, the stars were free to shine down on Danny and me with an intensity I found to be nothing short of intoxicating. So much so that I found myself craning my neck over the steering wheel to peek up through the windshield at the beauty of it all.

"You've had a hard time lately, haven't you, Frank?"

Danny was awake again, rattling my cage, making me think about things I'd rather have left alone. I thought about the implication for a moment, then answered.

"Uh huh."

"It's going to be OK you know. You're going to be OK." He said this as if he had inside information. As if the statement wasn't a mere opinion, but a verifiable fact.

"I guess."

I didn't completely believe him, but I didn't see any reason to resist the idea either. So I chose to go with the flow.

Danny repeated himself more insistently.

"I mean it. You're going to be OK. You're going to find yourself again." He was being kind, but he was adamant. My old friend had a point to make and this was the moment he'd chosen to make it, just as I was getting my first good look at the universe that had been hidden behind suburban street lights and downtown neon signs for my entire life. Danny babbled on, "The good news is that the few regrets you've got in life are the result of inactivity." He wasn't lecturing. He wasn't even looking in my direction. He was just casually chatting as he looked out into the darkness, as if he could see right through the night. "That's a relatively easy problem to fix, ya' know. It's not like you've lived a vindictive lifestyle, inflicting cruelty and violence on the world. That's a tougher nut to crack. You just need to recognize a simple weakness in your personality and make a change."

I was listening and thinking hard about what he was saying. Never having been particularly disposed to sitting quietly while being criticized, the fact that I was listening at all was pretty unusual. But Danny's assertion that the great truths in life were simple and basic made more and more sense as he related his ever-expanding list of the "rules of life." He shared those precious nuggets of knowledge one by one. He was in no rush. That much was clear.

According to Danny, people often become such thoughtless slaves to the pressures and distractions of the daily grind, they begin to believe life is complicated and unruly by nature. It isn't, though. Although he admitted, given the opportunity, we can and often do make life far more difficult than it needs to be. Peculiar as it may sound, Danny claimed it to be the preference of a great many of us. Apparently, the majority of us mistake being physically busy for being intellectually and emotionally engaged. As it turns out, there really isn't much of a connection there at all. It's all an illusion. It's a tremendously counterproductive illusion, too.

"Do you remember the way you were when we were younger?" It was a rhetorical question. "You were a completely different guy, Frank. Do you remember? You were confident. You believed you could do anything." Danny had my memory digging into a seriously deep, dark hole now. He was pushing me to remember tidbits of my life that I'd spent the better part of two decades trying to forget.

I snorted at the memory of the brash young man I'd been. The words that might convey my feelings about the me I used to be were nowhere to be found.

He was right, though. I really did believe I could do anything back then. I believed that Danny and I were going to be famous, wealthy beyond our wildest dreams. We'd be kings who traveled the world on a whim.

"That's an embarrassing thought," I said.

"What is?"

"The idea that we," I corrected myself, "that *I* could have gone on to do great things. That I could have been somebody of consequence."

I was truly ashamed for having allowed myself to live as only the superficial shell of a man. But at the same time, rediscovering the memories of when Danny and I were young and strong was enlightening, too. That was a wonderful time of life. When through that volatile combination of youthful arrogance and naivete, we'd developed an almost unlimited faith in our own abilities.

"First of all, it's fairly important that you learn to accept the fact that you already are a person of consequence." Danny's expression was stern. "Your future depends on it." He was lecturing now, like a college professor tutoring a promising but troubled student. "Everyone is a person of consequence, no matter what their station in life might be. Think about it. What's the alternative?"

I didn't feel any need to answer. Danny was on a roll.

"If they weren't, it would mean the world is populated entirely by two kinds of people, those who are worthwhile and those who aren't. You've got to know right off that's just not the way it is." Another one of those simple truths flew out of Danny's mouth as if it was nothing special, just a priceless jewel tossed into the wind for anyone close by to grab a hold of and treasure. "And in the second place, you did do something special. Something that anyone you've ever known would count as an accomplishment to be proud of. Even your Dad would be impressed with what you've done."

I looked directly at Danny, incredulous at his ridiculous assertion that I, in particular, was a man of accomplishment. His expression confirmed he was serious. He sat calmly on his side of the car, looking right back at me, as serene as could be.

"Are you out of your mind?" I shouted back. The emotional flood gates flew open, letting loose a torrent of pent-up frustration and anger I felt for the disappointment that my life had become. It all came pouring out in a tirade of expletives, spittle and raw emotional fury.

"I've never accomplished a single fucking worthwhile thing in my entire life," I shouted in exasperation. How could he be under the impression I not only had the capacity to do something worthwhile, but that I already had? "I was a lousy student in school because I didn't care. I didn't pursue music as a career like we'd planned, because when it came right down to it…I was afraid. I was afraid to go out into unfamiliar territory and put myself up against players and singers and writers who were so much better than we were." I caught myself in mid rant and corrected myself, "Better than *I* was."

"I know," Danny replied quietly, knowingly.

Tears flowed down my unshaven cheeks as I raved on, "I wanted to be so much more than this."

"I know," came the quiet response.

Lashing out with my right hand, taking a stab at the dash board, I carried on, "I was afraid, Danny. I just wanted to grow up and become a regular person. I didn't want to fail. I even took a job I hated because I thought it was the right thing to do."

"There isn't any such thing as a regular person," Danny said, impassively. "And you haven't failed. Not yet, anyhow."

"I took on a life that I detested," I cried out in pain. "Every single thing I've done in my life has been an absolute failure." I was screaming, pleading with myself for mercy. The tears continued to flow as flecks of spittle flew from my mouth with each new outburst.

Holding the wheel tightly, struggling to keep the uneasily vibrating Taurus in the right-hand lane, the slow lane, where a guy like me belonged, I was having an almost total breakdown. That was my reward for making the choice to relive the long, torturous series of events that led me to this, the low point of my life.

"How can you even imply that I've got potential, or that I can be anything other than what I am?" I railed on at poor Danny who sat passively, absorbing my tirade. He looked like a skinny little holy man, taking it all in. Never once did he raise his voice or argue back.

"And what are you?" he asked quietly, almost in a whisper.

"A failure!" I screamed. My station in life was as obvious as it could be, and now I was for the first time, admitting it out loud.

"Nnnoooooo," Danny corrected me, shaking his head lightly. The word dragged out long and slow, the extended length somehow imparting it with extra weight, a deeper meaning. "You're not a failure by any means. You've just made some mistakes. What you perceive as failure is really nothing more than an unfortunate series of bad decisions. That's all."

"Bad decisions. Yeah." The sarcasm was thick, and bitter. "So what am I supposed to do now, huh?" I was challenging my old friend, daring him to apply his "rules of life" to the almost surely insurmountable task of pulling the remnants of my life from the bottom of the ever-deepening pit I'd dug for myself.

"Make better ones," he replied. The words rolled off his tongue as if the answer was the most obvious thing in the world. Which upon reflection I realized, it was.

While his appearance conveyed the beating Danny had taken over the course of his own life, he was mentally as sharp as ever. Maybe even more so. He was at peace with himself, whatever his circumstances might have been. Unshaken by my temper tantrum, he appeared serene, absolutely at ease with the world around him. Throughout the entire ugly episode, he hadn't flinched.

It occurred to me that no matter how tough things got for him, Danny had no intention of giving up. If his way of looking at the world was more in tune with reality than mine was, maybe I shouldn't throw in the towel just yet after all. I felt compelled to at least entertain the possibility that my old friend knew a thing or two that I didn't. Which wasn't easy for me to do. But I resigned myself to accept his outlook as a working theory. After all, what did I have to lose?

Even in the darkness, with only the light reflected back from our own headlights and the pinpoints of stars above, I could see with each passing mile that Danny was becoming more mentally lucid and physically capable. Although, I also considered for the first time that perhaps it wasn't so much that he was being transformed as it was my perception of him that was changing.

Something was going on in that creaky old gray car as it rolled down the road. And it wasn't something I understood very well. It was strange. But it was good, too.

"Make better ones," I said, almost to myself.

"Make better ones," agreed Danny. He smiled, a warm smile that confirmed our friendship. I felt warm inside. For the first time in who knows how long, I didn't feel quite so alone in the world.

"Make better ones," I said again, with more cheer in my voice this time. Danny's lesson hit home. My life was mine to make what I would of it. Whether I started now, or next week, or next year, as long as I was drawing breath, I had hope of becoming a more substantial person than I had been.

Why wait? When the sun came up on a new day, I promised myself that I'd begin reinventing myself. It was time to put the past behind me and start to live again.

As simple as that idea may sound, it was an epiphany to me. News that I had every intention of acting on right away. But first, I needed to get off the road for a bit. I needed to rest. Maybe it was the hours upon hours of ceaseless driving. Or maybe it had more to do with the conversation requiring far more concentration than I was prepared for. Whatever the reason, I was exhausted.

A generic rest stop sign loomed out of the darkness ahead, the Taurus' headlights making it glow eerily green and white. Aiming the hood toward the next off ramp, I rolled into a long, sparsely populated parking lot and eased into a space far from the rest rooms and snack machines.

The engine groaned to a stop as I rotated the key counter clockwise. The machinery sounded as tired and worn out as I felt, but I was far too sleepy to care as I climbed into the back seat and curled up into a ball. Shortly, the darkness overtook me and I went willingly into the void.

CHAPTER 17

A Fender Telecaster guitar hung loosely from a leather strap across my shoulder. It felt perfect in my hands, solid and full of potential. Finished in custom metal flake white paint, it looked like a crystal-filled snowstorm was raging somewhere deep in its musical core. This was my favorite of any guitar I'd ever owned.

In the back of my mind, I remembered the day I first saw that guitar. It was winter and bitterly cold. The kind of cold that makes your nose hurt with each frigid breath. Wispy, white streams of water vapor seemed to emanate from everywhere. When it's that cold, manhole covers, sewer grates, even your own head is transformed into a steam manufacturing facility. Billowing clouds of warm, moisture-laden air explode from the nose and mouth with every exhalation.

We'd driven down to Cardini's Music that day, Danny and me. We both needed guitar strings and picks, but we were killing an afternoon as much as we were doing a necessary chore. I loved going to Cardini's. As a matter of fact, I considered it to be a life-affirming experience.

The store was a little family-owned shop on Burnside Avenue, not far from the apartment I'd one day call home, on Tolland Street. It's gone now. I don't know why. It just is. One day it was Cardini's Music Shop, the next it was empty. A few weeks later, it was remodeled and became a far less alluring store that sold vinyl siding and Pittsburgh Paints.

Life changes and you just have to adapt to it. To resist is futile. The harder you try to make the world around you remain the same, the more the world demands to be free to change at will. Remember this…however the world around you looks today, know that it didn't look that way 20 years ago. It won't look like this 20 years from now, either. You just have to accept that fact. Learn to embrace it. Change is in your future, like it or not.

This occurred to me as the memory of buying that sparkling white Telecaster replayed in my head. I held the guitar in my hands, feeling the weight of it, examining it with my fingertips as well as my eyes. I experienced a profound sense of satisfaction at being reunited with it again after so many years apart.

On that particular trip to Cardini's, when the air was so cold that the vinyl seats in Mr. Loughman's car crackled as we settled into them, I got more than I bargained for. Mr. Cardini was just hanging the Telecaster up on the wall as Danny and I walked through the door, stomping the snow off our boots and cursing the temperature for being as deficient as it was. The Tele was worn a bit, but not too badly. Its neck sat crooked, as if there was a foreign object wedged between it and the body, preventing it from lying flat and straight. Any reasonably proficient guitar player should have been able to spot that flaw right off. Luckily for me, Mr. Cardini was a drummer.

A quick but discreet visual inspection confirmed my suspicion that somebody had indeed removed the neck and left a small obstruction in the joint when they put it back together. As long as the screw holes weren't stripped, I was sure I could fix the imperfection. In every other sense that Tele was the finest guitar I'd ever put my hands on. The few scratches on its body only served to give it more character.

Almost immediately, I was bartering with Mr. Cardini to become that guitar's new owner. In my favor was the fact that Cardini liked Danny and me. We were loyal customers. Working against me was our familiarity and Cardini's knowledge that I didn't have much money to work with.

After a fair amount of haggling, the dangling carrot miraculously appeared.

"I could pull it off the floor for you if you'd agree to buy it for say, two hundred and twenty-five dollars," Mr. Cardini offered. "But I'll only hold it for a week. After that, I have to put it back on the floor, for sale."

"Oh, I can do that, for sure Mr. Cardini. Thanks a lot." I shook the diminutive man's hand enthusiastically. In truth, I had no idea at all of how I might come up with that much money in only seven days.

As agreed, the store owner removed the guitar from his showroom and carefully put the object of my affection away in its rectangular, hard-shell case for safekeeping. I decided against buying strings and picks that day, preferring to save my seven dollars and change for a larger purchase scheduled for one week away.

"I don't know how, but I'm going to come up with that much money in a week," I agonized as we drove through East Hartford's frozen streets.

"I'm sure you will," Danny replied.

I was about a hundred and ten dollars short on the deal. With only a week to come up with the rest, it seemed unlikely that I'd be successful. I scrambled though, calling in even the smallest debts from friends and family, then going back for small loans from the very same people. I was adding dollars to my nest egg daily, but I was still too far from reaching my goal to feel confident that success was in my future.

The arrival of a heavy and unexpected snowstorm two days before my window of opportunity closed, put me over the top. I got up early and stayed out late shoveling more than my share of sidewalks and driveways. But at ten to fifteen dollars a pop, I was getting closer to my dream guitar with each shovel full of snow.

Fortunately, that snowstorm produced only the feather light variety of frozen precipitation. Fast, efficient and full of youthful exuberance, I shoveled enough driveways to reach my financial goal before the sun set on the seventh day. I was overjoyed.

Luck was certainly on my side. If that storm had produced the much heavier, slushy wet snow so common in southern New England, I'm sure that Tele would have wound up back on the wall marked for sale again, while I'd have suffered debilitating lower back pain for the rest of my life. But as it was, I walked back into Mr. Cardini's shop exactly one week after we'd shaken hands, with enough cash in my pocket to cover the purchase price and the sales tax that he had no choice but to tack on.

"I knew you'd be back," said Cardini with a big smile as I sauntered through the door. He'd already moved the guitar to a safe place behind the cash register in anticipation of my arrival.

"There was never any doubt," I answered with as much self-confidence as I could reasonably fake. Although the truth was, I hadn't been absolutely sure I'd come up with enough money until almost the last minute.

That had all happened more than a quarter of a century earlier, while I was still in high school. But somehow that same guitar, long gone from my possession, was now hanging from my shoulder as an alarmingly loud musical assault blasted me from all sides. I was in the midst of the commotion, holding my favorite guitar. But I wasn't actually playing. I was standing as still as a statue. One deeply confused observer planted smack in the middle of an unrelenting sonic fury.

The band was The Mayfair's, my old group. My three bandmates had me surrounded as they ran through an arrangement in Danny's Burke Street garage. Marc Patnoe stood less than three feet from Bobby's bass drum. Marc was hunched over, his head down, watching the fingers of his left-hand walk back and forth across the fret board of his bass, just like he always did. As a person, Marc was shy and withdrawn. He hardly spoke to us at all when the music died out. And we were his closest friends. But when the music was playing, he was a critical part of the band. I think that's when he felt most comfortable, when he was lost in the zone of being a bass player, an integral part of a group.

Bobby Yount was set up in the back of the garage, facing the front. He played the drums with a ferocity that reminded me of nothing so much as a linebacker going after a loose ball. His entire kit rattled with each shock-inducing blow from his meaty 5B gauge sticks. They were good-sized sticks and Bobby was larger and stronger than the average kid. Drummers are commonly viewed as the timekeepers whose playing leads a band. But Bobby didn't just lead the band, he drove us. Hard, with a pounding beat that could make the neighborhood quake. Even when we weren't quite sure where we were going, his drums pushed us enthusiastically forward.

Bobby's contorted face ranged through a spasmodic barrage of maniacal expressions. Which is exactly how I remembered him. Arms flailing away, bashing his drums into submission, he was a loveable lunatic if ever there was one. The rack toms shook ominously on their mounts as he made his way around the kit. The cymbals shook in terror.

Danny sat against the wall directly across from me. His fingers noodling over the keyboard of a Fender Rhodes.

The Rhodes electric piano was unique. Instead of making its sound in the traditional way, via hammers striking strings, it used a series of tuning forks that sounded a lot like little bells. You might think of it as a carillon in miniature. Not content to be just a better-than-average guitar player, Danny had set his sights on being a great all-around musician. Even as teenagers, it had become apparent that he was well on his way to accomplishing that goal. Musically he'd surpassed us all by the time he was seventeen.

Something wasn't right. Something was very much out of place, but I couldn't quite put my finger on it. I loosened up a bit and began looking around with a more discerning eye. What was I missing?

Danny's fingers were dancing across the keys of his electric piano as he sang into a dinged up old microphone. I couldn't make out the words amid the din of the full-on rehearsal, but the tune sounded familiar. The effect reminded me of early REM recordings. The words, being nearly indecipherable, became a melody line unto themselves. Their meaning was entirely inconsequential to the enjoyment of the song.

My mind raced. My ability to think clearly was muddled. Something was wrong, profoundly wrong. But try as I might, I couldn't identify exactly what was amiss. It wasn't until I stopped trying to find the answer that the problem became obvious to me.

They were young, too young. And Danny's family had moved to Canada years ago. They didn't own or live in the house on Burke Street anymore.

"What's going on?" I yelled over the music at the teenaged version of Danny. His eyes were closed. He didn't hear me.

Looking down at my hands, which were still gripping the neck of my sparkling white Tele, I realized something else. I wasn't young. My hands were lined and showed obvious signs of use and abuse, like those of a man approaching middle age tend to be. My hands really were my hands. They weren't the hands of a teenager. I was no longer young. Death was closing in on me, while Danny, Bobby and Marc had somehow kept age and the future at bay.

Fear began to well up inside me. "What's going ooooonnn?" I screamed over the pounding beat, throbbing bass and swirling keyboards. Panic began to take over. My forehead was wet, the neck of my guitar became slick as my palms began to sweat.

"What's going on?" I repeated over and over again. Mumbling, screaming, sobbing as I alternately pleaded or demanded an answer from my old friends. They were all so timelessly and impossibly young.

Danny's eye's popped open and he drilled his gaze into mine, without missing a beat or a note as his fingers continued to dance across the keyboard. With our eyes locked together, he intoned with perfect clarity, "You're dreaming, Frank."

Yes, that was it. I was dreaming. Dreaming about the band, about my youth. And why not? Those were the happiest days of my life. The four of us weren't just together physically. We were together spiritually and emotionally too. We were a unit, like soldiers during wartime. It was our mission to push on, to build up a catalog of original material and head out onto the open road. We would entertain thousands upon thousands of adoring fans. We'd play on bills with big names like Bad Company and Aerosmith, working our way up that ladder to the point where we could headline a coliseum show of our own.

"Dreaming, yes, I'm dreaming," I acknowledged with relief. The realization freed me to enjoy the images and memories as they came to me. As disjointed and bizarre as they were, I reveled in the sense of reality dreams can impart. I remembered exactly how I'd felt during countless rehearsals in Danny's garage, rehearsals that were virtually indistinguishable from the one I was in the midst of now.

"This is great!" I yelled at the rest of the band. Danny smiled and nodded in agreement. Bobby kept pounding his drums oblivious to my newfound joy while Marc's eyes stayed glued to the fingers of his left hand.

We'd dreamed of coming back home to play the Hartford Civic Center and packing the place. We'd be conquering heroes, we agreed. Channel 3 News would interview us at their rooftop studio on Constitution Plaza. Local radio legend Brad Davis would play our records in heavy rotation on his show, broadcast on WDRC. Howard Stern at WCCC would feud with WHCN's morning men, Picozzi and the Horn for backstage interviews and exclusive chats with us in their studios. We'd be hometown boys done good. We'd have arrived.

That was the dream for the four of us.

But in real life, none of that happened. The roof of the Hartford Civic Center collapsed under the weight of a heavy accumulation of snow, missing its opportunity to kill hundreds, if not thousands of sports fans by only a few hours. Brad Davis got older and became inevitably less cool as his core audience aged along with him. WDRC changed. The new FM programming lost any edge it ever had in favor of dull and repetitive corporate style playlists. Howard Stern went to Detroit, then Washington, then New York and ultimately outer space, where he became the biggest thing in radio since Jack Benny. Picozzi and the Horn left WHCN, effectively bringing an end to the era of inventive, entertaining local talent. Even Channel 3's reign as the most powerful station in the area became a moot point with the advent of cable and satellite TV.

Life changed and The Mayfair's were no longer a part of it. We hadn't adapted to the world around us. Instead, we fell apart. We ceased to exist. We died.

The music in Danny's garage rehearsal space stopped, as if the needle had been picked up from a record. Bobby and Marc disappeared. The two of them vanished without leaving the slightest evidence they'd ever been there at all. Danny and I were alone in the garage.

"This is so cool," I said, loving the experience as it occurred to me.

"Yeah it is," he agreed, still tickling the keys of his Rhodes. The notes he picked out hinted at an abbreviated arrangement of the tune the band had been playing only moments before.

He looked great. This was just the way I remembered him, in the years before he was so worn down and beaten up by life.

"Pretty good, huh?" His tone implied great pride, almost as if he was boasting. The smile was back, his youthful eyes delicately crinkling in the corners.

"I'm sorry?" He'd caught me off-guard. I wasn't exactly sure what he was referring to. Which seemed odd, considering I'd realized that I was dreaming and was ostensibly in control of the direction of all the activity surrounding me.

"The song, it's pretty good," he was urging me to agree.

"Yeah, it's OK," I admitted, distracted as I was by the circumstances of the conversation.

"OK? It's a hit, Frank!" Danny was beaming with excitement, still twiddling away on the piano as he spoke.

"I've got to be honest with you Danny. I can't remember how to play it. I don't even know the words." I was somewhat embarrassed to admit that fact even if it was only in a dream. The melody was so familiar that I found it frustrating to have such difficulty placing it. I had to admit. It was catchy, though.

"I kind of like it," I announced boldly.

"I should hope so," he laughed.

"Why would you hope so?"

"Because you wrote it."

A ferocious clap of thunder snapped me awake. Yet my eyes popped open to find nothing but bright sunshine filtering through tall, bushy pine trees rising into the sky from all around me. There was no storm raging over South Carolina. As a matter of fact, there was hardly any sound at all. Only the soft rush of traffic mixing with the muted voices of fellow travelers who'd parked closer to the facilities during the night. I looked at my watch.

"Eleven-thirty?" I was amazed. How could I have slept so long, curled up in the back seat of a moldy old car?

"Welcome back," Danny piped up from the front seat.

"Why did you let me sleep so long?" I demanded, as if my sleep schedule was somehow my traveling companion's responsibility.

"Sleep is an important commodity my friend. You didn't have much in the bank."

"You can say that again," I agreed, the thought of my dwindling funds leaping to the forefront of my mind once again.

"I was talking about sleep, not money," Danny corrected me.

Yawning mightily and stretching my arms toward the ceiling of the car, I commented, "Of the two, I'll take the money." I winked in Danny's direction. "In my experience, it's a whole lot easier to grab a nap than earn a living."

"Be careful what you wish for, Frank," Danny warned. "There's a big difference between being a man of great wealth as opposed to being a person of substance."

"I know that," I replied sharply. Although to be honest, I had no idea what he was talking about.

"I'm not sure you do," Danny challenged, clearly skeptical of my claim. But he shifted gears quickly. Getting back to our current situation, Danny announced, "Whenever you're ready, I think we should get going."

"Absolutely, right," I said, sitting up and pulling myself out from the back seat for the second morning in a row. "Give me just a minute to clean up and I'll be ready to roll."

As I headed off to the Men's Room and a vending machine breakfast, I heard his voice in my ear.

"I'll be here," Danny assured me.

I realized I was humming as I entered the rest room. The song from my dream repeated over and over in my head, running like a loop, never starting, never ending. A mental 8-track tape cartridge of sorts. I still had no idea what the words were or where I'd heard it before. But it stuck with me, a hauntingly familiar melody that nagged at me well into the afternoon.

CHAPTER 18

By almost any measure, it was a good afternoon. The temperature was at least 30 degrees warmer than I'd have been experiencing if I'd stayed in Connecticut. With the windows rolled down and a strong breeze induced by highway speeds whipping through the car, I was trying hard to enjoy the scent of the sweet sappy pines that lined the highway, a thick wall of aromatic greenery. But try as I might to look on the bright side, a dark shadow continued to stalk me. I knew, even if only subconsciously, that malevolent forces were on my tail. Eventually, they would catch up with me. Exactly when and where fate might intervene was the question that nagged ever more furiously at my overtired mind. I had no answers, only ragged nerves.

The farther we descended into the south, disturbing signs of impending trouble caught my attention with greater frequency. The experience of starting the car that late morning back at the rest stop is a good example.

"And off we go," Danny announced with glee.

"Florida here we come," I replied hopefully, the key that would bring the Taurus's engine to life poised between my fingers at the ignition switch. And come to life it did, complete with an unnerving bang and a pop and an ominous cloud of black smoke, thick enough to almost completely block my field of vision in the rear-view mirror.

Pushing that event from my mind as best as I could, I pressed on, intent on reaching my destination on that, the third day of my journey.

The engine started out running rough, kicking and protesting against my desire to accelerate onto the highway. But I had hope, even as damaged and worn as the aged Ford was. That car had enough miles logged on the odometer that it had given up and refused to roll over another digit long ago. But I still fully expected this last day on the road to be capped off with the successful conclusion to our journey. We'd finally have arrived in the Sunshine State.

I tried to push the Taurus to 60 miles per hour, still working under the assumption that the faster I drove the sooner I'd reach my goal. But the overworked and poorly maintained drive train disagreed and resisted. The only result of my pressing ever harder on the accelerator was a sickly series of knocks and worrisome metallic gnashing sounds. The puff of smoke I'd seen at the rest stop was still with us, drawn out now into a long wispy trail of blue and white. Individually the signs were worrisome. Collectively they spelled almost certain doom.

Eventually accepting the car's limitations for what they were, I backed off and settled on 55 miles per hour as the fastest pace I'd be able to set. I was disappointed to be progressing so much slower than I'd intended to, especially on the pancake flat roads of the south. But being our last day on the road, I imagined I could put up with the minor inconvenience of rolling into my destination a bit slower than I'd hoped. It wasn't long before I realized that even my lowered expectations were almost assuredly beyond my grasp.

By the time we crossed the Georgia state line two hours later, our speed had slipped to 50. The clanking of the engine had worsened and while I wasn't positive, I thought I saw the high temperature light in the dashboard beginning to glow. In combination, they were ample warnings that the end was near.

"This isn't looking good," I muttered as I allowed the car to drift down to 45 miles per hour. The smoke trail behind us was persistent, the clanking of the engine ever louder. It became harder and harder for me to ignore the obvious.

"Things will work out," Danny responded simply.

"I'm not so sure," I replied with genuine concern, "I'm beginning to think the car's not going to make it."

"You've got to have faith, Frank. Everything will work out fine in the long run."

"Faith, huh?" I said dubiously. "You think this is the sort of situation where God is likely to intervene?"

"You never can tell," Danny said with a smile.

I was as skeptical as Danny was optimistic. Silently urging the Taurus to hold itself together for just a little while longer, I kept an eye out for signs counting down the miles to Savannah, then Jacksonville. We were closing in on our goal without a doubt. But we were by no means assured of success. The closer we got, the higher my anxiety level rose.

Two and a half hours after entering Georgia, we rolled gingerly across a low concrete bridge, leaving the Peach State behind us. Florida lay on the opposite side, festooned with palms and pines and a wonderland of vegetation of every imaginable shape and size. We were so close. So close to the end of the line.

A vibration that took the form of a steady hum passed from the engine through the frame of the car and into the interior. It transferred to my hands through the steering wheel, ultimately routing itself directly to my brain. Acutely attuned to each new bang or clunk or unexpected rattle, I became more convinced than ever that I was only moments away from being stranded. The Taurus was on its last legs. There was no denying it.

"Five miles to Jacksonville," Danny chimed in as a highway sign proclaiming that very fact drifted past.

Shaking myself alert, I shifted my concentration from the engine to the road, casting my gaze farther down the highway to where a full-blown city sat directly in our path.

Jacksonville was bigger than Hartford. Much bigger. And although both cities were built alongside a river, Hartford was designed in such a way that the city was abbreviated by its proximity to the Connecticut River. This most northern city in Florida on the other hand, had ignored the limitations the St. Johns River had presented it with, choosing instead to revel in the waterfront as glorious scenery and take advantage of the natural highway to the sea it presented. Jacksonville completely surrounded the lazily flowing waters of the St. Johns. The city rose up from the banks and stretched out to the horizon on all sides. The river and the city coexisted, neither of them impeding the progress of the other.

I felt so far from home. So completely out of my element.

"We're almost there now," Danny reminded me.

"Uh huh," I agreed nervously.

Florida stretches south for nearly 500 miles, from Jacksonville to Key West. A bizarre little town that just happens to be the southernmost point in the United States. Once again, my map-reading hobby gave me some insight into this unfamiliar territory. I was rich in generalities and trivia, but knew almost none of the specifics of where I was or where I was going. Gainesville, I knew, was only a little more than an hour or so from Jacksonville. But that estimate assumed a deeper knowledge of the area and a car that ran at normal highway speeds. I had neither of those things. A fact that was becoming pointedly obvious to me.

"No Good to Cry," by the Wildweeds came pumping out of the radio, mixing with the wind noise flowing through my open window. Hearing it so unexpectedly cheered me up somewhat.

The Wildweeds had never been a big success in the music business, even though they did knock "Hello Goodbye," by The Beatles out of the Number One slot in the greater Hartford area with this peppy little tune. Al Anderson, their guitar player, the man who wrote "No Good to Cry," went on to some fame and considerable critical acclaim as a big-time songwriter and a member of The New Rhythm and Blues Quartet, more commonly known as NRBQ. Theirs was the kind of band musicians love, but non musicians hardly seem to notice. What a shame. The "Q" was fantastic.

"No Good to Cry" sounds for all the world like a Motown production, complete with growling, sweet vocals, a bright, ringing guitar line and a strong beat that sounds like it was born in Detroit. In reality, Anderson was a chubby, white high school student from rural Connecticut. The band's bass player, Bob Dudek, could sing like nobody's business, too. He was also a white suburban kid. And he was blind to boot. I have no proof, but I think it's possible the band didn't find greater success simply because they didn't look anywhere near the way they sounded. Still, no matter how they looked, I loved the sounds they made in my head.

The sun was nearly gone behind the trees as we limped south past the city of Jacksonville, still on Interstate 95.

I was repeating the same words over and over to myself, like a mantra, "Just a few more miles down the road."

"Here you go," Danny piped up, pointing at a large green exit marker ahead of us. Exit 318, it read, "St. Augustine, Green Cove Springs." The sign also featured a black route number printed inside a white box, indicating Route 16 intersected with the highway here.

Rolling toward the exit at a steady 40 miles per hour, my blinker flashed for nearly half a mile before I found the off ramp, as if a forgetful retiree was at the wheel. The subtle orange glow of the setting sun was rapidly giving way to darkness. My mood sunk in unison as the last rays of light disappeared behind the trees. Dejectedly, I realized this would be my third consecutive night as a member of the great, largely invisible, American homeless population. Two idiot lights were glowing on my dashboard. One signaled the engine was overheating. The other alerted me to the desperately low oil pressure my engine had to work with.

Coasting down the ramp and around a tight corner, I pulled up to the pumps of a BP gas station. Fortuitously, a Denny's restaurant was located only a short walk across the parking lot. I picked my spot almost entirely based on it being the most efficient place I could find to get gassed up, fed and back on the road as soon as possible. I was consistent if nothing else.

There was a dim hope in the back of my addled brain that perhaps a short rest would cure whatever was ailing the beleaguered Taurus. But turning the ignition key to the "off" position didn't immediately result in the mill shutting down this time. The engine coughed, sputtered and shuddered for several seconds before finally going silent. I didn't take that as a good sign.

A hard, sharp ticking sound signaling excessive heat dissipating from the engine block caught my attention. Accompanying the ticking was a barely perceptible wisp of steam or smoke rising from under the hood. That delicate sign wasn't encouraging, either. It hinted at potential troubles that were likely to be far worse than a plastic bag stuck in the air cleaner.

The sky was totally dark. There were no moonbeams to lighten the landscape and only a handful of stars speckled the void above. But it wasn't late. The pumps were empty except for the Taurus and me. The Denny's parking lot, which was only 20 yards or so away, held only a handful of cars. More vehicles than would be driven in by the staff, certainly, but not many more. The restaurant's windows were almost completely obscured by posters heralding the wonders of breakfast being served 24 hours a day, effectively blocking the interior from view.

Dragging myself from the driver's seat, it felt good to stretch my cramped body. Pushing my palms toward the few stars that weren't overpowered by the pump lights, I shook and pulled and stretched as many of the kinks out as possible.

"Yaaaahhhhh," I let loose a powerful yawn, shook out my arms and stepped back to evaluate the Taurus under the artificial light bathing the gas station's island. What I saw surprised me.

Rust patches I hadn't noticed before were obvious and plentiful around the rear wheel wells. Paint was worn away in so many places that it was difficult to tell what the original color of the car had actually been. Several trim pieces were missing. Those that were still attached were bent and barely holding on. Disfiguring dents both large and small were everywhere.

"Whhheeewwww," I whistled softly in disbelief. Sitting before me under the clear, bright light of a dozen metal halide bulbs was an absolute wreck. Even the tires looked ready to give up. Most of the tread was gone.

Discouraged, I made my way to the hood, pulled it open and gazed inside. The rapid ticking sound continued as heat, far too much heat in fact, worked its way from the interior of the engine to the surrounding atmosphere. The wisp of steam or smoke I'd seen was gone, but nothing in the engine compartment looked encouraging. Everything was black with grease and dirt. Like the exterior of the car, the engine appeared to be just barely functional. The Taurus was dying. Whether it would survive long enough to make it through the last leg to Gainesville was very much in question.

I found a paper towel dispenser mounted to a steel pillar beside the pumps and pulled one free. Sliding the oil dipstick out of its holder I wiped it down, reinserted it and pulled it out again. The steel came back dry. The prognosis didn't look promising. For either one of us, frankly.

CHAPTER 19

When I was a kid, there was no such thing as a Self Serve gas station. Full Service was the way of things, with a strong emphasis on the word *service*. I looked forward to going to the service station on Saturdays back then. Tanking up the old Corvair was my kind of adventure at the age of seven.

My dad's Corvair was white, with a black vinyl interior. My sister and I thought it was about the coolest looking automobile in the world. I still think so.

Instead of a traditional shift lever, it had a stubby toggle switch on the dash for shifting the automatic transmission into gear. And the engine was air cooled. It was mounted in the back of the car, just like its air-cooled European cousin, the Volkswagen Bug. On chilly days, a pair of wide, steel heater vents were capable of spewing hot air from under the back seat, into the passenger compartment. More than once I remember Sharon and I having to lift our feet off the floor to keep from having them roasted off as our dad tooled down the highway, oblivious to nearly everything around him.

I absolutely loved that car.

Every weekend throughout the summer, my dad would stash a gas can in the trunk and head for the Esso station on Silver Lane. I was still too young to operate our old Briggs and Stratton lawn mower myself, but I was plenty old enough to tag along to get gas. In those days, I thought mowing the lawn was a young man's highest calling. I admired my father in those younger years too, for being so tall and smart and powerful. I desperately wanted to be just like him.

That was the way of things when I was very young. Before natural processes let loose by years of neglect served to create chasms between us that were far too wide to ever cross again. Within a few short years, my father had turned into a much smaller man who hated the world and everything in it, including me.

At the Esso station, we'd pull up to the pumps with a flourish. Sometimes my dad would honk the horn, if he was in an especially good mood and horsing around with me. But there wasn't really any need. A black rubber hose running across the cement, perpendicular to the pumps caused a bell to ring inside the station whenever a car rolled across it. The front tires made the bell ring once, then the back tires made it ring a second time. "Ding, ding," a customer is at the pumps. I remember that double bell as such a happy sound. "Ding, ding."

Identical twin brothers Roger and Barton Wheeler owned the Esso station on Silver Lane. Whenever a car pulled up to the pumps and made their bell ring "ding, ding," one or the other of them would appear from the bays wiping his big, rough mechanic's hands on a work rag. Pumping gas was something of a social occasion as I recall it.

Roger had a mustache. Barton didn't. I called both of them Mr. Wheeler, which was the custom for children who were addressing adults in those days. Apart from the mustache, I couldn't tell them apart.

Sporting a big Full Service smile, a Wheeler brother would always say, "What can we do for you today, Mr. Stevens?" as he hurried ambitiously out to the pumps.

Back then, people knew your name. Life wasn't nearly as anonymous as it is now. Week after week, month after month, service providers got to know you like a neighbor.

"Fill 'er up, Roger," my dad would reply in his deepest, fatherly voice. I inferred from these exchanges that my dad was a man of great power and influence in the world.

"You betcha," came the easy, confident reply. And with that, a Wheeler brother would uncap the fuel tank, insert a gas hose and pull the trigger to start that golden go juice flowing. While my dad and I sat and waited for our tank to fill, a Wheeler would squirt blue liquid on our windshield, then squeegee it clean. Taking care to wipe the residue from the squeegee with a soft, blue paper towel after each stroke. When Mr. Wheeler was done, he'd call to my dad, "Check the oil, Mr. Stevens?" To which my dad would always respond, "Why not?" If the level was low, Mr. Wheeler would offer to top it off while he was filling our tank.

Servicing the family car seemed like such an elegant and noble task when I was young.

Thirty-five years later and nearly a thousand miles away, there wasn't a soul in sight as I headed for the BP's convenience store to stock up on oil for my own heap. Thoughts of the Wheeler's Esso station flooded my head. I longed for the days when a driver could count on a friendly face and a helping hand at times like this. Me, I was more or less on my own.

The store was clean, well-lit and featured all the modern conveniences, including pay at the pump options that didn't require customers to interact with anyone at all during their fill-ups. The place was spotless. Although it occurred to me that the cookie-cutter approach that had made gas stations the pinnacle of industrial efficiency in the modern world had also deprived them of any personality. I knew instinctively that this wasn't the sort of place young boys dreamed of visiting with their fathers on Saturday mornings.

The world has changed so much. And it can never change back. Not in a million years. Life just doesn't work that way.

I found the oil display and gravitated to the least expensive brand on the rack. There wasn't much point in purchasing anything but the cheapest stuff I could find. Although, since the dipstick came out dry, I didn't have any idea how much oil I actually needed. My starving engine might need two quarts or three.

If I needed four quarts, the whole issue was probably a moot point. If I'd run the engine completely dry of oil, I was pretty sure the car wasn't going to run for long enough to get me to the end of the parking lot, let alone Gainesville. That's if it ran again at all. But I had to start somewhere, so I decided to look on the bright side. I picked up two quarts and carried them to the cashier's counter.

Behind bulletproof glass, under an overhead rack of cigarettes and framed on either side by displays full of antacids and pain killers, stood a woman I can only describe as angelic. Her name was Jessica, according to the tag she wore. She was alone, but appeared confident in her well-fortified position. I imagined it would take a substantial effort to breach her bulletproof bunker. Still, this woman gave the appearance of being far too precious to be alone at night, stationed beside a lonely stretch of highway.

"Did you find everything you were looking for?" she asked in a voice that betrayed an absolutely delightful southern accent. It was subtle, but it was there. Her flashing green eyes and genuinely warm smile were devastating.

"Uh, yeah. I think so," I said, a little off balance, after being surprised by her enthusiasm. I couldn't imagine her job was anything but mind-numbingly dull. Yet she seemed to have risen above it all somehow.

"That'll be $3.79," she cooed while making good eye contact. I fished a five out of my pocket and fed it through the slot. She slid the change back, still smiling. "You have a good night now, ya' hear."

"Thanks…I will," I stammered back.

As I pushed through the glass door and made my way back to the car, I realized I was feeling unusually self-conscious. I was embarrassed about everything, from the way I looked to the way I must have smelled after days at the wheel, to the stiff-legged gait I walked across the lot with.

She was watching me. I could feel it. Jessica had her eyes on me. The only other human being in sight.

I twisted the plastic cap off the first container of oil, removed the oil filler cap from the engine and poured the golden brown liquid in, spilling only a small amount in the process. I repeated the procedure with the second quart, and was proud of myself for not spilling even a single drop. As the engine swallowed up the contents of the oil containers, I found my thoughts drifting until they focused again on the girl at the counter, Jessica.

Her hair was sandy blonde and tied back in a very becoming ponytail. She wore a blue denim shirt with a white cotton T-shirt underneath. A thin gold chain hung around her neck. Even isolated from her as I was by the cashier's bulletproof defensive position, I was sure that if I were to stand next to her, I'd find that she wore just a hint of some intoxicating scent.

Screwing the oil filler cap back on and grabbing another paper towel from the dispenser, I pulled out the dipstick again to find it just as dry as it had been the first time I'd checked it. That wasn't good. Not good at all.

I was embarrassed to have to walk back into the BP for another couple quarts of oil. So I did my best to look casual and in control. I pulled a hose from the closest pump and began to fill the Taurus's tank. The handle didn't have a locking mechanism, so I held it tightly. Too tightly, actually. The safety catch clicked the pump off four or five times before I got the message and relaxed my grip. Finally the aromatic fuel pumped smoothly into the filler neck without interruption.

When I was a kid, I loved the smell of gasoline. I loved it so much that I once pressed my face close to the filler cap of our zippy little Corvair and took a deep whiff when neither my father nor the Wheeler brothers were looking. The cranial fireworks display and explosive coughing fit that followed changed my opinion of fossil fuels forever. Now, while I was aware of the aroma of the gasoline, I neither enjoyed it nor disliked it. It just was what it was. Much like myself.

Fourteen and a half gallons later, I hung up the hose and replaced my gas cap. Fishing for cash deep in the front pocket of my jeans, I snuck one more sad peek into the engine compartment as I rounded the pumps to pay up and purchase even more oil. Feeling a bizarre mixture of depression over the state of the Taurus and exhilaration at the opportunity to see the astounding girl at the counter again, I pushed through the heavy glass door and headed directly for the oil rack, giving a nod and a sheepish smile to Jessica as I passed. She returned a far more impressive smile along with a little wave and a cheerful, "Welcome back."

There were only two quarts of the cheap oil left on the rack. I grabbed both of them, figuring that adding only one more quart wasn't going to get the job done. I would almost certainly have to add another quart or two before I got to Gainesville. If the car would make it to Gainesville at all.

"You're not having a good night, are you?" queried Jessica, her lilting voice softening the stinging truth.

At first, I'd gotten the impression that she was quite young. Maybe in her early twenties. Now, looking at her more carefully, and for longer, I realized that she was older. She was still very beautiful, but delicate lines radiating from the corners of her eyes and mouth told me she was on the far side of her mid-thirties.

"Uh, no…no I guess I'm not," I answered, stumbling over my own words. I was busy thinking about things I had no business thinking about.

"That's $27.72 with the gas," she said with a grin that spoke volumes about her capacity for kindness to strangers.

"OK," I replied as I pressed a wad of crumpled bills through the security slot. A moment later my change rattled down a curved metal chute. She retrieved the coins and pushed them through to me.

"I like the song you were humming," she said. "It's familiar, but I can't quite place it. What's it called?"

I had no idea what she was talking about. "I was humming?"

"Yeah, you were humming a song," she reiterated somewhat sarcastically, as if she thought I was teasing her. "It goes sort of like…" and she proceeded to hum the tune back to me.

I just looked at her, feeling like the biggest idiot in the world. I didn't have the slightest idea what she was talking about. Although I could have happily stood there taking in her physique and listening to her hum all night long.

"I'm sorry, I'm a little tired," I said self-consciously. "To tell you the truth, I didn't even realize I was humming."

"Oh, don't apologize. I enjoyed it," she replied. Her eyes conveying a sense of real compassion. "I didn't mean to make you uncomfortable."

"I guess I'll have to pay better attention to myself in the future," I joked self-consciously. It was a vain attempt at humor that fell flat. But at least I tried. Which was better than slinking away with my tail between my legs.

I pulled the door open and stepped through it. Then, just before the door closed tight, I shot back, "Goodnight…and thank you."

Jessica waved and smiled from inside her protective cubicle. She looked so good that I wished with all my soul that I was another man, a better man. I yearned for the chance to spend time with a woman like Jessica. More time, under more pleasant conditions.

There's always room for hope.

The third quart of oil made the dipstick come back gooey. Wiping it off and rechecking it, I found that I was now less than half a quart low. The fourth quart finished the job, with the remaining pint and a-half going into storage in the trunk. I had no doubt I'd be using it before long.

The ticking of the cooling engine was still clearly audible as I closed the trunk lid and worked my way back to the front of the car. The overheating problem still awaited my attention.

I'd always been told that the best coolant to use in cars was a 50/50 mix of antifreeze and distilled water. Apparently, the minerals in tap water can screw up your engine over time. And up until that moment I'd always religiously used a 50/50 mix of antifreeze and distilled water in the radiator and reservoir of the aged Ford. But considering the circumstances, I knew I didn't have to worry about any long-term buildup of minerals on my engine's internal workings. I only had to worry about the next couple hundred miles. The Taurus had to last me another few hours, a day at the most. After that, I'd find a new automobile to worry about. How I'd come up with the money to buy a new car was a completely different problem. But I could solve that dilemma later. For the moment, I needed water. Tap water would be fine. I just needed enough to fill my radiator and reservoir and be on my way.

A long-forgotten quart bottle of drinking water laying amidst the clutter in the trunk had caught my eye. After retrieving it, I positioned the plastic container on my noticeably dented, badly rusted, and significantly discolored front fender. Holding a wadded-up rag to protect my hand from the still uncomfortably hot radiator cap, I pressed down hard, twisted the cap and stepped back.

There was an admonition printed on the cap that warned not to remove it when the engine was hot. Having just done that very thing, I immediately understood why the warning was there. A little too late, unfortunately. A geyser of steam erupted from the engine compartment, complete with boiling spittle spewing into the air. I jumped back, momentarily terrified by what I'd done. The cloud of steam grew, enveloping me in its warm, moist grasp. I stumbled backward, retreating toward fresh air as quickly as possible.

"Are you all right?" Jessica hollered. The timbre of her voice implied real concern. She sounded harder and stronger than she had earlier.

The Taurus was parked on the far side of the pumps, making it difficult for her to see exactly what had happened. From her perspective, the pumps had erupted into a billowing cloud of white, growing rapidly in size as it drove a frazzled wild man away at top speed. Her concern was sufficient to get her out from behind her cocoon of glass and into the main doorway.

"Yeah, yeah I'm OK," I yelled back in a voice that was both shaky and considerably louder than the situation required. Catching myself, I moderated my tone before uttering another word. "I guess it was hotter than I thought. I hope I didn't scare you." I'd certainly scared the hell out of myself. My heart was beating like mad, thump-bump, thump-bump, thump-bump. I felt like my chest could explode at any moment.

"Whew…that was something," Jessica chuckled, putting her right hand to her throat and taking a moment to catch her own breath. "I don't see much of that here. You know, most folks just get gas and get gone."

"I'm sorry," I replied. And I meant it too. She was the warmest, most compassionate, most approachable person I'd come across for a thousand miles and who knows how many years?

"No, that's OK. As long as you're all right." Then she did the unthinkable. At least it was unthinkable to me. Instead of disappearing back into her protective space by the cash register she walked toward the gas pumps, toward me. My overworked heart jumped, then stopped, then came back to life.

Jessica gazed into the engine compartment as the steam slowly dissipated. The sound of the radiator gurgling away was still noticeable.

"That doesn't look so good," she said.

"No, it really doesn't, does it?" I agreed. I caught myself staring at her soft, unmistakably feminine face without even the pretense of trying to be cool about it. I reached for my water bottle, still sitting precariously on the fender. I began twisting the cap off with the intention of pouring it into the radiator to replenish the fluids that had been so violently expelled.

"Hey, don't do that," Jessica said forcefully, grabbing my arm and firmly pushing it away from the radiator. "You've got to let it cool down first."

"Really?" I asked. I honestly didn't know that pouring cold water into an overheated engine was a bad idea.

"Really," she said somewhat insistently while maintaining a disarming smile. "You're going to have to let this puppy cool down for quite some time." Her head swivelled back and forth from Denny's to the Texaco station across the exit ramp and back to the Cracker Barrel on our side of the road. "You might as well come on in and wait with me," she said tugging at my sleeve. "You're going to be here for a while."

She pulled me toward the convenience store, leading me inside. As the door swung shut, she extended her right hand to shake mine.

"My name's Melanie," she grinned. Her grip was firm and confident. "Why don't you grab a cold drink from the cooler while you wait? On me."

"Melanie?" I queried, "But your name tag says Jessica."

"Oh I just put on whoever's name tag is laying around when I get in," she explained with the wave of a hand. "Sometimes it feels like it's a whole lot easier to deal with people if I'm somebody else, somebody other than myself." Squinting hard in my direction she queried, "Do you know what I mean?"

"No," I replied haltingly. The idea seemed a little loopy to be honest. But as it rolled around in my head for a bit it seemed to make more and more sense. "That sounds like an interesting policy, though."

I was smitten.

CHAPTER 20

I learned a lot that night about Melanie, the compassionate cashier. The two of us established a rapport fairly quickly. I laughed comfortably at her genuinely humorous way with words while she appeared to be enthralled by my stories about the odd characters I'd met over the previous two days. By the end of our first hour together, the conversation had shifted from superficial chit chat to far more specific details about our personal histories. We hit the high notes of the experiences that made us tick and then began to willingly delve deeper into the colorful incidents that had helped shape us into the people we'd become. I found the exchange to be a wonderful experience. She gave every appearance of being just as taken with our time together.

The Taurus cooled off as she predicted it would, but I was in no rush to leave, having been only recently welcomed into the company of the most alluring woman I'd met in a very long time. You might say I was stalling. Certainly, I found the I time spent with Mel to be far more appealing and substantially less stressful than I knew climbing back behind the wheel would be. As close as I was to my destination, I was more than happy to put off that final leg of my journey for just a little longer.

The real Jessica showed up just before midnight, as Melanie's shift was ending. She was tall, a strikingly beautiful woman. Her skin was smooth and cocoa brown. A thick bundle of long tight braids hung past her shoulders, a smattering of colorful blue and yellow beads woven into her locks. On first sight I'd have sworn she wasn't a day over 25. She was, in fact, more than 10 years past that age.

Mel beamed and gave her replacement a warm, welcoming hug as soon as she crossed the threshold. "Hey you," she said, "I've got someone for you to meet." She introduced the two of us as if I were an old and trusted friend. "Jess," she said, "This is Frank." Leaning in close and lowering her voice, she added, "He's in a bit of a bind." I was humbled by the attention they showed me, but I shook hands and exchanged pleasantries as best as I could.

Not being a particularly sociable sort of guy, I found myself to be surprisingly comfortable in the company of these two women. I felt warm and oddly protected in their presence. An emotion that was better attributed to their company than the bulletproof glass booth near the door.

Among the bits of information I'd learned during the hours before Jessica's arrival was that Melanie preferred to be called Mel. She explained the nickname as a tribute to her dad, whom she was named after.

It seems her parents had been that unfortunate sort of a couple who'd tried for years to have children, only to be repeatedly disappointed by failure after failure. Mel came along late in their lives, quite unexpectedly. But she introduced them to the joys and pains of parenthood, as babies are wont to do. Together, the three of them made a fine family unit.

It was Mel's mother who'd insisted their baby be named after her father. A quiet but level-headed man, the elder Mel appreciated his wife's devotion. But that didn't mean he was about to let his little girl go through life named Melvin. So the couple compromised on Melanie. A perfectly lovely name that satisfied both of them and fit their little girl just fine.

Mel's description of them was simple yet heartfelt. "They were wonderful, just wonderful parents."

Mel's father was more than 50 years old when she was born. Her mother was in her mid-40s. Rough estimates of their ages were all she knew. Apparently, approximations of their ages were as close as her parents could come, too. Fire had robbed them of the specifics of their lives.

As Mel told it, their small rural community's official records had been kept in a collection of wooden filing cabinets in the back of a cracker-style Baptist church located near the St. Johns River. "Late one night, that church just burned to the ground," she explained, "along with everything in it."

Fortunately, nobody was harmed in the fire. Although the loss of all those written records of births, deaths and marriages became a point of contention for a number of the locals forever after. Officially at least, their lives had gone up in smoke, along with the specifics of their exact ages and anniversaries.

Mel explained the situation as best she could, "Some of the old folks thought the fire was caused by lightning. More than a few said it was set on purpose. Whatever the truth was, nobody ever knew for sure."

Because of that long-ago tragedy, the markers at the head of Mel's parents' graves still don't have birth dates on them. Not to this very day. That information remains a mystery, lost to the ages.

Mel's beloved father died when his daughter was only 16 years old. He succumbed late one August afternoon to a heart attack brought on by smoke inhalation and heat stroke. He was a rural firefighter who'd become trapped by burning, falling pines while battling a raging blaze near a small town called Switzerland, which was and still is located beside the slow-moving but mighty St. Johns river. It was nearly an hour before his crew got control of the situation and rescued him. By that time, Melvin was unconscious. His breathing came only with great difficulty. Amazingly, he wasn't badly burned. The poor man went into cardiac arrest while awaiting the arrival of an ambulance. He died en route to the hospital.

Mel the daughter lost a lot more than her father that day. Her family lost the glue that held it together. Like a three-legged stool with one leg gone, the cornerstone of her whole world crumbled on that hot summer evening. Her simple life of contentment would never be the same again.

Her mother, like so many doting wives unlucky enough to lose their husbands without warning, faded away quickly.

"She became obsessed with the thought of daddy being gone," Mel explained. "She lost her will to get up and go about her business. Eventually, she lost her will to even breathe."

By November, Mel's mother had let go of her grasp on this life, too.

Had it not been for Jessica, the real Jessica, Mel might have been alone. Instead, the two women became family by choice, pressed hard by circumstance. They chose to become sisters who were born of different parents. Regardless of the fact there was no family resemblance between them, they were far more committed to each other than the members of most families I'd ever known were. Certainly far more than the members of my family ever were.

Mel and Jessica had known each other since childhood. Both being from equally poor families, they were on an equal social footing, even during the turbulent years when "Jim Crow" was still resisting being driven out of the south. Progress came ever so slowly, both for the girls and for the region they called home.

Still living within a few miles of where they'd grown up, Mel admitted they'd both wanted to leave North Florida and explore the world. But circumstances and a certain amount of trepidation about leaving the only home they'd ever known always seemed to keep them firmly rooted in place.

"It's not such a bad place to live," Mel intoned. "I'm sure we could have done a lot worse."

Jessica nodded in solemn agreement.

Mel's statuesque replacement didn't show up for work alone. She arrived with her boyfriend in tow. A tall, muscular white boy who really was only 25 years old. He was silent, sullen and gave no indication of having any interest in me at all.

Marshman Brown was a broad-shouldered young man dressed in blue jeans, work boots and a Molly Hatchet T-shirt. His lower lip bulged noticeably with a full load of chewing tobacco. In his right hand he held a large Styrofoam cup into which he spit tobacco juice on an alarmingly frequent basis. He looked every inch a redneck.

Looks can be deceiving.

The young man's name, Marshman, was a family heirloom that embarrassed him more than anything else. "Buddy" was the name he preferred.

On his upper right arm, he sported a black rose of a tattoo. Beneath it was a single word, "Jessica." Hidden underneath the rose, invisible to the untrained eye, was a previous tattoo he'd covered over. That artistic statement had also featured a woman's name, "Ebony," which was the moniker Jessica had been using professionally when they met.

Jessica and Mel had worked at the BP station, covering two-thirds of the business' 24-hour work day, five days a week, for almost five years. But being a cashier in a gas station/convenience store doesn't produce the level of income required of those who wish to own a home of their own. Which is exactly what the pseudo sisters had hoped to do. Home ownership promised stability. Something that had been sorely lacking in their lives for far too long.

Unfortunately, the rural, northeastern corner of Florida didn't offer Jessica, Mel or their backwoods neighbors many high-paying employment opportunities. Not many at all. But there was one possibility available, distasteful as it might be. That position did indeed offer the potential of high pay, in exchange for a certain, moral flexibility.

The hours were good and the money was exceptional, all things considered. After careful consideration, long hours of reflection and a couple strong gin and tonics, Jessica swallowed her pride along with her natural sense of modesty and took a job as an exotic dancer. She was known as Ebony. The name Buddy had originally tattooed on his arm, then covered up with another blotch of ink when he found out he'd marked himself with a pseudonym, a stage name.

"It's not something I'm proud of, you understand," explained Jessica, "but I'm not ashamed of it either." She casually looked out through the glass wall of the convenience store at Buddy, who was fiddling with my car at the pumps. "I got him out of the deal," she cooed, as she sat on a display stack of Diet Coke six-pack cans. Jessica's affection for the younger man was unmistakable. Mel smiled and affectionately massaged her friend's shoulders in a silent display of solidarity.

Jessica pointed out with considerable pride that her man was a better-than-average mechanic. Considering my situation, I was in no position to turn down well-intentioned offers of help.

"He's got a real flair for making things go," Jessica chuckled and winked at Mel in a way that made me think she wasn't talking about cars. Feeling a little uncomfortable about the possibility of verbally stumbling into a hornets nest, I let her comment pass without interjecting anything of my own.

Buddy showed no hesitation at all when Jessica asked him to do what he could for my ailing pile of rusty, dented steel. The request for assistance originated with Mel, passed through Jessica and ended with Buddy, who nodded silently before sauntering out to peer into my open hood. After a moment or two of poking and prodding inside my engine compartment, he retrieved a toolbox from his own trunk and got busy making repairs. I stayed inside, out of the way with the women.

Jessica returned to the story of her dancing days, keeping a casual eye on Buddy and his well-carved torso as she did so. Over the course of six difficult months, she was able to meet her financial goals and get out of the exotic dancing business. "It's one thing to earn a shot at a better life by doing a job you don't enjoy," Jessica explained. "It's another thing entirely to base your livelihood on the fact that you have breasts."

Buddy entered her life as a devoted fan who was far too shy to join the crowd of drunks stuffing her G-string full of dollar bills. He hung back. But as his infatuation grew, so did his confidence. Buddy began to make himself known, eventually even appointing himself as her personal bodyguard.

"He seemed a little creepy at first," she giggled. "But he kind of grew on me, ya' know what I mean?"

Melanie shot me a bright smile. I knew exactly what she meant.

Buddy watched over her at work, making sure nobody got out of line with his favorite girl. He walked her to her car when she left the club, warding off the occasionally amorous parking lot prowlers. He even began staking out the BP parking lot during her overnight shifts to keep her safe.

The "Ebony" tattoo was the first Buddy had ever gotten. A fat, sweaty, tattoo artist wearing a leather vest and no shirt stuck him with it in Jacksonville. The shop was located in a strip mall right next to a Chinese restaurant. Buddy could hear the cooks through the wall, shouting back and fourth in their native tongue as thousands of electric pin pricks shot through his skin.

Carefully peeling back the protective bandage, he showed Jessica the tattoo with great pride that evening.

"You're really something. You know that?" She laughed and rubbed his head teasingly while kneeling on the raised runway near the bar. His girl was completely naked and being ogled by a dozen strange men. But somehow, neither Buddy nor Jessica was at all aware of anyone else at that moment.

Later that night, she let her young admirer in on the little secret that virtually all dancers work under an assumed name. She confided her real name and kissed him on the cheek, saying, "You're so sweet." The kiss left a colorful, moist smear of lipstick on his face.

On the next night she danced, Buddy showed up again. This time with the rose on his arm, and her real name newly lettered below it. He slipped her a note instead of a dollar bill. The note read, "It's our secret. I'll never tell."

They slept together for the first time in the morning and had been a dedicated couple ever since, although they lived separately. Jessica had her house, which she shared with Mel. Buddy lived with his parents several miles away, in the farm house his grandfather built when the family migrated to north Florida from Georgia in the 1920s.

Neither Buddy nor Jessica had any illusions about how his family would react to the news of their relationship. It was impossible to know for sure what would offend them most. The fact that their little boy was seeing a black woman, or that the two of them had met in a strip joint where she was a featured performer. Whatever the case, they weren't likely to be understanding or supportive.

Jessica's short-term embarrassment aside, the income that had allowed her to become a property owner made her feel a whole lot better about the fact that there were hundreds, if not thousands, of truckers cruising the highways of America harboring a mental image of what she looked like naked. There were more than a few upstanding, local, churchgoing men among that group, too. But they were far more concerned that Jessica might tell their wives about their late night shenanigans than she was that they'd publically discuss her employment history.

Very few customers came through the station during the long overnight shift. Those who did roll up to the pumps paid remotely, using credit or debit cards to settle their bills. Not a single soul entered the convenience store during the nighttime hours. No one but Mel, Jessica, Buddy and myself, that is.

After several hours of conversation and with my stomach full of pre-packaged sandwiches and more than a few cups of coffee, the eastern sky finally began to lighten. The sun inched its way up over the highway, slowly arcing above the ocean that lay only a few miles to the east. The scent of the sea mixed with the aroma of gasoline and oil whenever the door to the convenience store swung open. Jessica and Mel shooed Buddy away in the early morning hours, calling out, "Go get some sleep." I sang out a thank you to him myself. But he didn't answer. He only waved lazily over his shoulder, tucked his toolbox back into the trunk of his Chevy Camero and headed wearily for home.

"It's only about 75 miles to Gainesville from here," said Jessica, still gazing out the window. "Right down this road." She stood motionless, watching Buddy's pimped-out Camero disappear into the distance.

"Route 16 will lead you right into Starke," Mel chimed in. "Turn left on 301, bear to the right as you come through Waldo and it'll take you right into Gainesville. No problem."

"Watch yourself in Waldo," Jessica warned sternly. "The whole damn town is a speed trap. They'll get you for going two miles an hour over the limit, and the speed limit there is sslloooowww."

Mel nodded her head in agreement. I scribbled the directions on a scrap of paper. Route 16 to 301, turn left, bear right through Waldo. It seemed easy enough.

"Just follow the signs," they said in unison, breaking out in playful giggles at the coincidence. "You'll be there in no time," Jessica assured me.

I said my farewells and was pleasantly surprised that Mel actually gave me a hug before I could get out the door. Momentarily overcome by a powerful sense of self-consciousness, I stiffened and took a half step backward. Thankfully, Mel took no noticeable offense at what could easily have been misinterpreted as rejection. I had no idea what to do under such unfamiliar circumstances. Fortunately, Mel did.

She reached out with her left hand and pushed a stray lock of hair from my eyes, smoothing it across my forehead. "I'll bet you clean up nice," she whispered through a dreamy smile. Returning to the counter, she grabbed a pen and a Post-It-Note, which she scribbled on. Turning back, she presented me with the yellow square of paper saying, "You call me when you can. I want to know that everything turns out all right for you."

We'd shared a lot of personal information overnight and I sensed that Mel and I had made a fairly serious personal connection in the process. I didn't trust my feelings entirely though. My track record for reading signals was spotty at best.

"I will," was all I could think of to say. I pushed the note far down into my pocket for safe keeping.

As I cranked up the car, I was pleasantly surprised to find that it sounded reasonably healthy.

Mel and Jessica were at the window waving good-bye as I pulled out of the parking lot. Waving back politely, I thought I saw Mel blow a kiss. The idea intrigued and excited me, but considering my situation, I chalked it up to being nothing more than my imagination playing tricks on me. Then again, maybe it wasn't.

There's that hope thing again.

Sitting in the driver's seat, tooling down the road, my eyes felt heavy. My thoughts came slowly, laboriously. Even though I was near exhaustion, I'd resisted falling asleep all night just to be near Mel for a few moments longer. There had been plenty of convenience store sandwiches to fill my belly and enough coffee and cola to make sure I had a good strong caffeine buzz going by the time I left the BP. But sleep is an important prerequisite to rational thought and I hadn't had nearly enough of it since my journey had begun. Fortunately, knowing that Gainesville was less than two hours away kept me alert and upbeat. Or at least I hoped so. I was counting on my trials being over soon. The fact that I had the phone number of a new friend in my pocket only served to speed me on my way.

Things were looking up.

Thoughts of Mel played on my mind, hanging there as peacefully and easily as the early morning fog floating only a few feet above the fields stretching out along both sides of the road. With each passing minute, I was ever closer to 301, the speed-trap town of Waldo and my ultimate goal — Gainesville. These facts boosted my mood considerably.

The land surrounding the two lane stretch of road was flat and green. Occasionally, we'd travel through a small hamlet that was just waking up to the brightening morning, but for the most part, we rode along arrow straight roads surrounded by open green fields, thick with vegetables and fruit-laden trees.

Connecticut seemed so far away and terribly long ago. The humid warmth of the Florida morning relaxed me. Especially considering that I was deep in a time of year when I knew my barren apartment in East Hartford would be cold and gray. I thought about how much I'd dreaded getting out of the shower during the winter months up north. The persistent chill on wet skin was an annoyance that I didn't care to experience again. Florida was looking and feeling increasingly desirable from my point of view.

Danny shifted in his seat, stretched his arms far out ahead of him and let loose a powerful, falsetto yawn that announced his awakening to the world. Rubbing his eyes with his left hand, he sat silently for a moment, thinking, searching the landscape.

"Where are we?" he asked.

"Route 16, my friend, south of Jacksonville. Maybe only an hour and a half or so from Gainesville." I was proud, as if I'd really accomplished something. "Down this road, a left on 301, hang a right as we slide through Waldo and we're there." I was truly, immensely happy as I repeated the directions the girls had given me in a grossly exaggerated style. "You're nearly home, my friend. As I promised you would be."

Danny smiled, gazed out the windshield at what I assumed must have been familiar sights and settled comfortably back into his seat. "Good," was all he said.

Danny hummed along with the radio. The Rolling Stones tune "Before They Make Me Run," was playing. I remembered it from the Some Girls album. As I recalled the story, the song came about as the result of a serious drug charge being leveled at Keith Richards in Canada. One that could have sent him to jail for a long, long time. As a founding member of the group, Keith is arguably the soul of the Rolling Stones. Without his participation, many fans believe the band would cease to exist. I count myself among that crowd, absolutely.

Keith wailed forlornly, acknowledging that he wasn't looking his best, but admitting in the same breath that he was feeling as if he was on top of the world.

I could relate, completely.

CHAPTER 21

A blueish-white cloud of oily smoke continued to follow us down Route 16. It traced our path all the way to Highway 301. The Taurus, while running again and covering ground at a reasonable pace, was clearly on its last legs. Despite Buddy's best efforts, the car made its objections known by clunking and groaning as we made our way along the two lane highway, audibly protesting each rotation of those balding tires. But for all its bluster and clattering the car kept rolling along. A fact that pleased me to no end. Mercifully, the distance between the dilapidated Ford and Gainesville became less with each passing minute.

My fixation on where we were and how short the distance we still needed to cover was broken by the sound of a plaintive acoustic guitar coming from the radio's speakers, followed by the delicate vocals of Neil Finn, the timelessly boyish singer and guitar player from Crowded House. The song was "Better be Home Soon." A classic as far as I was concerned.

"Oh, I love this song," I blurted out as I sat up straight, newly invigorated by the melody filling the car's interior.

"Absolutely," agreed Danny.

I listened intently, enjoying every nuance of the music. The instrumental break introduced a swelling mass of vibrato notes as they flew free from the organs pipes. Those ethereal tones blended seamlessly with a harmonious symphony of guitars, bass and drums that filled in behind them. The effect made it impossible for me to remain detached from the emotion of the moment. In unison, Danny and I joined in for the next verse, singing as if we were teenagers again, belting out the high notes, emoting for all we were worth.

"Man, I haven't heard that song in years," I said, suddenly feeling tremendously nostalgic.

"Yeah, that's a good one all right."

"Sure is," I replied.

A wave of exhaustion swept over me like a wave crashing onto a beach, catching me by surprise, crushing my exuberance in the blink of an eye. I was running out of gas. The car had three-quarters of a tank left. But I felt shaky all of a sudden, as if I was on my last legs. I fell silent, my capacity for conversation having left me over the course of no more than a couple heartbeats.

"Life is a lot like a song ya' know," Danny opined. I looked at him from the corner of my eye, dubious, but curious where he might be going with this line of reasoning. "People are always trying to figure out what songs really mean. They're convinced that songwriters are putting secret messages into them, hidden, deep down in the mix where only the most astute listeners will be able to discover and decipher the secret clues."

I supposed that might be true, but he launched off on a continuation of his theory before I could comment.

"Was Paul McCartney already dead when Sgt. Peppers Lonely Hearts Club Band came out? Who was the Walrus, anyway? Is Mick Jagger the devil? Is he *really* a Satan worshiper?"

The examples he was citing might seem ridiculous today, but I remembered a time when people seriously pondered those same questions. Danny plowed forward. My old friend appeared to have been rejuvenated. He represented an unrelenting tide of ideas, hardly stopping to take a breath. I on the other hand, sat nearly motionless, doing no more work than the task of driving absolutely required of me.

"In reality, the songs mean whatever you want them to mean," Danny continued. "It's not much different than your life, really. These things only have as much value as you give them." He paused momentarily, looking me over. He was very definitely back on his soapbox, acting the part of the teacher to my student. This time, I didn't take offense. I merely listened, compliantly.

"What the songwriter thinks the song is about is no more valid than your interpretation is. There's plenty of room for both of you to be right, even if you completely disagree." That concept threw me for a minute. I remember thinking that I'd have to spend a fair amount of time pondering his suggestion before I really understood its meaning.

"Your life doesn't have to be a reflection of what someone else thinks it should be. You can make it your own. You *should* make it your own. Define your own value system. Figure out what's important to you and put your heart into it. Make it your reason for living, even if the thing you live for seems unforgivably stupid to everyone else you know." I had to admit, that seemed like sensible enough advice, even if it was a bit extreme.

"This is your shot, Frank. Make it count."

A sign drifted by on the right side of the road that read, "Gainesville City Limits." I caught it in my peripheral vision as we passed. Finally, we were only a few minutes away from Danny's front door.

"We're almost there," I said, pointing over my shoulder at the sign.

"Almost," replied Danny reverently, "almost."

CHAPTER 22

We were cruising through the center of the city when Danny piped up again.

"Turn left on 441," he instructed. My old buddy was hyper-alert, looking intently ahead as if he were trying hard to pick out a single familiar face from an endless sea of humanity. He was enthusiastically taking in the full spectrum view as we made our way through the bustling college town. As he'd suggested, I turned left at the intersection and headed south.

Highway 441 is a four-lane blacktop that leads right through the heart of town and keeps on going. Danny, the failing Taurus and I followed that river of asphalt through the heart of the downtown area and out the other side, to where the buildings became shorter and fewer until there weren't any buildings at all. We were back in the boondocks.

This was the part of the trip that I'd tried to put out of my mind for the past few days. Finding Florida hadn't been particularly difficult. However, finding a specific house in Florida, located in the outskirts of a town I'd never been to before, now that was going to be a trick. It had occurred to me that I might be driving around searching side streets for hours. But I chose instead to stick to the main road, finding comfort in the wide swath of blacktop that I'd become so much a part of in recent days.

A street sign flew past at highway speed, then another and yet another. It was with some difficulty that I searched my memory, until I found a faint glimmer of an idea about where I might be and where I might be going.

"109th Place, right?" I nudged Danny, double checking my memory.

"Right," he replied.

"Well then," I announced proudly, "If I'm not mistaken you're just about home."

A reflective green street sign marking 109th Place appeared from behind a clump of live oaks on our left. I was a little surprised to see Danny's street and realize it was hardly more than a strip of sand jutting off from the main road.

I slowed the car and turned carefully onto the white sandy path. The earth was soft and loose beneath our tires. The front wheels slipped momentarily in the shifting grains and lost their traction, only to find it again, allowing the car to proceed lazily forward.

The twin wheel tracks that lay ahead of us twisted and turned around clumps of live oaks and scrub palms for a hundred yards or more. Beyond that was a mystery. The road disappeared around a bend. How far it led beyond that turn was anyone's guess.

The trees overhanging the road were thick with Spanish Moss, which hung low enough to scratch at the car's roof as we passed. The scratches wouldn't do any harm, I knew, but I began to wonder if I was about to find that Danny lived in a rusted-out trailer. Or maybe he made his home in some fallen-down, wood-framed shack with a tin roof. My mind drifted to those ramshackle hovels I'd seen bordering the tobacco and cotton fields of the Carolinas. We were several miles south of downtown Gainesville. I hadn't seen any structures in the area that left the impression they were either modern or solidly built. Doubt crept into my psyche.

A fresh wave of anxiety shook through me. More than a shiver, but less than a full-blown panic attack. The almost debilitating reality of my situation crushed down on me all at once, making me sink deeper into my well-worn seat. The smoke-belching Taurus was about to die any minute, and here I was, a thousand miles from the only home I'd ever known. I was down to my last few dollars and had no place to call my own. My outlook suddenly seemed as bleak as ever, despite the long drive and Danny's promise of repayment.

I breathed deep, blowing a long, thin stream of air through my lips in an effort to prevent this nerve-shattering realization from escalating to an even more uncomfortable level. I turned to speak, but Danny cut me off before I could get the first word out.

"Drop me off here," he said, indicating an ancient-looking, single story building on the right side of the road. I pulled up along side it.

Three wooden steps led up to the open front porch. Both the steps and the railing were unpainted and worn by age and weather. A deeply faded but carefully hand-lettered sign hung from the porch roof. It read, "Townsend's Store."

The weather-beaten door was little more than a rectangular wooden frame with a screen covering it. There were three rocking chairs lined up on the porch. Two were empty. One was filled by a heavyset man in overalls who held a Coke bottle to his lips, inverted, its bottom to the rafters. The bottle caught my eye. It was one of the old style six and a-half ounce bottles I remembered pulling out of a bright red vending machine when I was a kid. The bottles were made of thick green glass back then and had the name of the bottling plant they came from stamped right into their bottoms. I didn't even know they made them anymore. Maybe it was a regional thing, I postulated.

The man in the rocking chair stared at the ceiling, draining his soda bottle without giving my smoking, clanking, wreck of a Taurus any notice at all. We rolled to a stop directly in front of the steps.

"You're getting out *here*?" I asked, more than a little alarmed at the prospect of being left alone in unfamiliar territory.

"Yeah, I have to settle up a few things before I go on." He opened the door and slid out of the car, settling his feet gingerly into the white sandy soil. "The house is just up around the bend there. Go ahead up and let yourself in."

"I can wait for you," I offered hopefully. I wasn't anxious to leave him in order to search for a house I'd never seen, somewhere along a road I'd never driven.

"That's all right. Go ahead," he replied, encouraging me to move along. He was smiling broadly, white teeth flashing brightly. His eyes were clear and alive. They crinkled at the edges.

"I don't mind…really," I implored him. I was in no hurry to leave Danny behind.

"It'll be all right," Danny repeated in a soft, reassuring tone of voice.

Realizing there was no point in arguing, I swallowed hard, turned my attention to the road ahead and accepted my fate.

"Just up here?" I pointed along the white, sandy lane, speaking the words haltingly.

"Just up the road," Danny confirmed. "It's not far at all."

"You'll be along soon?"

"Frank, it's all right. Really, it is."

His tone was warm and comforting, almost as if he were talking to a frightened child. I felt close to him, as if he were the brother I'd never had. Which of course, he was.

It occurred to me all of a sudden that Danny looked absolutely vibrant. Young, enthusiastic and full of hope, he was the picture of health. This Danny bore only the faintest resemblance to the man I'd discovered on my porch a few days before. The change took me by surprise, even though there had been signs of his rejuvenation all along our route.

Searching for a rationale, I realized that I hadn't slept in nearly 24 hours. Adding to that the fact I hadn't eaten a decent meal in well over a week, it wasn't at all difficult to admit to myself that my senses might be a little frazzled. I chalked the illusion up to a combination of sleep deprivation and low blood sugar and put it out of my mind as quickly as it had slipped in.

I lightly pressed down on the accelerator, adding a bit of extra pressure at first, in order to push the dead weight of the Taurus through the soft, forgiving sand. Danny stepped back, slapped the roof twice and waved me on. He called out, "Thank you, Frank," as I rolled away. The sentiment caught me off guard. He didn't sound like he was shouting out an offhand remark. It sounded more heartfelt than that, as if he were saying good-bye. But I ignored the thought and put it in the same category as my minor hallucination involving his appearance. I'd had far too many hours at the wheel during the past few days. The idea of spending the night in a real bed with soft fluffy pillows and crisp, clean sheets began to dance around in my brain like fireflies. A hot shower would be a welcome change of pace too.

I drove on toward the bend in the road, watching and waiting for Danny's house to appear.

CHAPTER 23

The house was hidden behind a wide canopy of live oaks and an impossibly thick clump of head-high underbrush. As I rounded the curve, I could see it sitting alone in a clearing. Danny's home was a beautiful thing.

An old style cracker house, two stories high with seven windows across the upper floor and a full screened porch downstairs on the other side, it was far larger than I'd imagined it might be. Beyond the house was a lake. A big lake, no doubt full of fish and swimmers and young lovers paddling canoes to and fro.

The driveway from the main road led to the back of the house. Its front was designed to take advantage of the lake view on the other side. The place was idyllic. There are no other words I could use to describe it.

A detached carport to the left of the main building held enough spaces for half a dozen cars. It was mostly empty, with only two vehicles parked underneath its shady roof. One was a Jaguar, a newer one. I'd always had a penchant for the old Jags with the long curved hoods and the big round headlights flanking a sparkling chrome grill. This one was more squared off and modern. But a Jag is a Jag. The evidence suggested that Danny was apparently doing a little better than I'd thought.

The other car was a Volkswagen Jetta. A perfectly reasonable car that was no more than two years old, I guessed. Its finish still had a deep luster to it that implied the car had been well cared for and often protected from the elements.

Considering these new clues, I thought it odd that Danny had showed up at my place looking like he'd been living off the land and stuck out in the rain. I shrugged off any questions for the moment and headed for the door, which was positioned dead center in the back of the house. Like the door at

Townsend's Store, it was nothing but a wooden frame covered by a screen. A pick-up truck was backed up to the door and parked only a few feet away. A large cardboard box had been carefully placed on the ground to keep the screen door propped open. Two others were stowed in the back of the pick-up.

I knocked on the frame tentatively, but got no response. Stepping inside, I stopped and announced myself.

"Hello," I called, a little weaker than I'd meant to. My second attempt was louder and more forceful.

"Hello!"

Hearing no reply and seeing no signs of life, I made my way further into the house. The kitchen was to the right, painted a bright yellow. The room was well appointed, containing an impressive collection of expensive looking built-in appliances. To the left was an office. Floor-to-ceiling shelves lined three walls. A dark brown antique desk was positioned in the middle of the room. Atop it were a telephone, a picture frame and laptop computer.

I kept going, deeper into the apparently uninhabited house. Moving through an open doorway I found a large living area complete with couches, an enormous entertainment center and a baby grand piano in the far corner. French doors to the right led into the dining room. A duplicate set of doors straight ahead led out onto the front porch. Beyond the porch, a concrete path ran straight as an arrow down the length of a long, well-manicured lawn. Beyond the path and the lawn was a dock that began at the water's edge. A small vacation house appeared to have been built on stilts there, a good two feet above the water level.

Seeing nobody to announce myself to, I turned my attention to the living room. In addition to the piano I found an electric guitar, an electric bass and an acoustic 12 string guitar positioned on stands along one wall. A compact rack filled with a mass of high-tech recording equipment as well as another computer was tucked into an open cabinet immediately behind the piano. What I'd initially assumed was a gun cabinet in the corner turned out to be a storage unit for microphones and microphone stands.

I was amazed. Danny had a full-blown home recording studio built right into his living room.

"This must have cost a fortune," I said out loud, in wide wonder.

The house and the expansive grounds were a far cry from our boyhood ranch-style houses on Burke Street. It was even farther from the claustrophobic, barren apartment on Tolland Street Danny had found me living in.

All indications were that Danny Loughman had made something of himself.

"Good for him," I thought to myself. "Good for him."

More cardboard boxes were stacked in the dining room. They looked to be the same size and type that I'd seen in the back yard on my way in. Some were flat, having yet to be shaped and taped into useful receptacles. Others were packed full and sealed shut.

The walls were bare of paintings, photographs or prints. I found it curious that all the table tops and shelves had been stripped clean as well. In retrospect, it's surprising I didn't put more thought into those peculiar observations. They were signals that should have alerted me to something being out of whack. Maybe I was just too overwhelmed by so much new information to process it all adequately. I was, after all, quite tired.

Glancing through a window toward the lakefront, I noticed a couple making their way up the walk from the dock. I hadn't noticed them earlier when I'd taken my first look at the lakefront. Concern rattled my brain and motived me into a state of near panic.

Scrambling to the windows on other side of the room, I scanned the back yard, hoping to see Danny sauntering around the bend, returning from the store. No such luck. Like a nervous teenager about to meet his date's father for the first time, I had no idea what to do or how to act. My level of discomfort grew at an alarming rate.

Stuffing my hands deep into my pockets, then pulling them out again, I shifted my weight from one foot to the other. Nothing seemed to help. I was at a loss.

"Plan B" had me trying to settle naturally into a chair, but the action felt forced as I tried desperately to appear confident and at home in such unusual surroundings. Finally, I settled on taking up residence at the piano.

I'd just begun plinking out a few painfully incompatible notes when I heard the front door open and footsteps fall on the wooden planks of the porch.

I coughed, as if to announce my presence in an even more decisive way than my abysmal piano playing could. The footsteps halted, then shuffled, then came tentatively forward. The first head past the doorjamb belonged to a man. He appeared to be in his mid-40s, with reddish-blond hair and a full beard. He was tall, perhaps a little over six feet and undeniably handsome. He wore jeans, a University of Florida sweatshirt and a pair of white Nikes that looked to be brand new. My first impression was that he may have been a retired model, or a news anchor.

Tentatively, a woman stepped into the room from behind him. Neither hiding behind her companion or showing signs of anything I'd describe as fear. She didn't strike me as the sort of woman who needed a man to shield her from danger. It looked to me as if the man had dutifully taken up a position in front of her in an attempt to be protective. She allowed her counterpart the illusion of chivalry, although her expression gave no indication that she felt she needed protection. There was no mistaking from their body language who was in charge.

I nodded in their direction, making eye contact, then breaking it immediately.

"Who are you?" asked the man with some trepidation.

"I'm Frank," was my answer, delivered as cheerfully and casually as was possible under the circumstances.

"Frank?" the man asked quizzically.

"Yeah, Frank Stevens," I responded while continuing to select and play an assortment of horribly discordant notes from the keyboard in front of me. My heart was beating hard. The blood rushing to my ears drowned out much of the ambient sound in the room.

"I'm waiting for Danny," I added by way of explanation

"Danny," the man repeated in a sarcastic tone, arching one eyebrow. The woman behind him looked equally curious. She wore jeans as well, along with a pair of leather work boots and a white tank top covered by a green striped button down shirt. The outer garment was noticeably too large for her. She reminded me of a little girl who playfully enjoyed wearing her father's discarded shirts.

"Danny Loughman," I said with some conviction. "We're old friends." It was at that very moment I realized I hadn't looked for Danny's name on the mailbox. As a matter of fact, I hadn't seen any identifying information anywhere. What if this wasn't Danny's house? What if this was Danny's neighbor's house? What if Danny was scamming me and didn't own a house at all? I swallowed hard and took a stab at feeling out these two for some more substantial information.

"He lives here, right?" Industrial strength doubts were creeping into my psyche from all directions.

The man looked at me with an expression of profound pity. Still, he didn't appear to be motivated to the point of taking a physical risk in the interest of empathy. Not until he had more information about this interloper sitting so arrogantly at the piano, anyway. The two of them held their distance, while I did my best to stand my ground.

He spoke the next few words as if I was none-too-bright. Which I couldn't blame him for a bit. I wasn't all that sure of my mental capacity at that moment, either.

"You're telling me that you're a friend of Danny Loughman's. Is that right?" His expression telegraphed a deep sense of skepticism.

"Exactly," I said hopefully, doing my best to appear confident and relaxed. I was in fact, experiencing an uncomfortable surge emanating from the exact opposite end of the emotional spectrum. "I gave him a ride home."

The man looked quizzically in my direction.

"When?" he asked suspiciously.

"Just now. Well, it's been about three days really. Maybe four, I really can't remember. Ya' see, he showed up at my place in Connecticut asking for a ride, and I know that's a long way from here…and no, I hadn't seen him in a long, long time, but he looked like he could really use a hand, and well…it's sort of a long story, but the short version is, I gave him a ride, like he asked me to."

I was blathering away like a cocaine addict on a week long bender. The words were flying out of my mouth fast and furious. Whether I was making any sense or not was another matter entirely.

I pushed the piano bench back slightly in an attempt to get more comfortable and gain some much needed space. I was hoping it might help control my breathing, too, which was becoming a little bit difficult. A loud, shrill squealing sound rose up from the feet of the bench as it scraped across the hardwood floor. The tension between the three of us was becoming obvious, even to me.

The room began subtly throbbing, bowing in and out as if the walls were flexible. No matter, I kept up my rapid fire prattle until the man waved his hands in the air with sufficient energy to signal that he wanted me to stop. The woman appeared to be lost in thought. She wasn't even looking in my direction anymore. Her eyes were closed, her left hand pressed to her temple.

"Let me be clear about this," the man said deliberately, "Are you saying that you think you gave Danny Loughman a ride, here, today?" His expression and tone indicated that he regarded me as a complete idiot.

"Yes, that's exactly what I'm saying," I replied indignantly. I was annoyed. Clearly this guy knew Danny or he would have thrown me out or threatened to call the police by now. "I just dropped him off," I said insistently, pointing toward the back of the house, the dirt road and the store around the corner. "I'm sure he'll be here any minute."

"Where exactly did you drop him off?" he condescended.

"Townsend's Store, just down there."

The woman shot up straight, rigid as a board, as if high-voltage electric current had been passed through her body.

"He said he had a few things to do and he'd be right here," I said. Then, with all the insolence I could muster, I added, "He told me to wait here. It's not like I broke in or anything."

"Townsend's Store?" the woman asked in a deeply hushed voice. I nodded, which was apparently the signal she'd been waiting for to scream venomously in my direction.

"You dropped Danny off at Townsend's Store?" She was infuriated, and obviously dubious of my claim.

"Yeah," I shouted back. I was feeling out of breath, my heart was pounding mercilessly in my chest. I wished Danny would walk through the door, effectively ending the inquisition. I was tired and wanted to lie down more than anything in the world. Sleep was what I needed most, not this pointless give-and-take that was leading us nowhere.

The room throbbed more strenuously, tilting slightly on its axis. I felt perspiration forming on my forehead.

The woman stood absolutely still, silently staring at me as if she didn't have the first idea what to do with me. One thing was clear however. She didn't care for me or my story one bit.

She was pretty. Even with almost no makeup and wearing her casual gardener's outfit, it was apparent that she was a stunning woman.

The man stepped back, took her arm and whispered discretely in her ear. She whispered back. The two of them sequestered themselves as best they could and held a short, intense conference right there in the doorway to the porch. It wasn't hard to figure out what the main topic of conversation was. She maintained eye contact with me the whole time, casually rubbing her counterpart's shoulder as she did. There was a noticeable affection between them. It wasn't overtly romantic, but it was obvious they cared for each other.

"How do you know Danny?" she asked finally. Her quivering lip movements indicating that she was working hard to control her emotions.

"We grew up together, in East Hartford," I answered with as much breathless strength as I could muster. "We were in a band together when we were teenagers. I hadn't seen him in years, but we were pretty good friends in the old days. Once a friend always a friend, I guess."

I couldn't help but smirk. The color began to bleed out of the room.

"What was the name of the band?" she asked defiantly.

It was a quiz question. She knew the answer. She was checking to see if I knew or if I was trying to snow her. My eyelids were heavy. Each breath seemed to take more and more effort. My head ached so badly.

"We were in The Mayfair's," I said with a tone of resignation. "It was me and Danny, Bobby Yount and Marc Patnoe."

My answer met with dead silence. The room was completely still except for my occasional, irritatingly erratic selection of stray piano keys.

"Look, I can understand how you might think I broke in here. But I'm telling you, Danny will be here any minute. He'll straighten this out." More silence.

"I just dropped him off, for Christ's sake."

I was disgusted, tired and out of ideas as to how I might convince these two that I wasn't an intruder looking to steal Grandma's good silver. I began to hyperventilate.

Finally the woman spoke again. Her tone was soft and surprisingly kind under the circumstances. Her eyes lost the hard edge they'd had only moments before. She looked like she was about to cry.

"Oh, Frank," she said haltingly, as if the words she was searching for were hard to say. Tears were welling up in her eyes. She brushed one away with the back of her hand before it broke loose and coursed down her cheek. "I don't even know where to begin."

She struggled to find the words. Her lips moved but no sound came out. She was almost pleading, straining to make me understand something that she wasn't quite able to articulate. I felt like I was supposed to be reading between the lines, but I wasn't even sure where the lines were.

Eventually, she found her voice again. She began to speak, forlornly.

"Danny lived with a lot of guilt over a wrong he'd done to you…a long time ago."

The mood in the room had shifted noticeably. The pair in the doorway were no longer suspicious of me. They pitied me. All things considered, who could blame them.

I shrugged.

"He never mentioned it to me." In truth I didn't have any idea what she was talking about. "It's all water under the bridge now, anyway. When he gets here, I'll forgive him if it makes you feel better." I was serious too. I'd have forgiven him for whatever was bothering her in a minute. "Hey," I forced a chuckle, hoping to bring some levity to the moment, but I botched the faked emotion badly. There was no humor to be found anywhere in the room. "I don't know what he thinks he did, but whatever it was, I never noticed it. It's no skin off my nose."

"Frank…" she choked up again. The emotions were thicker now, harder to cut through as the reality of the situation bore down on her like a great weight. Tears were running down her cheeks. Even her male companion was looking uncomfortably choked up.

"Danny died." Her voice broke as she pushed the words out. "He died…of Leukemia." She paused, both to let that crushing news sink in and to give herself a chance to regain her composure before adding the coup de grace.

"That was three months ago, Frank."

I sat quietly on the piano bench trying to process the information she'd just shared. The couple in the doorway took a moment to comfort each other, although neither of them took their eyes off me completely.

Staring dispassionately at the keyboard in front of me, her words rolled around in my head like steel balls in a pinball machine, crashing this way and that, causing bells to ring and lights to flash as they went about their business. The idea occurred to me for the first time that I very well might be completely insane. Certainly I was in a great deal of trouble. But whether that trouble was legal, financial, automotive or spiritual wasn't entirely clear to me. The only thing I knew for sure was that the keys of the piano were growing in size. Slowly at first, then with incredible speed, they rushed up and enveloped my entire field of vision.

I felt two or three of the thin, black, raised keys bang into my forehead, the result being a horrendous sound that was in no way tuneful or pleasing. My entire world exploded in a flash of light, then went black. Somewhere in the distance, the cacophonous sound of the piano resonated on. It swirled around in my head, blocking out the sound of the pretty woman's words, filling my ears completely with a surprisingly welcome mishmash of off-key fury. The darkness felt good. It felt peaceful and safe.

What more can a hallucinating vagrant hope for?

CHAPTER 24

The first rays of morning sun came streaming through an expansive kitchen window. I stood alone at the sink, enjoying the solitude of the moment while occasionally sipping at a hot, sweet mug of Folger's finest. The soft whooshing sound of the shower running in the bathroom was the only distraction of the morning so far. It was a Sunday.

Half-a-dozen horses grazed in the pasture below, oblivious to me and my wandering eyes. They grazed continuously, casually, paying little attention to the world around them. And why should they, I reasoned? Horses are bright enough to know they're just as comfortable in this place as they'd be in any other pasture, munching grass in another town. Life goes on. Sometimes it goes on in another place. But it goes on just the same.

Horses are a lot smarter than people give them credit for, I think. I really do.

A few hundred yards away, traffic was building up on Highway 441. The occasional glint of sunlight off the windshields of stray cars produced a strobe effect. The reflected light was neither offensive nor enjoyable. It was just there, then it was gone. Very much like Danny had been.

It had been a year, almost to the day, since I'd head-butted my old friend's Steinway and collapsed to the floor beneath it. I'm pleased to say that I'd learned a great deal during the course of those 12 months. Much more than I ever learned during the 12 years I spent in public school, or the more than two decades since, while I'd been drifting aimlessly through life.

For instance, I'd learned to take the time I'd been given and whatever opportunities I might discover in life much more seriously. I'd learned a bit about making friends and maintaining relationships too. Important skills, all.

Still, there were questions that remained. Questions that I wasn't at all sure I'd ever know the answers to. But I was patient. The answers would come one day, at least I hoped they would.

The bearded man, the one I'd first seen in the doorway of Danny's living room, emerged from the house next door and began moving fluidly toward a spot directly under my second story window. He wore faded jeans, a blue and orange ball cap and a University of Florida Gators sweatshirt.

The thermometer outside my kitchen window edged up toward 60 degrees. Another sip from my coffee cup aided the rising sun as it warmed me. The coffee worked from within, the sunshine from without.

The bearded man's gait was slow and sure as he flowed gracefully across the lawn. On his feet were a pair of black cowboy boots. Bright and shiny silver tips flashed in the sunlight as he walked across the short grass. In his left hand was an insulated coffee mug made of brushed stainless steel, which he raised in a casual salute before disappearing from view. A silent "Good morning," offered from one neighbor to another.

I raised my own cup, reciprocating his greeting. He missed my response as he climbed into the driver's seat of his car, parked 10 feet beneath my feet. His was the Jaguar I'd seen at Danny's house when I first arrived in town.

His name was Dale Albritton. A total stranger a year before, he'd since become a rock solid stabilizing force in my life. He'd also become a good and valued friend.

My life was turning around. There was no doubt about that.

After being released from Shands Hospital, which is where I spent a few days recuperating after my unfortunate incident at Danny's house, I learned that Dale was a lawyer, a gentleman rancher and one heck of a nice guy.

While I was still at the hospital, on the mend, Dale did some checking up on me. Which I have to admit, was completely understandable. Considering how we'd met, my background and mental state were certainly worth taking a peek at. He wasn't secretive about the idea of looking into my background at all. Which was refreshing, frankly. I didn't take the least offense. I was just glad he wasn't threatening to press charges or have me immediately transferred to a mental institution. Either of which would have been perfectly reasonable options from my perspective.

The two most important facts he learned from his investigation of me were that I really was who I said I was and that I was absolutely dead broke. Unfortunately, there really wasn't much more to learn on the subject of Frank Stevens.

It was Dale who solved my homelessness problem by suggesting I move into an apartment on the second floor of his barn. Having virtually no other option, I accepted the offer, of course. Which is how I came to live directly next door to Dale's own home, just above the stables. My modern, fully furnished two-bedroom apartment came complete with cable TV, a stocked refrigerator and a computer work station with high-speed Internet access. It was nothing short of palatial compared to any place I'd ever lived before.

Even more unbelievable was the fact that I'd never been asked for a dime in rent. *Never.* It hadn't even been suggested that I write a check or begin to think about moving on. As far as Dale was concerned, his home was my home. The man even gave me an allowance of sorts. A few bucks spending money now and then. He claimed he owed me for doing chores around the property.

It appeared that Dale Albritton had set his sights on being my full-time guardian angel. A function that he performed flawlessly, I must say.

Our original meeting turned out to be a complete stroke of luck for me. I learned later that his presence at Danny's house was coincidental to my arrival. But having been Danny's lawyer and best friend, it was virtually guaranteed that we'd have met eventually. And while I wished with all my heart that I could have made a better impression on our first meeting, I had no complaints about how things were turning out.

The water in the shower stopped whooshing. The apartment fell silent.

A second man hurried from the house next door, ran to the Jaguar and jumped into the passenger's seat. He wore his sun-bleached blond hair razor sharp and short. A trim, stylishly dressed middle-aged man, Stephen Pierce, earned his living as a doctor specializing in sports medicine. He was employed by and taught at the University of Florida, which was located nearby. Stephen was also Dale's partner, his significant other.

Quick, light footsteps padded across the tile floor behind me. A mass of cold, wet hair slapped against my back as Mel's arms closed tightly around my middle, nearly causing me to drop my coffee mug into the sink.

"I'm freezing," She chattered her teeth for effect, exaggerating the early morning chill. "Warm me up."

"It's not that cold," I teased. "In an hour it'll be in the 70s."

"Seems pretty chilly to me," she chided. Still damp from the shower, a thick terry cloth towel was her only protection from the not quite brutal onslaught of autumn in Florida.

"You big baby," I teased.

From the moment I'd met her, Melanie had made a powerful impression on me. Fearing the worst but hoping for the best, I made the drive back up to the BP station in Jacksonville as soon as I was able, tracked her down at the house she shared with Jessica and made it clear that I was interested in her for more than her ability to secure free sandwiches and soft drinks.

I didn't make this bold move completely of my own volition of course. I was pushed. The therapist I'd been referred to while still at Shands Hospital suggested I make the trip and tell this intriguing woman how I felt about her. Which I did, as ineptly as can humanly be done, I suspect. But much to my surprise, I found that telling the truth actually worked. The object of my affection admitted quite readily that she was as attracted to me as I was to her.

A relationship was born.

Mel and I began taking turns commuting on weekends to see each other. Within a couple of months, the weekend day trips became weekend sleep-overs. I can only speak for myself, of course, but I was deliriously happy with the way things were working out.

This time around, I was taking my personal relationships a lot more seriously than I'd done in the past. With more than a little help from Dale, Stephen and my newfound psychologist, Dr. Patel, I learned to actually listen to Mel and honestly care about what she said and how she felt on a daily basis. I took the time to explore her emotional attachments, her motivations, fears and goals. The process wasn't nearly as intimidating nor as mysterious as I'd imagined it might be. It wasn't the least bit boring either. And in the end, I found I had a far more complex and interesting woman in my life than I'd ever imagined was possible.

Sometimes progress just sneaks up on you. It certainly did in my case.

"Where are they off to so early?" Mel asked, pointing at the Jag as it wove through the pasture below toward the highway.

I held up the coffee pot and a fresh mug, offering her a cup. She nodded thankfully and grabbed a carton of creamer from the refrigerator.

"Antiquing I think." I knew almost as much about the buying and selling of antiques as the average receptionist knows about molecular biology. "Stephen thinks he's tracked down something interesting at some shop in Leesburg, or Ocala," I waved away the question with my free hand.

Mel smirked and gave me a playful elbow in the ribs, "Oh, you're a big help."

"You'll have to excuse me," I said feigning embarrassment, "but this dumb Yankee doesn't know diddly about antique collecting."

"No kidding?" Mel mocked good-naturedly.

She accepted the coffee from my outstretched hand then reached up on her tip toes and planted a soft kiss on my lips. We held each other for several minutes, savoring the vividly powerful sensations of being together, committing the moment to memory. For while we spent as much of our time together as we could, it was far more common that we were apart. A fact that neither of us cared for much.

"Can you stay for a while longer?" I asked hopefully.

"I can't," she said with genuine sorrow. "I promised I'd be back to take the afternoon shift today. But I'll be back Thursday morning for sure."

"Ahhh, Thanksgiving with the neighbors," I sang out.

"I can't wait. Is Jean coming too?"

"Yeah, I talked to her briefly the other day. She said she wouldn't miss it for the world."

Jean Eldridge had been Danny's fiancé. She was the woman with Dale on the day I'd so inauspiciously introduced myself at Danny's house.

"Actually, she was being a little secretive, in a playful sort of way," I went on. "She said she's got some news that she can't wait to tell us about."

"News for us?" Mel asked, stirring creamer into her coffee.

"Well, actually she said she had news for me, but I was trying to be polite and include you in the festivities."

"Oh, what a gallant man you are."

"That's me all right," I agreed with gusto. "Everybody says so."

"Well then, I guess I'd better not be late," Mel teased as she danced back to the bedroom. "I wouldn't want to lose my date to one of your many admirers."

I laughed out loud as she disappeared behind the bathroom door. But a sense of melancholy colored my otherwise upbeat mood. In 20 minutes, Mel would be gone. Four days would pass before we'd see each other again. I could only hope the time would pass quickly.

CHAPTER 25

By the time Dale and Stephen rolled back through the main gate, the sun was hanging low over the tree line to the west. Rather than sulk over Mel's early departure, I'd kept myself busy with farm work all day. More than anything else it was that newly acquired tendency to do physical labor whenever I felt down or prone to slipping back into my old self-destructive ways that had carved 10 pounds of flab off my mid-section. The habit had also given me time to think, to plan and imagine my future. Something I'd rarely done in the past.

During the course of the day, I'd managed to muck out five of the six stalls in the barn below my apartment. I was just getting started on the last one when I heard the Jag's throaty rumble as my neighbors pulled up to the wide front door and switched off the engine. Dale and Stephen crawled out of the low-slung XK coupe, both with empty hands and long faces.

"Couldn't find anything worth pulling out your checkbook for, huh?" I queried in my friendliest tone.

Dale rolled his eyes. Stephen looked sullen, then announced with annoyance, "It was a bait-and-switch fiasco. I still can't believe it. On the phone, the man says he's got a piece of early 20th-century Steuben art glass. But when we show up at his shop, all he's got are shelves full of tacky green ashtrays, old soda bottles and a handful of chipped electrical insulators."

Of the two, Stephen was clearly more upset. Continuing on, Stephen affected a mock whisper to add, "And the soda bottles were off-brands. Not an original Coke bottle in the bunch."

Still not knowing anything about antiques or understanding the compulsion some people have to buy them, I said sincerely, "I'm sorry it didn't work out for you."

"Thank you," Stephen gratefully acknowledged my sympathy.

"So anyway," Dale interjected as tactfully as he could, "Mel's still planning to come down for Thanksgiving?"

"Yeah, she'll be here. She asked me to thank you again for the invitation."

"Not at all, not at all," Dale gave his assurance, "we're thrilled to have her."

Daydreaming of a hundred different details about her that had so affected me, I toed the dirt under foot and muttered, "So am I."

Dale and Stephen exchanged a quick glance, leaving me with the impression they'd discussed the progression of my love life before. Which is no big deal. Friends do that sort of thing, I suppose.

"We were planning on whipping up a couple steaks quick and making an early night of it," Stephen explained, apropos of nothing. "Would you like to come over for supper?"

Giving myself a quick once-over, I recognized I was a long way from being presentable enough to accept even the invitation of a close friend. "Thanks guys, but I think I'd better sit this one out. I've got one more stall to finish up anyway. I wouldn't want to throw off your night."

"Oh, you'll be fine," Dale urged, "Come on over and have dinner with us."

I've never found it easy to turn down a heartfelt invitation. Perhaps because I'd had so little experience receiving them before this.

"Thanks, really. I appreciate the thought, but I'm going to finish up here, clean myself up, microwave something reasonably nutritious and crawl into the sack."

"OK, if you're sure," Stephen gave me one last chance to accept.

"We'll see you Thursday then," Dale tossed over his shoulder as he began to make his way across the yard.

"Two o'clock, OK?" I queried.

"Works for me," Dale called back. Stephen nodded enthusiastically before disappearing around the corner of the barn, leaving me and my pitchfork to clean out one last stall in solitude.

I truly felt bad for not accepting Dale and Stephen's dinner invitation. Over the course of the year I'd been living above their barn, I'd averaged at least three dinners a week at their house. The food was always good, but the after-dinner conversation was even better. We talked about politics and religion, personal histories and celebrity gossip. Nothing was off the table. As a matter of fact, it was during those after-dinner conversations that I learned most of what I know about Danny and what he'd been up to after leaving East Hartford, and me, behind.

Initially, Danny had gone west, to California. His attempts to start up or join a successful band failed miserably. As Dale related the story, Danny was close to packing it in and heading home when he somehow wrangled a job playing piano in a West Hollywood bar. It was there that an industry bigwig heard him, offered him a publishing deal and launched Danny's career as a songwriter. It was something of a shock to learn that my old friend Danny had written a fair number of the songs I'd been listening to over the years. That talent had made him a rich man. He was apparently a much sought-after commodity in the entertainment business.

Danny had made it. What we'd dreamed as kids had come true for him. Knowing that gave me a tremendous sense of relief. Although it didn't come close to explaining why I was still under the impression we'd spent the better part of a week together driving down Interstate 95. Even Dr. Patel hadn't been able to help me figure that mystery out yet.

Tired of the pressures of the business and worn out from almost constant work, Danny came to Gainesville to get away from the never-ending commotion of the music business. By his mid-30s he was ready to settle down, which by all accounts, he did quite well. After buying a house in town, Danny hired a local lawyer to help him invest his substantial royalties and set about the business of becoming semi-retired. The lawyer he hired was Dale Albritton.

Red wine and good whiskey were always on hand and liberally dispensed after dinner with Dale and Stephen. Not that any of us were hard-core, fall-down drunks. But Stephen and I had on occasion been known to knock back a few. Jean wasn't shy about hoisting a glass or two either. Danny's fiancé might have been petite and pretty, but she was no demure flower of a girl, all appearances to the contrary.

Dale was another story. He never said anything about our drinking one way or another, but he rarely indulged. Even when attorney Albritton did accept a glass of scotch or a cold beer, he rarely seemed to get anywhere near the bottom of his glass.

"No, I'm good," was his standard response whenever offered a refill. More often than not he'd nurse a single glass of Jack Daniels for hours, sometimes through the entire evening. He conducted himself almost as if he was the designated driver for the rest of us, even though he was already home and none of us was likely to be going anywhere. I only lived across the lawn, and whenever Jean made the trip for dinner, she almost always ended up staying overnight in the main house.

I chalked my observation up to the fact that Dale was just a 24 hour-a-day, responsible guy. The sort of fellow who always feels like he's on duty, that he should be in top form all the time, just in case. He was, in effect, a self-imposed chaperone.

Of the pantheon of men and women in human history I admire most, Dale Albritton definitely makes my Top Five.

My mind wandered freely as I shoveled soiled straw from the floor of the last stall. Even considering the health benefits of my willingly accepted farm chores, the ability to daydream at will was the real reason I'd taken so enthusiastically to regularly doing manual labor in the barn and on the grounds. Ideas for the future mixed effortlessly with reflections on my past as I toiled away. My mind wandered aimlessly, until it fixed on an issue of importance. Being otherwise disengaged from the actions of my body, my thought processes were free to consider the various facets of my new life, to analyze them until I found either acceptance, or a resolution that worked for me and my rapidly developing system of values. Included among the topics I struggled with in those days was the crystal-clear realization that my situation in life had been improved immeasurably due to the kindness of two men who owed me absolutely nothing.

I was also aware that to some degree I owed a fair portion of the credit for my second chance at life to Danny. Although I'd not yet been able to figure out exactly how he figured into the big picture.

There was no doubt, my childhood friend had expired as the result of a long and difficult battle with Leukemia. He was physically gone long before I found him weaving on my front porch like a drunken sailor. There was no way, absolutely no possible way that he had accompanied me on a thousand-mile road trip to Florida. And yet, as I tossed one pitchfork full of fresh straw after another into the last stall, I entertained vivid memories of him sitting beside me in the car, alternately sleeping and jabbering away as I drove ever southward.

Nobody could explain exactly what had happened. Not yet at least. And it seemed that with the significant number of inconsistencies in my recollection of the chain of events, there wasn't much chance that my story ever would make sense. Not to me at least. Probably not to anyone.

I hadn't seen Danny Loughman in more than 20 years. And I can say with complete confidence that as I sat in my empty apartment in East Hartford, slowly wasting away, I didn't know the first thing about where he lived or what he'd done with his life during those intervening years. But somehow, I'd driven more than a thousand miles, directly to his front door and wandered right inside his home. I couldn't even begin to explain that one.

Even more peculiar, I distinctly recalled dropping Danny off at Townsend's Store with such clarity that I could still visualize the old wooden porch, the steps that ran up to it and the loose fitting screen door that led inside.

But as I learned firsthand on the day Dale drove me back to pick up the Taurus more than a week later, there was no Townsend's Store. Danny's house was the only structure on 109th Place. It sat exactly where I remembered it, at the end of a pair of sandy tire tracks behind a bend in the road, shielded from view by a thick stand of live oaks and underbrush. But between the main road and Danny's house, there was no wood-framed store with a screen door and three rocking chairs on the porch. There wasn't even a ratty old tool shed I might have mistaken for a general store. The spot I remembered dropping Danny off at turned out to be nothing more than an empty space between two young saplings.

The piece of the puzzle that disturbed me the most though had to do with my old, road-worn Taurus. Dale and I went to retrieve it not long after I'd been released from Shands. This was only one day after I'd moved into the most beautiful apartment I'd ever seen.

The plan had been to drive the car back to Dale's house. Not that the car was much to write home about, but the rationale was that at least I'd have possession of something familiar. Something that might provide me with a sense of independence. As shaky and worn out as my poor old car was, at least I'd have the illusion that I could pack up and go whenever the mood struck me. My psychologist, Dr. Patel, thought that aspect of recovering the Taurus might have some therapeutic value for me.

It was worth a shot, anyway.

The reality turned out to be something entirely different. In the daylight, with the benefit of a week's rest and a series of solid, well-balanced meals, it was obvious that the Taurus was way past the point where it could be driven safely, if at all.

I turned the key, hoping with all my heart to hear the engine leap to life. Instead, the result was a horrible, slow grinding sound. Metal grated on worn out metal. The starter motor tried in vain to turn the crankshaft. The crank resisted, then it refused.

"I don't think this thing's going anywhere under its own power," Dale intoned.

"No, apparently not," I agreed sorrowfully.

The interior of the car reeked of sweat, stale food and moldy fabric. The dashboard lights flickered on and off, seemingly without any logic to their she-nanigans. The turn signals didn't work, nor did the interior light. The electrical system was shot.

More important than any of that however, the radio was silent. I pressed the power button repeatedly and cranked the volume all the way up. Still, no sound escaped the car's weary speakers. I punched the preset buttons to no avail.

It was dead. As dead as Danny Loughman. Even though I had crystal clear memories of music coming from that radio, keeping me company, providing me with memories and motivation for a thousand miles.

I didn't have a clue where reality ended and fantasy began.

For the second time in a week, it occurred to me that I might be completely insane. I didn't pass out that second time, though. At least that's something.

Dale silently drove me back to his house and my new apartment above the barn. He invited me to dinner then too, but I declined.

"I'm not really in the mood," I begged off.

"Of course not, another time then," Dale patted me warmly on the shoulder and left me to my own devices. Once inside, when I was alone and felt secure enough, I broke down and cried.

The next morning, I woke up with a whole new attitude. I decided that my newly discovered mental health specialist, Dr. Patel, was right. It was time for me to pull myself together and start my life over again.

Knocking on Dale's front door with some trepidation, I asked if I could work odd jobs on his little farm until I figured out what I was going to do, where I might go.

"Sure," Dale answered simply enough. "You can stay here as long as you want. We're in no rush to see you leave."

That gracious statement was as close to a "Welcome Home" as I ever thought I'd come. My anxiety level dropped to its lowest point in years. I began to feel surprisingly comfortable in what were otherwise completely foreign surroundings.

But even with my housing issue dealt with and my steadily improving men-tal health in the hands of a capable professional, I still had one hurdle to clear before I could start with a clean slate. I needed to talk to Mel.

I didn't set out to find her for another couple weeks. But when I did, I told her my whole story right off the bat. If she was going to reject me, I wanted it to happen right away. As I saw it, there was no point in putting off the pain. If it was going to come, let it come.

It took a good 15 minutes of talking to get the whole story out. But by the time I'd finished, she'd heard everything, from the moment Danny had landed on my doorstep right up to the point where I decided to find her again.

"Hmmm," was all she said.

"That's it?" I asked, "Just hmmm."

"Well, I don't really know what to say," she replied thoughtfully. "I've never heard a story quite like that."

"Danny was with me for the whole trip," I reiterated. "At least I believed he was. I still believe he was, I think. Do you remember seeing him when I stopped, on the night we met?" I asked, hopeful but nervous about what her answer might be.

Mel furrowed her brow and thought hard. She weighed the question seriously, searching her memory for any glimmer of a detail she might have forgotten. "I just don't remember, Frank. With all that steam blowing up out from under your hood, I'm not sure if I ever looked inside the car at all."

"Yeah, I guess that's true," I said, my dejection showing.

"We were in the store for most of the night anyhow," she added.

"Um hum."

Sensing the downturn in my mood, Mel tried to counteract it.

"Hey, don't you worry. If you believe it happened, I'm going to believe it did, too."

"Why would you do that?" I asked skeptically.

Mel took a deep breath, looked me directly in the eye and forcefully launched into a quiet tirade,

"Because I was orphaned as a teenager and I need something to look forward to, that's why. I work at a gas station convenience store, and believe it or not, that's the best job I've ever had. It might be the best job I'll ever have. My best friend bought the house we live in with tips that a bunch of sweaty old truckers stuffed into her G-string while she danced around a pole naked for their entertainment. Her boyfriend is a semi-literate redneck whose family would probably lynch the both of them if they knew what their baby boy was doing, and from the moment I laid eyes on you, I found myself being strangely attracted to you for reasons I just can't explain. A man who I now know to be doubting his sanity because he may have seen a ghost."

The litany sounded like it might go on forever.

"Considering all that, I hope you won't be too offended if I choose to be a 'glass half full' girl and have a little faith in you and a bit of hope for my own future."

"You make an interesting point," I replied, somewhat intimidated by the outburst, but intrigued more than ever by the woman it came from.

"I'll grant you, your story's a bit odd, Frank. But I for one think you're a long way from the loony bin."

"You do like to look on the bright side, don't you?" I suggested hopefully.

"What do you say we just start off clean then?" Mel asked, answering my question with one of her own.

"From right now?" I asked.

"From right now," she agreed.

For a moment we were silent, sitting in the deep green grass, under the shade of a big old stately tree in front of Jessica's pale yellow cement block home. Mel smiled playfully and gave me a little wink, nudging me with her shoulder.

"Hi, my name's Frank," I said, putting my hand out to shake hers.

"Hey there Frank, my name's Melanie, but all my friends call me Mel," she took my hand in hers.

"Well I think I'd be very proud to be counted among your friends," I said sincerely. Our palms pressed together lightly, her fingertips tracing the outline of my hand.

"Well I'll just bet you would, Frank." And at that moment Mel kissed me for the first time. I can still feel her lips whenever I think about that moment. So soft and warm, pressed lightly against mine.

"So you wouldn't mind if I called you then?" I asked, suddenly sure of myself.

"You'd better do a whole lot more than call," she answered, smiling mischievously.

CHAPTER 26

Mel arrived by 10:00 AM on Thanksgiving morning, immediately announcing that she was free to stay until Sunday afternoon.

"Really, we get to spend an entire three-day weekend together?" I beamed.

"Four days," she replied, ticking off a finger to represent each day, "It's a four-day weekend."

"Even better!" I exclaimed.

I'd spent the better part of the previous week pining away for Mel's company. Four days spent apart had seemed interminable at times. The days took far too long to pass. Just as I knew our four days together would zip past us all-too-quickly. Mel had gotten under my skin during the time we'd been together. In a good way, of course. She'd become the focal point of my existence. How I might express that to her was still beyond my grasp, but I was working on it.

After a great deal of effort and a fair amount of time on Dr. Patel's couch, I'd come to grips with the idea of being on my own. In time, I'd learned to become comfortable, even content in my own company. Still, humans are generally social animals. And while I hadn't developed any driving compulsion to press myself into situations that involved large crowds, I had found that my mind was more or less fixed on thoughts of Mel during my waking hours. In truth, she was a featured player in a fair number of my dreams too. I was enamored.

"I'm so glad you're here," I said. "I've been thinking about you all week."

"Me too," Mel responded without hesitation, plopping herself down on the living room couch. "I mean, I missed you too." She patted the cushion beside her, inviting me to sit close and snuggle. I greedily accepted her invitation. Within a matter of seconds, we'd transitioned into a flurry of hands and lips and heavy breathing.

A few moments later, as we unwound ourselves from the tangle of clothing, hair and throw pillows disturbed by that momentary fit of passion, Mel and I stretched out lengthwise on the couch, holding each other in a firm embrace. It was at that moment that I made my first attempt to broach a subject I'd always found far too intimidating to delve into. But this time I was driven. I was ready to move ahead. I was also, unfortunately, almost incomprehensibly tongue-tied.

"Have you given any thought to where we...I mean, where you and I...where we're going?" I stammered pathetically.

"You mean Stephen and Dale's house?" Mel guessed innocently.

"No, no, no." I waved my hands as if to erase the misunderstanding from the air, backtracked mentally and quickly decided I'd be better served to start over. Launching into a new direction, I tried again.

"I've been putting a lot of thought into my future." Immediately recognizing the self-serving appearance of what I'd said I blurted out, "Our future! I meant our future." The correction felt weak and late.

Mel picked a stray throw pillow up off the floor and hugged it close. Her sandy blonde hair hung in glorious disarray, framing her face with a golden glow as the morning sunlight filtered through those tousled strands. She'd kicked her shoes off and untucked her pink cotton shirt. I knew without a doubt that she was absolutely the most beautiful woman I'd ever seen as she gazed at me curiously from her position on the couch. I paced the room as I rambled on. Mel said nothing.

Still too stupid to put down the shovel, I continued to dig a deeper hole for myself.

"I'm not saying this very well. I know that. I'm sorry." My mind raced, searching for perfect words, magical words that would articulate exactly what I intended, clearly, poetically. I was thinking Dean Martin but acting Jerry Lewis.

I turned to face her, my hands clasped together as if in prayer, my eyes closed in hopes that the dark might help my concentration and smooth over my inability to speak clearly. "Mel, I've been thinking about us a lot and I want to..."

Whomp!

The pillow Mel had been holding bounced off my face like an oversized marshmallow. I opened my eyes. Quick as a cat, Mel stretched out toward me, grabbed my hands and pulled me back to the couch. She wrapped both arms around me with enthusiastic affection.

"Can we talk about this later, loverboy?" she cooed, kissing my neck with abandon. "You've got unfinished business."

"I do?" I asked, laughing.

Mel's eyes darted from my own to the bedroom and back again.

"You've got to learn to finish what you start, mister."

"Ohhh, OK," I answered as the big light bulb clicked on above my head. "But we're going to get back to this later on, right?"

"Umm hmm," she mumbled, kissing my neck and chest voraciously.

"Do you understand what I'm trying to say?" I asked sincerely.

"Oh shut up and kiss me," was Mel's reply.

"Yes ma'am." I picked her up and carried her to the bedroom.

CHAPTER 27

Considering my family history, I didn't have a whole lot of experience with what most people would consider happy, holiday celebrations. But I did have certain expectations about how the rest of the country celebrated big national holidays, including Thanksgiving. As Mel and I made our way from the entryway of Dale and Stephen's expansive executive home to the dining room near the back, it was clear that my assumptions were way off-base. At least in the context of how my new circle of friends saw things.

Instead of the traditional turkey dinner I'd anticipated, our hosts had laid out a feast of southern delicacies. The table was piled high with slabs of barbequed ribs and heaping bowls of sweet potatoes, mashed potatoes, collard greens, snap peas, a mass of corn bread, fluffy white biscuits and icy tall glasses of sweet tea. I knew immediately that it was a safe bet pumpkin pies weren't on the dessert menu.

"I hope you're not disappointed," Stephen said as he led us to the dining room table. "We tend to depart from the mainstream on Thanksgiving." Jean and Dale were already seated, chatting away as old friends are prone to do. No one bothered to ask why Mel and I were nearly a half hour late. I'm sure the reason was obvious.

I was genuinely glad to see Jean again. The two of us weren't particularly close, but we were getting there. She'd taken Danny's death harder than Dale or Stephen had, understandably enough. And while she'd warmed up to me considerably, I was of the impression that she still harbored a certain amount of trepidation about how nutty I really was. Which, all things considered, was completely understandable.

"Good afternoon, Jean," I said festively, "you remember Mel."

"Oh yes," she replied warmly, pulling herself upright to shake hands with each of us. "It's good to see you again, Mel."

"Good to see you too," my girl was the soul of propriety. "Thank you so much for the invitation, Dale, Stephen. This is wonderful."

"We're just glad you could make it," Stephen beamed, gallantly pulling a chair out for my date to settle into. Dale grinned royally and raised a glass of iced tea in salute to his new guests.

Based on our previous dinners together, I knew that Jean typically brought a bottle of something special with her. In more refined company that might suggest she was carrying a fine wine or some sticky sweet after dinner liqueur. But that's not Jean. It's not very true to the traditions of the south, either. A one-liter bottle of Jack Daniels Tennessee Whiskey plunked down in the middle of the table attested to that fact.

"Would you care for a drink with dinner?" Jean asked, hoisting the bottle of "Jack" in the general direction of Mel and me.

"Sure," I answered without hesitation. It was a holiday after all, and I was in a particularly good mood.

"That would be nice, thanks," Mel responded politely. Of the two of us, Mel was almost always the more eloquent and diplomatic.

"Everybody's here now," Stephen called from the kitchen, "so you might as well dig in."

"You don't have to tell me twice," Dale called back, piling an impressive selection of ribs, potatoes and corn bread onto his plate.

For the next hour, the five of us ate and talked, laughed and commiserated with each other over the successes, near misses, trials and tribulations of the past year. We reveled in each other's company, making it ever more clear to me that we were in a sense, forming a family unit of our own.

All five of us were orphans of a sort. Some through the physical loss of our parents, as was the case with Jean, Mel and me. Or in the cases of Dale and Stephen, because they had been more or less cast out of their biological families, shunned because their romantic interests diverged from those of their parents and siblings. Neither of them was lucky enough to have been born to parents who could find it in themselves to be sufficiently open-minded to keep their families together. And so Dale and Stephen, two of the kindest, most caring men I'd ever known, were as much orphaned as the rest of us were. More cruelly perhaps, considering their losses were intentionally imposed on them. At least Jean, Mel and I had the consolation of knowing we'd been dealt emotional blows by mere chance. That took at least some of the sting out.

The greatest Thanksgiving gift I could have hoped for was that realization; I was once again part of a family. I had friends to cherish and be cherished by in return. None of us were alone any longer. We had each other.

All of which was true. But it was far from the biggest surprise of the night. That was still to come. The ripples of which extend through time right up until today. Even now, years later, I can hardly believe it.

As the ribs, corn bread and potatoes disappeared, so did the whiskey. The combined effect of which lubricated the conversationalists among us and raised the volume of the room considerably. It was during the course of that chat-fest, before we'd even had the chance to push ourselves back from the table and adjourn to the screened porch, that tiny bits of my personal mystery began to reveal themselves.

The whiskey hadn't hit me hard yet, but it was making its presence known. I wasn't alone in feeling its effects either. With the exception of Dale, none of us was being shy about refilling our glasses whenever we got the urge.

Jean began to reminisce quietly about her life. Her memories of Danny and the life they shared together all too briefly.

"I loved him so much," she said softly between bites. "I loved that house too." She raised her head and locked eyes with me, then Mel as she related her story.

"I used to play there when I was a little girl, you know. My grandmother and I planted hibiscus bushes around the stand of live oaks next to the walkway when I was 10." She closed her eyes and leaned her head back, reliving the memories as she spoke. "Danny and I cleaned them out and planted new bushes there." She rocked forward, leaned into the table and found another mouthful of cornbread. Jean paused to chew then added, "Three years ago we did that."

"Wait a minute," I don't think I was slurring my words, but a burst of giggles coming from Stephen suggested otherwise. "You used to play in the yard at Danny's house when you were a kid? Before you met him?"

Jean nodded vigorously as she put away a mouthful of mashed potatoes, "My grandparents owned the house before Danny did. They bought it back in the 1920s. When I was a little girl, I'd stay with them during the summer."

The tone of Jean's voice conveyed her love of the property and the memories it held for her.

"It was a wonderful place to spend a childhood. Granddaddy would get up early and walk to work and Granny would let me run loose pretty much all morning. Later, the two of us would bring Granddaddy's lunch to him at noontime."

Jean was becoming increasingly lost in her vividly realistic dreamworld as she spoke. So much of what was important in her life seemed to be lost to her memory alone. She obviously cherished those remembrances as much as she did the physical world.

"I loved bringing Granddaddy lunch. It made me feel so important. We'd sit side by side in rocking chairs out on the porch while he ate his meal. He was always telling me some wild story or other, always swearing that it was absolutely true, no matter how far fetched it sounded. Then, Granny and I would carry that wicker basket back to the house where I could play in the yard until he came home at the end of the day."

"How weird is that?" I asked rhetorically. "Your family owned that house before Danny did."

"Yes, I practically lived there as a kid," Jean confirmed, "I've always loved that house," she repeated.

Her face turned upward to the ceiling again, her eyes momentarily closed. Even without knowing exactly what she was thinking, I could tell her mind was filled with images that were nowhere to be seen on Dale and Stephen's ceiling,

"I have a lot of happy memories tied up in that place."

"I thought somebody'd told me that Danny bought it from the estate of an old widow," I said, searching my memory for details of what I knew.

"He did," she replied, her spell broken by my intrusion. "That was my grandmother, Granny Townsend."

The name hit me like a bolt of lightning.

"Your grandmother's name was Townsend? Like, Townsend's Store, Townsend?"

"Yeah, Townsend's Store belonged to my grandfather." Jean commented nonchalantly. "Before there were Wal-Marts or CVS drug stores or Publix Supermarkets, there were little general stores like my grandfather's all over the place. They're all gone now. The stores, I mean. Well…the owners and customers too, I guess. It was a long time ago."

"I thought your last name was Eldridge." Mel challenged curiously, picking up on my thought process exactly.

"Oh, no. That's not my maiden name. Eldridge is the result of a very short, unhappy marriage from my college days." Jean threw a theatrical frown in Dale's direction, who shrugged in response. "I'm a Townsend originally."

The revelation was profound, momentarily causing the whiskey-induced cobwebs in my head to clear. "Then there really was a Townsend's Store," I marveled.

"Oh yeah, but it burned down a long time ago, when I was about 12 I think," said Jean.

"Was it right there, around the bend from Danny's house?"

"Um hum, it was there all right," she confirmed, picking at the last of her slab of ribs.

"That's kind of freaky," Mel interjected.

"Tell me about it," answered Jean and I, nearly in unison.

"How much do you know about Danny?" Stephen asked, looking in my general direction. "I mean, how much do you know about his life down here."

"Not much, really," I replied. "I know he was a songwriter and that he was successful enough to make a living at it."

"That's for sure," Stephen chuckled. It was a curious comment. But even though the subject piqued my interest, I didn't follow up on it. After all, I wasn't entirely in command of my faculties at that point.

Dale picked up the conversation, addressing Mel and me directly. The information he shared was already common knowledge to Jean and Stephen.

"Danny wasn't just a songwriter," Dale explained, "he was a *very* successful songwriter. He also produced records for a number of other artists whose work sold quite well." He listed a few names, but they were all unfamiliar to me. They were afer my time I imagined. Mel knew most of them, though. She appeared to be quite impressed with Danny's resume as Dale ran it by us.

"He also become a fairly astute businessman after he got off the road and dedicated himself to settling down," Dale continued. "Once he'd decided to more or less retire from the music business, he branched out into new areas of investment and speculation. He had a real knack for identifying good investments. Among other things, Danny got into real estate. And like everything else in his life, when he got involved, he got involved in a big way."

"No kidding," I remarked in amazement. "So, what happened to it all?" It seemed an innocent enough question.

Jean raised her hand, modestly. "He left it to me."

"All of it?" Mel asked, fascinated by the events as they were unfolding.

"All the real estate, anyway. Which is plenty, believe me," she replied with a unique mixture of pride and humility.

"So are you going to move back into the house someday," Mel pressed, then backtracked, suddenly concerned that she'd overstepped her bounds. "I'm sorry. I don't mean to be nosey. Curiosity got the better of me."

I felt like I was sitting at a writer's conference table in the midst of a planning session for a daytime soap opera.

"No, no, that's fine. I don't mind talking about it." Jean poured herself another Jack and Coke as she explained why she wouldn't be moving back into the house she loved so much. "I'm converting it into a sort of a halfway house. I'm calling it Loughman Hall." A crooked smile crept across her face as she related the name.

Jean went on to explain that her own short, unhappy college experience had taught her a lesson she hadn't soon forgotten. And now that she had the means to do something that might lighten the load for those unlucky few who would almost certainly find themselves in a similar situation, she felt it was a moral imperative that she do so.

Gainesville is home to a major university. As a matter of fact, the student body of the University of Florida makes up a substantial portion of Gainesville's overall population. With all those bodies packed into close quarters, combined with all the pressures and activities inherent to college life, there are bound to be mistakes made. Some more lasting, more damaging than others.

Jean knew firsthand how vulnerable, even gullible, young women can occasionally be when they're away from home for the first time. In an attempt to combat the effects of those unavoidably unfortunate, impulsive, horribly flawed decisions she knew would be made by young women on campus, Jean had established a charitable foundation. It was to be based out of Loughman Hall and was designed to feed, clothe and house young women who found themselves to be suddenly and unexpectedly homeless, penniless or perhaps pregnant. The foundation's focus was to aid young women who were enrolled in college, to make it possible for them to still reach their goals. Her intention was to create a safety net that would make it possible for them to stay in school, whatever their short-term personal difficulties might be.

"That's fantastic," I exclaimed."What a great way to live your life, helping people to become more productive and secure. That's just great!"

I truly envied Jean for what she was setting out to do. It was obvious how much thought and heartfelt emotion had gone into her plans. Even the name of the home she'd founded was important. It was a tribute to Danny, who had, in effect, funded the program. It was also designed to sound collegiate. As Jean reasoned, it was important the name didn't raise questions in the minds of far-off family members who might become curious about a housing facility that sounded more like a treatment center than a dorm.

We all sat quietly, soaking up the emotions of the moment, sipping our drinks, lost in our own thoughts. Stephen was the one who finally broke the silence.

"Dale, you've got to tell him."

Dale shushed his partner with a waving motion of his right hand. In his left was a tumbler containing two fingers of golden brown whiskey. He hadn't touched a drop all night. Being the only other 'him' in the room, I realized that Stephen was alluding to me. A fact that caught my attention immediately. I tuned in to their exchange.

"He's entitled to know," Stephen reasoned. "He's come a long way, geographically and emotionally. It's time he knew the truth."

Dale sagged in his chair. He wasn't disagreeing, but he was clearly uncomfortable with the subject matter.

"I don't think this is the time or the place to do this," he mumbled at his mate.

"No, Stephen's right," Jean chimed in. "He should know."

"Look, I'm not saying he shouldn't be told," Dale argued, "but at least two of us are a little drunk and I'm not at all sure this is the best environment to bring up a subject of this…magnitude." Dale gestured in the direction of Jean and me as he described our condition.

Mel giggled, being a little tipsy herself. Jean and I exchanged glances and smiled. It wouldn't be until the next morning that I'd realize we'd been smiling for completely different reasons. In my case, being pleasantly inebriated, I was amused at the fact that I was among friends, true friends who were arguing politely about some news that I may or may not be about to hear. I'd had just enough alcohol to feel loving and warm. I was everybody's friend at that moment.

Jean, on the other hand was smiling because she knew something I didn't. Something she was lobbying for me to hear right there and then. News that it would turn out had the power to change my life forever.

"The only people directly involved are all in this room, Dale." Stephen had the floor. "You're the executor, they're the beneficiaries, it's that simple. He deserves to know." His argument was measured, logical and a total mystery to me. It was fun to watch him work though.

Dale glared at his partner, not in anger, but in a way that conveyed his displeasure at being put into a position there was no graceful way out of.

"Tell him, Dale," said Jean firmly.

Mel squeezed my hand under the table.

Dale exhaled heavily in defeat.

"OK, ok, if you both want to do it now, we'll do it now."

He put his drink down on the table, still untouched, shifted in his seat and made solid eye contact with me. His posture and demeanor said that he would be addressing me alone. The fact there were others in the room was incidental. Dale, the friendly, jovial host was gone. He'd been replaced by Attorney Albritton, the consummate legal professional. His voice shifted to a deeper tone. His steely eyes and rugged face now displayed the stern countenance of a father preparing to tell his maturing child something of great importance.

I made a valiant attempt to return his gaze with a similar sense of sobriety, but I failed miserably, only managing to look confused and tired.

Dale began with a warning of sorts.

"You're going to have questions about this. Quite a few questions, I would imagine. So I want you to know that I'm available to offer you as much advice as you need in order to deal with this news intelligently."

I almost laughed, a drunken and totally inappropriate reaction to the mood of the room, which had changed so dramatically in only a matter of seconds. Dale continued.

"The only thing I'm going to ask of you tonight is that your questions wait until tomorrow. You can come to my office for a more substantive discussion of the details regarding your situation."

"That sounds fair," I said flippantly, my tongue heavy with the effects of alcohol. For all I knew, Dale was about to tell me I had a piece of spinach stuck between my teeth or that he and Stephen had decided to begin charging me rent. No matter, I was in a good mood. I was pleasantly buzzed and not the least bit concerned about whatever he was about to share with me.

Dale began, "You know that Danny felt a great deal of guilt about how the two of you parted ways."

"Yeah," a wave of warmth passed over me. I felt compelled to talk, so I did. "He shouldn't have felt bad though. It wasn't his fault."

Liquor is a remarkably effective lubricant for the tongue. I should have just shut up and listened, but I wasn't capable of being quiet for the moment.

Dale interjected, sternly, "Something else that bothered him a great deal, and something that you apparently haven't been aware of, was the fact that the first song he sold as his own was actually one you wrote. The result being that he felt as if his entire career was based on a lie."

"Ahh, that's no big deal." I waved at the air, as if I could soothe Danny's guilty conscience with a flourish of my hand. "I wouldn't have been pissed off at him for that."

I really didn't think I would have been mad either. After all, I might have written it, but I didn't do a damned thing with it, not ever. If not for Danny, nobody outside of East Hartford ever would have heard that song at all. Hell, I didn't even remember it consciously. Or at least I didn't think I did.

"Well, regardless of how you may feel about it, Danny hoped that he could make things right by providing for you in his will." Dale presented his case in a serious, formal, legal fashion. He wasn't chatting with me as a friend. He was informing me as a client.

The urge to laugh returned with a vengeance. I had to bite my lip to keep from bursting out in an explosion of nervous energy. The evening was turning out to be the strangest Thanksgiving dinner of my life, without a doubt.

Recovering my sense of decorum, I suggested sincerely, "That was really nice of him." I smiled across the table at Jean and patted Mel on the knee. Jean continued grinning back, studying my face through eyelids that hung low, the result of one Jack and Coke too many, I imagined. Perhaps I was sporting that same look, I thought to myself. Certainly I'd had as much to drink as Jean had. I tried to mentally tally how many drinks I'd put away since dinner.

"Danny left you the entirety of his publishing rights, Frank," Dale explained calmly.

"Man, he didn't have to do that." Truthfully, I didn't know the difference between Danny's publishing rights, the Bill of Rights or the right-on-red law. Unlike Dale, I didn't have what you might call a passing familiarity with the law. I knew even less about business finances.

"By conveying his publishing rights to you, he transferred any and all income derived from CD sales, the playing of his music live or for broadcast, the future recording of his music by other artists as well as income generated from the inclusion of his music in movie soundtracks, television programs, commercials and a variety of other media."

"Wow," was all I could think of to say.

I was really enjoying spending time with my new family, these friends of mine. I felt like I was the center of attention. Everybody in the room was looking directly at me. Two were smiling like idiots. I'm sure I was too. Mel was supportive, but she was as far out of the loop as I was. I felt great though, as if I was the life of the party. A sensation I'd rarely felt in the past.

Of the five of us, only Dale wore a serious expression on his face.

"It's a substantial amount of money, Frank."Dale's desire to make his point intruded on my dreamy mental wanderings.

In an effort to be a polite guest, I tried as hard as I could to focus on what he was saying. The resulting facial expression was comedic, I assume. Stephen began giggling again, this time uncontrollably. Dale soldiered on through it all as if he were in his own office, talking to a perfectly lucid client sitting across from him at his desk.

"A trust was established for you several months before Danny died. Our intention was to protect your holdings until you could be found. But as you know, you showed up somewhat unexpectedly and found us first." Dale seemed slightly embarrassed by that turn of events. Again, I waved away the emotional baggage of the moment with one hand and attempted to say something witty to ease my host's discomfort. Unfortunately, I only managed to screw up my face and make a peculiar huffing sound with my lips. Further convincing Dale that this was indeed the wrong time to attempt to convey any truly important information. He rolled his eyes toward Jean sitting across from me at the table. She offered him no salvation however, urging him to continue.

Fighting on through my inebriation, Dale continued to the best of his ability.

"I'm sorry this is the first you're hearing of this, but it seemed prudent to wait, considering the shape you were in when we first…encountered you." He sounded so professional. I'd never heard a lawyer at work before. Not in real life anyway. The effect was remarkably entertaining.

"Ironically, the reason I'd gone to the house on the day we met was to talk with Jean about hiring a private investigator to track you down. Which is why we were so suspicious when we found you sitting at the piano." A bit of information that would have made obvious sense had I been in better control of myself. But at this point on that particular Thanksgiving night, my skull had been bullet proofed by enough Jack Daniels and Coca-Cola that I suspected I was going to have difficulty navigating the stairs to the second floor of the barn later on. It occurred to me that I could avoid that problem by merely going to sleep right there on Dale and Stephen's back porch. An idea that made all the sense in the world to me at that moment.

Oblivious to my mental machinations, Dale kept right on talking.

"You were claiming to be a man none of us knew at all. We didn't have the first idea where to begin looking for you. Then suddenly, *boom*, there you were sitting in Danny's living room, big as life, like a ghost popping up out of thin air."

"That must have seemed pretty weird, huh?" I smirked.

Jean crinkled her nose, grinning with an intensity that implied she might explode soon, or possibly pee her pants.

"Frank, if you handle this well, you'll never have to work again for the rest of your life."

That woke me up.

"No kidding?" I asked in amazement.

"No kidding," Dale replied without a hint of humor.

"You're talking about a lot of money then? Danny left me a lot of money?" The concept escaped me.

"Ballpark figure, its current value is somewhere around $9 million," Dale reported in a monotone so bland that it delayed the impact of the number for a second or two.

They say everything goes into slow motion when you're involved in a horrible accident. You can see every little detail happening, but you can't move fast enough to do anything to prevent it. That's pretty much how I felt as my alcohol addled brain struggled with that new, life-altering information.

I dropped my glass. I saw it slipping away from my fingers and slowly rotating, the golden brown liquid spilling out in a swirling dance as the glinting crystal headed for the hard tile floor with all the force gravity could affect it with. Yet I never felt it leave my hand. I tried, but I couldn't manage to do anything to prevent its fall. On impact with the imported tile the vessel shattered, sending splinters of glass rocketing outward in a tiny display of crystal fireworks. The miniature light show shot out a foot in every direction.

Raising my head, I attempted to work my jaw to speak, but nothing came out. Jean was laughing audibly, although she was working hard to stifle the sound behind her hand. An effort that made her snort loudly, which made her laugh even harder. Stephen headed for the kitchen where he grabbed a broom and dustpan. He continued to giggle in fits as he returned to the table and clapped me on the back with far more energy than his slight frame would imply was possible.

"Don't worry about it," he said.

I wasn't at all sure if he was talking about breaking the glass and spilling my drink or the fact that in the space of a few seconds I'd just gone from being a helpful but friendly ne'er-do-well to a multimillionaire.

Mel continued to squeeze my hand under the table. As I recovered my wits, she leaned over and kissed me lightly on the cheek.

Looking her in the eye, still in shock I said, "I don't know what to say."

"Who would?" was her perfectly reasonable response.

"I'd like to talk about this in greater detail at my office, tomorrow. Would that be all right with you?" Dale's eyes remained riveted on me.

"Uh huh," was my only response. I got up unsteadily, feebly waving good-bye as I did. Somehow I made my way out the door, across the lawn and up the stairs to my apartment. Mel followed behind, guiding me as best she could, keeping me from wandering off into the woods or giving up and laying down to sleep on the dew-soaked grass. I wobbled and weaved considerably, but with Mel's able assistance, I made it to my apartment unscathed.

As we crossed the lawn I could still hear Jean laughing hysterically. Stephan's giggling floated on the light evening breeze, too. And while I can't be sure, I thought I heard one, single burst of relief come from Dale as well.

I may have gone to sleep right away, or I may have closed my eyes for the night several hours later. I really don't know. Time is apparently as relative as Einstein said it was. Or at least it was in my case, on the night I learned the news that I was wealthy beyond my wildest dreams. And in all likelihood, would remain so for the rest of my life.

CHAPTER 28

True to his word, Dale Albritton carved two hours out of his schedule for me the following morning. Sitting in a high backed, red leather chair, behind a broad, dark, highly detailed antique desk, Dale struck me as being somewhat regal. Much as he had the night before when he presided over Thanksgiving dinner from the head of the table. But that was his home life. Here, in his well-appointed, private office, I felt privileged to see him work in the room that served as his seat of power. Deep piles of legal-sized papers were arranged neatly on the desktop. A splash of color was provided by an assortment of pot-ted plants and fresh-cut flowers that dotted the room. I did my best to relax into a thickly padded armchair across from my gracious landlord. But try as I might to settle down, I fidgeted constantly, my right knee pumping up and down as if driven by a hydraulic ram.

Dale casually laid out a mind-numbingly long list of what he referred to as, "revenue streams." He went to great pains to use language that was clear and concise for my benefit. Yet, somehow I couldn't quite seem to absorb it all. What he labored to describe so carefully entered my brain as a vast and almost incomprehensible jumble of information. To me, it was nothing but a whirl-wind of numbers, names and technical details that tangled together into a sort of financial white noise. I was lost, way out of my depth. The possibility that I could screw all this up and lose the entirety of Danny's accumulated fortune dawned on me for the first time.

Who knew that inheriting immense wealth could be such a daunting expe-rience?

Raising an index finger to signal a pending question, I leaned forward in my chair. Dale paused in anticipation.

"Did Danny set all this up by himself?" I asked cautiously.

"No, no, not at all," Dale chuckled. "This all came together over a period of years. There were accountants involved from several companies, a handful of lawyers and Danny of course."

"And you?" I guessed, hopefully.

"Yes, I had a hand in organizing things too," he admitted.

"Well, who kept all these balls in the air? Was that Danny or you for the most part?"

Dale was quiet for a moment, pensive. When he spoke his tone was soft and warm, but firm.

"Danny and I were good friends, you know. We had a business arrangement, or course. He brought me in to handle the legal details and a good deal of the financial management that was required. But I wouldn't represent the success of all this as my doing. It was more of a collaborative effort between us." Dale fixed his eyes on me with an intensity I'd seldom seen. "I had a lot of respect for Danny. I'd like to think he felt similarly about me."

"I'm sure he did," I responded, still somewhat awed by the enormity of what faced me.

"Look," Dale interjected, lightening his tone a bit, "It's getting close to lunch time anyway. You wanna grab a bite?" Maybe he was truly hungry, or maybe he was hoping for a brief respite from trying to educate me about an empire I was clearly never going to understand completely.

"Yeah, yeah I would," I answered. "But first let me ask you a question." Dale was standing behind his desk, adjusting the cuffs of his shirt as I forged ahead. "What are the odds you'd consider doing for me what you did for Danny? Handling all this, I mean."

"Extraordinarily high," my new lawyer replied with a satisfied grin.

"Then let's get something to eat. And when we're done, if you'll promise to explain things in painfully simple terms, I'll do my best to keep up with you."

"Economics 101, huh?"

"Something like that, yeah."

"Sounds like a deal to me," Dale grasped my hand and we shook on the terms of our loose agreement. Three days later, we made the arrangement official.

CHAPTER 29

The sun rose up from behind the trees, a flaming orange ball possessing enough power to bring the entire world back to life after a short hibernation in darkness. The color of the sky shifted by the moment from black to deep purple to a brilliant azure blue. Contentedly alone, I watched the whole show gloriously unfold from my quiet perch atop the uppermost rail of the long whitewashed fence surrounding Dale and Stephen's pasture. Christmas was only one week away, and I was overjoyed to know that every important person in my life was gathered together, either upstairs at my apartment or next door at my landlord's place. All but one that is. A glaring omission that would be corrected soon enough.

Mel's old roommate and best friend Jessica was upstairs. Through the oversized windows I could see her pacing back and forth, biting her nails as the tension of the morning grew. She and her hopelessly devoted boyfriend Buddy would be magically transformed from two singles into a committed couple within an hour. The groom was hungrily eating breakfast next door. He'd arrived separately from Jessica, his limousine trailing only minutes behind hers. Wearing a big goofy grin as he climbed out of the car, he looked every inch as if he'd just won the lottery.

The ceremony was scheduled to take place right there on the lawn of the Albritton ranch. Only a dozen yards away from the spot where my latest acquisition was parked. This most recent expenditure took the form of a second hand recreational vehicle large enough for two to travel and live comfortably in. It would depart for a California honeymoon before lunch time. With any luck at all, the happy couple that traversed the continent in it would be spending Christmas in Apple Valley, California. But first things first. There was still a wedding ceremony to get through.

A justice of the peace drove in from Ocala to preside over the nuptials. His name was Cletus T. Romer. I'd never laid eyes on him before, but Dale recommended him highly, which was all the endorsement I needed before phoning the man and hiring him, at a premium, to perform the ceremony so early in the morning. He pulled through the gate right on time, rolled up beside my spot on the fence in a brand-new Jeep Cherokee and parked.

"Good morning," I called out cheerfully as he climbed out of the gleaming vehicle.

"Mornin', son. Are we doin' this right out here?" Cletus wore his white hair longer than I'd expected. He looked like the good ol' country boy he was. And it suited him. He was dressed in a crisp white shirt with a black string tie. Against the early morning chill, he'd worn a well-tailored black suit jacket with red and yellow stitching on the lapels.

"Yes, sir. That's the plan."

"Well, whenever you're ready to go, let's do it."

And with that, I clambered down off the fence and disappeared, gathering up the handful of people required for the big day to begin.

Mel's high heels tap, tap, tapped down the stairs in a syncopated rhythm along with Jessica's. The two of them were angelically beautiful, equally nervous and nearly ecstatic with thoughts of what was to come. Their tea-length gowns matched, blue/green brocade on white satin.

Buddy appeared from the doorway across the yard ahead of Dale and Stephen, both of whom had opted for formal tuxedos. Buddy wore a navy blue sport jacket and khaki slacks. I was in cowboy boots buffed to a high shine, Levi jeans and a corduroy jacket with leather patches on the elbows. The jacket was a gift from Mel. Under the circumstances, it seemed the appropriate thing to wear.

The six of us gathered in a semicircle around the justice of the peace, beneath the branches of a wide, ancient magnolia tree. It had lost almost none of its deep green, glossy leaves throughout an unusually mild fall. Buddy and Jessica stood together in the center. Stephen and Dale were to their right. Mel and I took up our positions on the left.

Cletus considered the situation facing him for a silent moment, closed the book in his right hand and spoke extemporaneously.

"I find a certain amount of satisfaction in my work each and every time I'm involved in helping a couple make their relationship a permanent one. But in

all my years as a Justice of the Peace, this is the most unique marriage ceremony I've ever been invited to perform."

Cletus took a moment to look the six of us over. We in turn smiled back in
his direction, held hands tighter and each felt a few butterflies in anticipation
of what was to come.

"With your permission," the white haired JP continued, "I'd like to stray a
bit from the standard reading I usually do at a time like this."

Jessica nodded at the stately old southern gentleman, somewhat timidly
conveying her agreement. Buddy shrugged his consent while the rest of us
grinned in silence. Cletus T. Romer took his cue and launched into an impro-
vised ceremony that included some of the kindest, most heart-warming words
I'd ever imagined I'd hear. He alternately looked each of us directly in the eyes
while relating his take on the importance of marriage, personal responsibility,
love and respect. The emotions involved and the institution itself were all connected as far as he was concerned. An opinion that was shared heartily by all
six of us as we listened raptly to his dissertation. Smoothly, almost without
anyone noticing, Justice of the Peace Romer flawlessly segued into the familiar
wedding vows. At the appropriate time, Jessica audibly said, "I do." Stephen
and Mel echoed those critical words too, nearly in unison. A moment later,
Dale, Buddy and I took our turns uttering the most important syllables ever to
escape our mouths. To which a jubilant Cletus T. Romer pronounced with a
proud yelp, "Y'all are married then. Congratulations!"

Certainly we were all aware that only two of our three couples had entered
into marriages that would be recognized by the courts. But marriage is a big
step for anyone, regardless of outside influence or official acceptance. At its
most personal and human level, marriage is an emotional leap of faith and
commitment of such enormity that it requires no outside acknowledgment.
There is no court, no state seal of approval that can render the promise of
affection and dedication from a willing spouse any more solemn. And so I was
a married man. A blissfully, happily, ready-as-I-ever-needed-to-be, married
man. And so were my closest friends, and Mel's too.

Cletus said his good-byes and left the six of us to celebrate on our own. Dale
tried to slip him a check as he strode to his car, but the old man refused.

"I may be the only JP in the country to have presided over a gay marriage, a
biracial marriage and a conventional marriage all at the same time. That's
reward enough for me," he explained. "I've got bragging rights for life. Ain't
nobody gonna top that."

The remainder of the morning was thick with stories, jokes, more stories and a general sense of satisfaction on the part of all concerned. Even Buddy came out of his shell after a time, proving to be far funnier and much brighter than I'd ever expected him to be.

We were finally home. All of us.

CHAPTER 30

Mel disappeared into the RV after breakfast, where she showed off her new rolling home with great pride. Newlyweds Jessica and Buddy took the tour with gusto, even settling into a pair of cushy chairs to watch the *Today Show* on the television mounted in the galley.

I resumed my position on the top fence rail, enjoying the smell of the grass, the sight of the horses grazing and the brilliant Gainesville sunshine for the last time. At least that would be the last time for the foreseeable future. Mel and I would be leaving soon. I had no idea when, or if, we'd be back. A growing sense of melancholy mixed uncomfortably with my lingering euphoria. I'd never felt so emotionally torn. I'd become attached to Dale and Stephen as much as I had to their little ranch. As excited as I was for the adventure ahead, I was sorry I had to leave that magnificent place in order to pursue my destiny.

Dale sauntered up and leaned on the fence beside me, quiet as a mouse. "This has been quite a morning, hasn't it?"

"Yes, sir. It certainly has," I replied, my gaze fixed on the thin line of cars passing by the drive, meandering down Highway 441. Mel and I would be joining that line shortly.

"You ready?" Dale asked, hopefully.

"Sure, you want to do it now?"

"Might as well. You and Mel have to get on the road soon. I imagine Jess and Buddy will head out shortly too." Dale's demeanor was subdued. I imagined that he was suffering from some of the same mixed emotions I was. Brothers 'til the end, I guess.

"Let's go then," I replied, jumping down from my roost on the fence.

Jessica and Buddy were just stepping out of the RV as Dale and I made our way up the drive. Mel and Jessica were crying, as brides do, I'm told. Buddy stood in the driveway a few feet away, taking in the scenery and no doubt marveling at the turn his own life had taken during the previous few days.

"Buddy," Dale called out, waving the younger man toward us. "Can we see you for a minute?"

Buddy nodded and shuffled across the sand driveway for ten yards to meet us.

"Before we all head off in our own directions, Frank and I wanted to give you a little something," said Dale, smirking like a little boy hiding a big secret. He reached inside his tuxedo jacket and withdrew an envelope, handing it to Buddy. The younger man looked surprised, almost stunned as he accepted the slim package. He tucked it into his own jacket pocket and shook hands with Dale and me in turn.

"Thanks ya'll. I don't hardly know what to say," Buddy exclaimed.

"It's our pleasure, Mr. Brown," Dale assured him.

"Absolutely," I chimed in. "We just wanted to give you something to help you and Jess get started on your new life together."

"Thanks," Buddy repeated sincerely. "Thanks a lot."

Dale and I stood together and watched with amusement as Buddy excitedly hurried back to his bride and hugged her. As they bid Mel farewell and promised to write and phone each other as often as possible, Dale leaned in and whispered to me.

"Do you think he's got any idea?"

"No," I answered confidently. "I'm sure he thinks that envelope has a couple hundred dollar bills inside."

"He's gonna shit when he opens it, you know."

"Oh yeah. I have no doubt about that at all."

I threw my arm around Dale's shoulder and steered him back to the house. It was time for me to say my own good-byes and I knew if I didn't get that chore done soon, my emotions would get the better of me. Grooms aren't supposed to cry on their wedding day. Although in my case, that was rapidly becoming a very real possibility.

"Stephen, they're going now," Dale yelled through the front doorway. The sound of drawers closing and pots rattling echoed down the long hallway from the back of the house. Stephen appeared in a matter of seconds, scurrying down the hall toward us, wiping his hands on a dish towel. His tuxedo was gone, replaced by jeans, a lightweight University of Florida sweatshirt and a long white chef's apron.

"So soon?" he protested. "You're going so soon?"

"Well, we've got a lot of ground to cover if we're going to make it to Apple Valley in time for Christmas Eve," I replied.

"Does she know you're coming?" Stephen whispered dramatically, as if my sister Sharon might hear him across the 3,000 miles that separated his doorway from her own.

"Yes, she knows. I called her last night. We talked for a good hour. I told her everything. Mel got on the line with her, too." A lump began to form in my throat. My eyes were becoming wetter than I was comfortable with.

"That's so sweet," Stephen melted with emotion, grasping my hands in his. "A broken family comes together for the holidays."

I hugged him lightly while trying to force myself to shift into a quick change of mood. Tears would be flowing soon if I didn't do something immediately to avert them. Changing the subject as a defensive measure, I stiffened and blurted out, "Well off we go. California awaits."

"Before you do," interjected Dale. "*We've* got something for *you.*" He removed another envelope from his breast pocket and slipped it smoothly into my hand.

Thoroughly surprised, I still had enough control of my faculties to open the flap and peek inside. The word "Deed" appeared on the top of a legal-sized sheet of paper. I looked at Dale, stunned, a hundred questions leaping to mind.

"We had the property subdivided," he shrugged. "The barn and the apartment above it is yours now."

Stephen nodded enthusiastically. He didn't say a word but was grinning like the Cheshire Cat.

"But…why…I don't…," words failed me.

"We've all lost friends and family over the course of our lives, Frank." Suddenly it became evident that Dale was on the verge of tears himself. "And we've always been happy here, Stephen and I. But when you came into our lives, we found out what it meant to really have a home." The two men clutched each other's hands affectionately, like the newlyweds they most certainly were.

"You gave us a great gift. One we'd like to keep if possible. So we'd like it very much if you'd consider this to be your home." He waved in the direction of the barn next door. "For you and Mel."

The three of us hugged there in the driveway, tears streaming down our faces, even as genuine laughter, driven by runaway emotions, shook our frames.

At that very moment, the thought occurred to me that during the course of a single year, I'd been almost magically transformed from a homeless, lonely wreck of a human being to a wealthy, happy, married man with family and friends running from one coast to the other. I was acutely aware that I hadn't accomplished this feat on my own. In fact, it would have been impossible for me, or anyone else for that matter, to alter a life so completely without the aid of a truly compassionate outside influence. I'd been blessed. And I knew it.

Perhaps the most surprising realization for me was knowing that the greatest gift I'd received in my new life didn't come in the form of papers describing my worth in the millions of dollars. It was the caring of strangers who had become my friends, my new family. The greatest gift I'd received was hope. And unlike monetary wealth, hope, I realized, can be passed on, multiplied and shared endlessly without eroding the principal in the least.

I was a remarkably lucky man. I had a wife I loved dearly. I had a family both by blood and by choice. And I now had a mission as well. I knew what I was going to do with the rest of my life. Right there, right then, it came to me.

What wonderful opportunities this life presents us with.

Epilogue

It was a warm, June morning when Lois Hunt got the phone call that changed her life. A rare scheduling error had left her with an entire day off. She was free of any obligation to serve meals at the diner or hand out toll tickets on the New Jersey Turnpike. Twenty-four hours of free time was a welcome rarity that Lois took advantage of by sleeping later than she had in months.

The bedside phone rang five times before Lois finally gave up her attempts to smother the sound under a pillow. She picked up the receiver with great effort and said simply, "Hello?" Her voice sounded tired and rough.

"Mrs. Hunt?" came the reply. The caller was a man. He sounded vaguely hopeful, betraying a subtle southern accent.

"Yeah," Lois replied flatly.

"Mrs. Hunt, my name is Dale Albritton. I'm a lawyer in Florida."

"So," her natural skepticism kicked into high gear.

"Mrs. Hunt, I've been instructed by an anonymous benefactor to arrange for the purchase of a home for you and your three children."

Silence came from the New Jersey end of the connection.

"If this is a bad time, I'd be happy to call you back when it would be more convenient, Mrs. Hunt."

"Is this a joke?"

"No ma'am, I can assure you this is no joke. I've got specific instructions to find and arrange for the purchase of a home for you and your family." Dale cajoled the now fully-awake woman. "How would you feel about Wee-hawken?"

Dale had sent me a tape recording of the conversation, with Lois's permission of course, so Mel and I could share in the sense of joy our first project brought the recipient. We listened to Lois's squeals of delight repeatedly while marveling at the spectacular light show put on by the night sky above the Arizona desert. Our RV sat nearby. It remains our only home to this day, aside from the second floor apartment we consider to be our winter residence in Gainesville.

In the glove compartment of our home on wheels, I keep all the usual paperwork. Insurance cards, AAA membership forms, maps, maintenance records and a collection of paper napkins are all neatly stuffed into the glove box. There's one additional item I keep in there, too. It's a letter. In fact it's the last letter Danny sent me. The same letter that launched me on this long, wonderful odyssey and changed my life so dramatically. I think of it as something of a good luck charm, since it was that letter that led me to Mel and Dale and opened up the world for me again. I keep it sealed in a plastic bag for safe keeping. Tucked away where I can get to it whenever the urge moves me. It's opened, as it was when I found it in my shirt pocket after being released from the hospital. But I haven't read it since the day it was delivered, when I was sitting at my folding card table in an otherwise empty apartment on Tolland Street, in East Hartford, Connecticut. I remember not one word of what it says, if I ever even knew. But I keep it in case I feel brave one day and decide I'm ready to attempt to solve the one great mystery left in my life.

I know for sure I'm not that brave yet. Maybe one day I will be. Maybe not. Either way, I've got plenty to do in this life, finally. I'm useful, needed and appreciated. What more could I wish for?

Aside from Lois, Mel and I have made something of a career of making similar attempts to find and offer assistance to those who deserve it. My old co-workers, Mildred Hanrahan and Ted Winters included.

Mildred, as it turns out, has a daughter with a keen mind, a strong desire to be a woman of substance in the business world. Her greatest unrealized dream was to earn an MBA from Yale. Unfortunately, her mother, whom I had seen all those years ago as little more than a human cash machine, had nowhere near the sort of capital or credit it would take to make her daughters dreams come true. Or at least she didn't. Dale and his investigators found Mildred right where I'd left her, more or less. After a few phone calls and a letter or two, a very proud Mildred capitulated and accepted a financial aid package being offered by a foundation she'd never heard of before. Stephanie, her daughter, is now enrolled in New Haven's most famous institute of higher learning. She begins classes next term.

Ted Winters, who so professionally handled the job of firing me on that dreary July afternoon, was himself let go only three years shy of his planned retirement. From what I've been told he handled that shock to the system with characteristic stoicism. He saw the move for exactly what it was, nothing personal. Even if it did affect him adversely.

Ted's departure from the company was precipitated by the purchase of our old employer by a larger, far more profitable entity. The new owner is a corporation that owns a diverse network of high tech manufacturers. The home office is now located in the far off exotic land of Cincinnati, Ohio.

Ted, who left quietly and without comment, was replaced by a much younger and far less experienced man who I'm told is prone to oddly erratic outbursts, suffers from a multitude of nervous tics and occasionally launches into full-blown temper tantrums at the office. It's been said that his position in the company and the fact that he's the nephew of the parent corporation's founder is merely coincidental.

Personally, I have my doubts.

As for Ted, he's comfortably retired now, with the slightly reduced value of his 401k having been augmented by an unexpected but very welcome infusion of cash from what Ted believes was a long forgotten investment that finally caught up with him again. Which in a sense, it was. He now lives in a relatively luxurious seaside home with his wife, Adriana, near the Mexican city of Tampico. It seems Adriana grew up in that region. Being no fan of New England's colder months, she'd wished to return to her Central American home for several years.

Who knew?

Originally Mel and I included Sal in our plans, too. You may remember him as the gas station attendant from New Jersey. I had a little run in with him over the topic of self serve gasoline. Our efforts to find him were to no avail however. From what I understand, he's beyond help.

As fate would have it, and unfortunately so for him, there are other people looking for Sal, too. Among those interested in his whereabouts are the New Jersey State Police, who are hoping to incarcerate him for selling crack cocaine and methamphetamine from a vacant, tumbledown house in a seedy neighborhood of Atlantic City. From what Dale's investigators reported back, it would actually be in Sal's best interest for the police to find him. Virtually nobody else working to ferret him out is the least bit interested in his long-term well-being. Sal owes people money, apparently. Bad people. The sort of people who tend to make their enemies disappear.

The news from Dale suggests it's unlikely Sal will ever be seen or heard from again.

Most of the stories I hear from Gainesville have happier endings, though. The world is full of people who need a break, or a little nudge to get them headed in the right direction. Mel and I have found more than a few of them as we wander across the landscape. And so we help, to the degree that we can.

It's what we do.

We're comfortable knowing that we'll probably never settle down any more than we already have. Certainly, we won't have children of our own. We're far too old for that now. But we'll fill our time well. Like doting parents we're paying college tuition, and making down payments on homes, and helping hardworking people who deserve a leg up in the world to make the transition from struggling to stability. Our family is large and growing. Even if most of them don't know we're a part of their lives.

We enjoy what we do. As a matter of fact, you might even say that our work defines us.

Through the wonders of the Internet and cell phones, Mel's been able to keep up a regular correspondence with her old roommate and closest friend, Jessica. Even as we travel the two of them chit chat back and forth on an almost daily basis.

Jessica and Buddy are expecting another child in December. They've had two girls so far, aged three and 18 months. The idea of a new baby in the family thrills Mel to no end. Whenever time and place allow, she's out scanning store shelves for baby outfits and children's toys to bring back to Florida with us. She's the ultimate aunt.

From what Jess tells us, she and Buddy have been doing spectacularly well with the garage, too. Jessica handles the phones and the books while Buddy turns wrenches out in the maintenance bays. By the second year they found the workload had grown enough that they had to hire an additional mechanic. Buddy's got three mechanics working for him now. He's an American success story. Which is exactly what Dale and I were hoping when we bought the garage for them as a wedding present.

Incidentally, Buddy's garage has been the only purchase I've made without Mel's knowledge. But then, Dale and I made the arrangements for that before we all tied the knot. So, no harm done.

In addition to our wedding vows, I've made only one promise to Mel. Which was this; with every decision I make and every person I aspire to help, Mel will be completely involved, or at least to the degree she wants to be. After all, what we're doing isn't a job, it's a lifestyle. It's a quest to make a difference in the lives of those around us. Sometimes that difference is considerable, as in

Lois Hunt's case. Sometimes it's less noticeable. But it's what we do and what we intend to keep on doing.

As long as we're doing it together, I don't see how we can possibly do anything but succeed.

Perhaps best of all, I've realized that if I ever feel even the slightest twinge of doubt about what I'm doing or where we're going, all I have to do is turn on the radio. Like everyone else, I occasionally sing along, tap my foot or play a quick line or two on my ever present air-guitar. But beyond the aural pleasures of the music I encounter across the dial, I know for sure that salvation is in there somewhere, hidden in the melodies. Redemption awaits me on the FM band. And so does my old friend, Danny Loughman, who, without a doubt, saved my life and gave me the chance to create a new one.

If the price for knowing that means I'll be spending the rest of my days prowling the highways of North America with Mel, searching out good people who've fallen on hard times…well, that seems like a pretty fair trade to me. Things could be a whole lot worse, all things considered.

If asked to describe myself at this point, I'd have to say that I'm a lucky guy. A very lucky guy, indeed.

About the Author

Like so many thousands of young men of his generation, Jamie Beckett took up the guitar at a tender age. Fueled by dreams of fame and fortune, he and his band, The Broken Hearts, played throughout the northeastern states, building a respectable following. In 1985, the group relocated to the Greenwich Village section of New York City.

While working as a professional musician until the eve of his 30th birthday, Jamie was fortunate enough to see, meet and in some cases play with a number of the musicians mentioned in Burritos and Gasoline.

Today, Jamie lives and works in central Florida, where he's a columnist for a daily newspaper and occasionally contributes content to regional and national magazines.

His web site is located at: http://jamiebeckett.com

978-0-595-40912-9
0-595-40912-1

Printed in the United States
64379LVS00005B/313-459

9 780595 409129